G000065426

Sextuplet and the City

MISHA BELL

♠ MOZAIKA PUBLICATIONS ♠

This is a work of fiction. Names, characters, places, and incidents are either the product of the author's imagination or are used fictitiously, and any resemblance to actual persons, living or dead, business establishments, events, or locales is purely coincidental.

Copyright © 2022 Misha Bell
www.mishabell.com

All rights reserved.

Except for use in a review, no part of this book may be reproduced, scanned, or distributed in any printed or electronic form without permission.

Published by Mozaika Publications, an imprint of Mozaika LLC.
www.mozaikallc.com

Cover by Najla Qamber Designs
www.najlaqamberdesigns.com

ISBN: 978-1-63142-755-8
Paperback ISBN: 978-1-63142-756-5

CHAPTER

One

"I WANT to sniff The Russian's tights." I set my mimosa on the table with a stern finality. "Now, will you help me with the break-in?"

The confused expressions on my sisters' faces are almost worth the humiliation. "Almost" being the operative word. The three of them are about to have a lot of fun at my expense.

"You mean that ballet dancer you're crushing on?" Blue, one of my five littermates, asks. Her green eyes, the same ones I see in the mirror every day, sparkle as she adds, "He's not a spy, by the way. I checked. Nor is he Russian for that matter. He was born in Latvia."

Of course. Blue is the family spook, so she assumes every foreigner is part of the intelligence community.

"I didn't ask you to snoop on him, but yes, I'm talking about the ballet dancer," I say. "Why else would a man wear tights?"

I ignore the part about his birthplace. According to his online bio, he grew up in Moscow. More importantly, "The Russian" is from *Sex and The City*, while "The Latvian" isn't.

Blue shrugs. "Because he's a hipster? To keep his legs warm during cold *Latvian* winters? Because his pet bear doesn't like the sight of hairy legs?"

Gia, my older sister who has one littermate of her own, waves one pale hand to shut Blue up. Leaning on her forearms, she peers at me intently. "What does your weird fetish for men's undergarments have to do with us?"

My left eye twitches. "I don't have a fetish."

Gia's grin is devious, as always. "Hey, I'm not kink-shaming."

I resist the urge to argue further, as it will only encourage her. Instead, I take solace in the fact that Gia is stumped by my request. As an older sister and a magician, she's used to being the one who mystifies, so the reversal must chafe.

Honey, another littermate of mine, takes out a flask from her leather jacket's inner pocket and pours some more champagne into her mimosa. Like Blue, she has my face, albeit a thinner version of it. I'm by far the curviest of the sextuplets. "Can everyone shut the fuck up and let Lemon explain what she wants?" she snaps.

I give the prickliest of my sisters a grateful nod. "To achieve my goal—"

"And by goal, she means those fragrant tights." Gia looks so happy I half expect her to pull a rabid rabbit out of a hat—and she's not even wearing a hat.

I blow out a frustrated breath. "Yes. To get to *the tights*, I'd like to sneak into his dressing room during a

2

ballet performance." I look at each sister in turn. "The three of you have the skills I need to avoid ending up on the evening news."

Actually, Blue alone probably has all the skills I need, but I've been dying to have a *Sex and the City*-style brunch for a long time and thus needed three accomplices. Too bad my sisters don't map neatly onto Samantha, Charlotte, and Miranda. It's more like James Bond for Blue, Lisbeth Salander from *The Girl with the Dragon Tattoo* for Honey, and G.O.B. from *Arrested Development* for Gia—except Gia also looks like Morticia Addams, if said character were to turn into a vampire.

Blue thrusts her glass at Honey, who pours her some champagne from the flask. "I think I speak for all three of us when I ask: *Why?*"

I scan our surroundings.

Good. We're the only ones sitting outside here at Brunchicka, so I can speak freely… or as freely as is possible given the minefield that is this subject. "As you know," I begin, "I have a bit of an obsession when it comes to The Russian."

Gia snorts. "Sure, if by that you mean you're on the verge of going *Fatal Attraction* on his tights-clad ass."

I roll my eyes, a Hyman family default when dealing with Gia. "Only some of you"—I glance at Honey—"know this, but most of my encounters with men, such as they were, ended as soon as I smelled them."

I fully expect snarky remarks along the lines of, "Did you try sniffing their butts? It works for dogs with a sense of smell as keen as yours." But the mocking doesn't come. All three of my sisters are looking at me with pity—which might actually be worse—and they don't even know the full extent of my problem. The main reason I insisted we sit outside is because smells are more concentrated indoors, often to an unbearable extent for me—and that's with my special nose filters that dampen my olfactory acuity. The list of smells that drive me crazy is longer than Gia's list of germs to avoid. I even hate the scent of lemon—which must be some sort of self-hate, with my name being Lemon and all. On the bright side, if there's ever a fire, I will always sniff it out and survive. Who knows, I might even become the first human to detect carbon monoxide—an allegedly odorless gas that defeats even dogs.

I clear my throat and pick up my mimosa. Orange scent is thankfully different from lemon, not having been overused in cleaning products. "Long story short: I don't like being obsessed," I say. "I want this guy out of my head, so I can focus on more realistic prospects."

Like my ex, who has a case of germaphobia that would put Gia's to shame. When we were together, he showered so often that he never had any body odor, only extremely dry skin. To tolerate him, all I had to do was convince him to use only unscented products. Too bad his lack of scent didn't help our lack of chemistry. Maybe I'll find another germaphobe who'll suit me better. I keep silent about that plan, though, so as not to offend Gia. She's showing herculean restraint by not mocking me at the moment.

Honey fondles a stud in her ear, one of her million piercings. "So, if I understand it right, you want to conduct an exorcism of sorts. Sniff his tights, get grossed out, and thus end the obsession?"

I bob my head. "Exactly."

"In that case, I'm in," she says.

"Me too, but on one condition," Blue says with a grin. "The codename of this operation is Big Sniff."

Fucking skunks. How long before they realize it makes a nice acronym?

Honey smirks. "I second that, but let's shorten it to BS."

Okay, so a millisecond, that's how long.

"Hmm." Gia mimes neatening a nonexistent goatee. "If you need my help with Operation BS, I also have one condition."

There's a churning in my stomach that isn't due to my craving for French toast... or at least, not only that. All Hyman sisters barter in favors to some degree, but Gia could probably teach the Godfather a thing or two about the technique.

I rub the back of my neck. "What's your demand?"

"Demand? More like a reasonable request." Gia's angelic expression doesn't fool anyone—unless we're talking fallen angel. "Lemon, you know what each of us does for a living, so all I want is for you to tell us what it is that *you* do."

"You're a genius," Blue says to Gia in an overly loud voice. "I've been wondering for a while and was about to start seriously sleuthing."

"What a great use of taxpayer money that would've been," I mutter under my breath. "Spying on your own family."

Honey slides to the edge of her chair. "Sorry, Lemon. I've been curious too. Dish."

I debate whether coming out is worth their help. Maybe. Maybe not. The truth is, I've been wanting to open up to someone, and these three are a decent focus group if I want to know how the rest of the family will react to my chosen profession.

"Fine. I'll tell you." I down the mimosa and gulp in a deep breath—a mistake because the smell of something delicious nearby makes my belly rumble. Ignoring that, I take another breath and say, "My work is masturbation."

CHAPTER
Two

THEY GAPE at me as though I've pulled down my pants and started auditioning finger puppets in front of them. At the same time, the smell of delicious food grows stronger despite my nose filters—that or the stress is making me hungrier.

"Did I hear 'masturbation?'" Blue asks, still speaking too loudly.

"Yeah," Gia says even louder. "But maybe that's an acronym for something, like a Master's degree in Urban Planning?"

My eye starts to twitch again, but I calm myself by mentally adding another euphemism for female self-pleasure to my existing list: Master's in Urban Planning, or MUP. But wait. Shouldn't it be Mistress's of Urban Planning since we're emphasizing the female-ness of the act?

"I'm pretty sure she's talking about diddling herself," Honey says, grinning widely.

Okay. Now my left eye is twitching so hard I wouldn't be surprised if it were sending Morse code messages to my sisters: two dots and a dash, then three dots and another dash—which stands for FU.

"If you would just let me get a skunking word in edgewise," I grit out, and they turn to me, eyes widening. I take another breath. "I did mean what I said. I'm a professional masturbator."

A throat is cleared behind me, and the smell of yummy food is the strongest it's been since we sat down, which makes me understand why my sisters are bug-eyed.

It wasn't my words but something else.

Something worse.

Flushing, I glance over my shoulder to confirm my suspicion.

Yup. Our matronly waitress is standing behind me, and if it weren't for the tray of food in her hands, she'd be clutching her pearls.

"That's right. I write a blog about masturbation," I say, lifting my chin as I turn back to the table.

When life gave me lemons—a.k.a. men whose smells I couldn't tolerate—I made lemonade by becoming so good at pleasuring myself that I don't even need a man at this point. In general, WLGYL is my personal motto, for obvious reasons. Speaking of that, my name is the one thing I could never make lemonade from: "Lemon Hyman" sounds like the virginal membrane of a sourpuss.

The waitress plunks down our plates so fast I'm sure

she's expecting me to pull a dildo from my pussy and make her suck it.

Oh, well. No point in backing down now. Raising my chin higher, I continue. "Self-pleasure empowers women. Allows them to safely release sexual tension, reduce stress, and improve sleep. It raises self-esteem and enhances body image, relieves cramps, strengthens muscle tone in the pelvic and anal—"

The waitress loudly plops the last plate—my French toast—in front of me and rushes away in a huff.

Gia grins. "Good going. Now she'll spit into whatever else she brings us."

Honey's eyes turn into slits. "I dare her."

Blue smirks at me. "Do you realize how much you just sounded like Mom?"

Ugh, she's right. The benefits of orgasms are our matriarch's favorite subject. When it comes to our parents, I haven't told them about my profession because of how much unsolicited advice they'll feel compelled to dish out.

I pinch the bridge of my nose. What's done is done. These three know now. I give each sister a hard look. "Can I trust you guys to keep this between us?"

Given how this is going, I don't think I'm ready to come out to the rest of the family just yet.

Blue puffs up. "Oh, please. I keep secrets for a living."

"And I'm a magician," Gia says. "I keep even more secrets than Blue."

Honey scoffs. "I'm the only one you should've told

—and the only one you need for Operation BS for that matter."

Okay, good. The Hyman sisterly competitiveness will work in my favor for once. Relieved, I grab a bottle of syrup and drown my French toast before taking a bite.

Nope. Not sweet enough.

I sprinkle on powdered sugar and give it another taste.

Still something missing.

With a sigh, I look at Honey and nod.

Eyes gleaming with satisfaction, Honey pulls out a plastic bag filled with a mixture of M&Ms, raisins, little marshmallows, and candy corn.

I make sure the waitress isn't looking and dump the contents of the bag onto my plate.

Finally, the French toast is sweet enough for me. Unfortunately, I've just encouraged Honey's obsessive frugality. As expected, to avoid paying extra for the toppings, she brought them with her to the restaurant. Earlier, she insisted we order orange juice that she turned into mimosas with the champagne from her flask, and I fully expect her to whip out a coupon for the meal itself when the bill arrives.

Yep, my badass sister makes Scrooge McDuck seem like a big spender in comparison. Of course, if someone says something about it to her face, she'll cut a bitch.

While I'm dealing with my toast, Blue studies the eggs on Honey's plate with suspicion. My brave spy sister fears and hates anything to do with birds. Her need to mock me eventually prevails, however. Looking up, she pins me with an intent stare. "Now that your diabetes is assured, can I ask a few questions about your work?"

Gia, who was also eyeing Honey's eggs disapprovingly, no doubt worried about salmonella or some other germ, glances at Blue with interest. "Do you mean Operation Big Sniff or the jilling-off blog?"

"The paddling-the-pink-canoe blog." Blue turns to me. "Why a blog? Are we in 2003?"

I sigh. "I've tried making videos on social media, but most platforms are prudish and limit what I can say on the subject. Also, for reasons known only to search engine algorithms, my blog is semi-popular."

Gia arches a black-dyed eyebrow. "Search engine algorithms?"

"If you search 'jilling off,' I'm one of the top results. Same for 'female masturbation.'"

Honey looks impressed. "Does that translate into lots of money?"

I give her a glassy stare. "Yeah, I rent a shithole in Staten Island just for kicks."

"You could be doing that because you like saving money." Blue furtively glances at Honey.

I grimace. "I wish. I'm drowning in credit card debt. Banner ads barely put food on my table. The way to make real money is by getting a sponsor, but that hasn't happened for me in a while."

"Then why do it?" Gia asks.

"Because it's my passion," I say. "Out of everyone, you should understand that."

Instead of making more masturbation digs, Gia nods

solemnly. For the longest time, her love of magic didn't pay much either, but her fortunes have recently changed.

"All I know is I'm not giving up," I say, and I'm not sure if I'm trying to convince my sisters or myself. "I just need to find a big sponsor and—"

I gag as the stench of aftershave defeats my nose filters and begins molesting my nostrils. Turning, I see the offender, a waiter carrying a pitcher of water.

"We don't need that, thanks." I wave him away, like a stink bug.

"You realize he was cute?" Honey asks.

I make another gagging sound. "He must've soaked in a bathtub of Old Spice for a couple of days before reporting to work."

"The horror," Gia says with an eyeroll.

"Perfumes and colognes are like farts that cost money," I say.

Blue opens her mouth, no doubt to say something snide, but karma lands right in the middle of our table —in the form of a cute little green parrot.

With speed even James Bond would envy, Blue dives under the table.

The bird hops over to a plate with plain toast and pecks at it as if we don't exist.

Gia stares at the bird, wide-eyed. "This must be someone's pet, right?"

"No fucking way," Blue says, her voice muffled by the table cloth. "That's a monk parakeet. They're wild."

She says "monk parakeet" the way most people would say "tarantula" and imbues the word "wild" with a sinisterness usually reserved for the likes of Voldemort.

"Wild?" Gia jumps to her feet, no doubt remembering all the germs a wild bird might carry. Then, as if by magic—at least the performative kind—a bottle of hand sanitizer the size of my head appears in Gia's hands, and she squirts the bird with it.

Yuck. The smell of alcohol and cheap faux mint is like a smack to my nose.

The parrot agrees with me. It makes a screech that sounds as if a chainsaw and the most annoying alarm clock had a baby, who was then tortured in hell by deaf demons.

"Make it go away!" Blue screams from under the table.

Out of thin air, a deck of playing cards appears in Gia's hands, and she throws them one by one at the bird, like ninja stars.

The bird screeches again but doesn't leave. Paper cuts must not be an issue when you have feathers.

"Please, guys," Blue says. "This isn't funny. Get rid of it."

"Okay, okay." Honey pulls out a butterfly knife and opens it in the flashy manner I associate with professional killers.

"No!" I shout. "Don't kill the poor—"

The bird spots the knife and screeches again, then takes flight, looking indignant as it disappears into the distance.

Honey awkwardly hides the butterfly knife in her purse. "I was just going to scare it."

13

Yeah. Sure. Like she scared that mean girl back in high school who had to get stitches in her forearm.

Blue climbs out from under the table, looking sheepish. "If you'd killed it, anyone with a brain bigger than a bird's would agree it was self-defense."

Gia squirts the foul hand sanitizer everywhere the bird's little feet touched, killing what remained of my appetite.

I push my plate away. "Can we get to the business at hand?"

"Yeah." Blue returns to her seat. "What's the venue?"

"New York City Ballet," I say. The ticket ate a big chunk of my blog's earnings from last month, but it'll be worth it to see The Russian live instead of watching his performances on YouTube. And, of course, to get him off my mind.

Blue takes her phone out and does something for a minute or two. When she looks up, her devilish smile reminds me of Gia's. "I can make it so you won't show up on any cameras." She gives Honey a challenging look. "Still think you're all she needs?"

"I'd say she needs me more than either of you," Gia says. Her tone turns professorial as she looks at me. "The key to getting into places where you don't belong is to not look guilty."

"She's got a point," Honey says. "I can walk into any nightclub by boldly pretending my stamp got smudged."

I take out my phone and make my first note: *Look bold*. Of course, that's easier said than done. I check to

14

make sure no waiter has somehow slipped past my nose and say, "There might be doors I'll need to open. Locked doors."

As if they've rehearsed the move for a year, my three sisters pull out lockpicks and then chuckle at each other.

"You want to do the honors?" Honey says to Gia. "You were the first to learn this."

Gia grins. "You have more practical experience."

Before Blue blows some smoke up Gia's ass too, I say, "I don't care who does it. Just teach me."

"Fine." Honey picks up a zigzag thingy. "This is a tension wrench."

———

The lesson takes triple the time it should because my teachers keep arguing about random minutia. Finally, I feel confident enough for Operation Big Sniff, so I wave at the waitress to bring the check.

As expected, Honey whips out a coupon, and the waitress has to go back to recalculate the bill.

"This is on me," I say when the check comes back.

"No," Gia and Blue say in unison.

"You just told us you have cashflow problems," Honey adds.

"Fine," I say with a sigh. My credit card *is* reaching its limit. "We split it this time, but if I get a nice sponsor, I'm taking you all out for a fancy dinner."

"Deal," Gia says. "So long as it's a clean place, like this one."

"Sure." I fight the urge to roll my eyes. "It will not serve any poultry either." I grin at Blue.

I even debate if I should reassure Honey that it will be a place she can find a coupon for, but I decide not to risk my skin with that knife in her purse.

Operation Big Sniff will be dangerous enough.

CHAPTER

Three

THE BALLET I'm watching is *Swan Lake*, and my crush's role is that of Prince Siegfried.

Damn it. I'm jealous of that crossbow he's holding. Given that my goal is to get this man out of my system, seeing him live might've been a step in the wrong direction.

His muscles—especially on his powerful legs—would make a statue of a Greek god weep in envy. His gleaming eyes are pure melted chocolate, and dark chocolate is also what his slicked-back hair reminds me of. His face is angelic, with cheekbones so sharp-edged they look like the hard layer of Crème Brûlée after you break it with a spoon. Oh, but all of that pales in comparison to the bulge in his pants—a feature of so many of my masturbation fantasies that I've even named the contents of it Mr. Big.

So, yeah. Seeing all this is the opposite of helpful—and if I activate the vibrating panties I'm currently wearing, it will make everything that much worse.

Originally, I put on the masturbatory panties because I figured this is my last chance at a ménage à moi with The Russian. If sniffing his tights works as intended, I'll have to resort to some other visual aid for visiting the bat cave—like *Magic Mike, 300,* or *Charlie and the Chocolate Factory.*

Then again, I shouldn't be selfish. This adventure would make for an amazing blog post. I don't usually get naughty in public, so this might be educational for my followers.

Yeah. I'll do it for them. It will be my last hurrah with The Russian—made that much more interesting because I'm seeing him live.

I scan the nicely dressed people sitting around me. The coast is clear. They're focusing on the spectacle in front of us, as they should.

I fish out the little remote that activates the vibration.

Last chance to change my mind.

Nope. The Russian flashes me the perfection that is his butt, with a gluteus maximus that I want to lick like rock candy.

I press the "on" button and grin as my underwear begins to vibrate.

It's DIY time.

Even at the lowest speed, my clit is instantly engorged, and I have to hope the electrical components inside this technological marvel are waterproof. Soon, I have to painfully bite my tongue to keep from moaning. Tchaikovsky's music is genius, but it wouldn't drown *that* out.

I had no idea it would be this hard to keep quiet. Must be The Russian's hotness in action.

Panting, I turn off the device to give my clit a chance to cool off. If I get caught doing this, I'll be escorted out and banned for life for being the pervert that I am.

When I think I can stay quiet, I turn the thing back on again.

Nope. Just as The Russian performs a particularly mouthwatering *fouetté*, the desire to be vocal is back with a vengeance.

Fuck. Me.

Whoever designed these panties should win some sort of a prize. They do to my nether regions what the Swan theme song does to my ears, or The Russian to my eyes.

An orgasm of cosmic proportions builds inside me, and staying silent takes an effort of will I know I don't possess, so I turn everything off once again, for good this time.

Fucker. Now I'm just really frustrated and cranky.

As if to sharpen my frustration, the ballerina playing Princess Odette shows up.

Can you say "impossible standard of beauty?" Translucently thin on top, she looks like someone who's never tasted a croissant in her life, yet her legs are powerful and seem to go on and on.

I know, I know. My jealousy is as green as a St. Patrick's Day donut. In my defense, her character is supposed to be sweet, noble, and guileless. She, however, dances the part with seduction, like Odile, the evil black swan. Speaking of *Black Swan*, it's all too easy

19

to imagine this woman stabbing someone with a shard of glass, the way Natalie Portman's character did in the movie.

That's it. Decided. Henceforth, this ballerina will be Black Swan in my mind.

As the ballet continues, I cringe each time The Russian touches Black Swan—which is often, especially during the *pas de deux*. In fact, things get so bad that when Princess Odette meets her sad end, I find it hard to empathize.

I'm just glad the show is over. Watching it live was definitely a mistake.

Fighting the exiting crowds, I make my way to the bathroom, where I lock my stall and climb on a toilet to hide my feet as per Blue's instructions for Operation Big Sniff. Her instructions are also why I'm wearing all black—dressy pants appropriate for the venue, a button-up shirt that's slightly too tight on me (I bought it a few pounds ago, so sue me), and a pair of ballet flats that have seen better days but are the fanciest shoes I can run in.

Taking out an earbud, I stick it into my ear and dial Blue.

"Hey, sis," she says. "The crowd is dispersing as we speak. Hold tight."

As I wait, Blue fills me in on all the juicy family gossip, making me wonder how she gathered all this information. No doubt using the same nefarious methods as Big Brother in the dystopian world of *1984*.

"The Latvian Elvis has just left the building," Blue

finally says. "And I turned off the cameras in your way, so you can start the op."

"Thanks." I move to hop down from the toilet, but my foot slips and I headbutt the stall door.

Ouch. I see stars in my vision—shaped like urinal cakes.

Worse still, I hear a sploosh.

No! Please no.

Sadly, it's yes.

My phone is swimming in the toilet bowl. Yuck.

"Hey," Blue says in the earbud through crackling static. "Is everything o—"

The rest is an unintelligible hiss.

My poor phone is dead.

I debate fishing it out, as gross as that would be. I've heard you can stick these devices into rice to dry out, and they may resurrect themselves. In the end, I decide against it. The phone is so old it's a stretch to call it "smart." It's better off drowning in the toilet with some dignity, even though I'll have to skip about a hundred trips to Cinnabon to afford a replacement.

The question now is: should I call off the operation?

I no longer have Blue in my ear, but I *have* splurged on this ticket and I don't know when I'll be able to afford another one. Besides, I've gone through all the trouble of learning how to pick a lock, and Blue has done her part already.

All right, I'm going for it.

Taking in a calming breath, I sneak out of the stall.

No one is around.

Good.

As I creep to my destination, I'm glad I memorized the layout of this place instead of relying on the schematics on my phone.

The first lock in my way is easy to pick, and the second door isn't even locked.

When I get to the last corridor, I realize I'm jogging, and by the time I stop next to the door of what should be The Russian's changing room, I'm panting.

Yep. "Artjoms Skulme" is what the tag on the door says. I'm in the right place.

I take out the lockpicks, and the lock yields to my newfound skills without much fuss.

Heart hammering, I step inside. In the large mirror in front of me, I look frightened, like Blue would in a bird's nest. Even my shoulder-length hair appears frazzled and pale, the strawberry-blond of my strands more ashy blond in this light than anything close to red.

Chewing on my lip, I look around for the tights. I've made it this far, and I'm not leaving without completing the operation.

Hmm.

I don't see tights anywhere.

Just my luck. He's a neat freak.

Wait a sec... I see something. Not tights, but possibly even better. Although also a bit creepier if I think about it too deeply.

I hurry over to the chair on which I've spotted the item—an article of clothing known in this industry as a dance belt.

Except it's not an actual belt.

Designed for ballet dancers with external genitals

that can flop about during vigorous jumps, this under-garment looks suspiciously like a thong.

I fan myself.

Just picturing The Russian wearing this butt-floss without tights makes me want to re-enable my vibrating panties.

But no. No time for muffin buttering right now.

I pick up the thong—I mean, dance belt. It feels nice and soft to the touch.

Must be made of boyfriend material.

I peer at the dance belt like I'm trying to charm a snake inside of it. A snake named Mr. Big.

Am I really going to do this? And if I do, does that mean I'm like one of those peeps who buy worn under-wear online?

No. I don't have an undies-sniffing fetish, more like the opposite.

Yeah. If anyone asks, that's my excuse.

With determined movements, I rip the filter from each nostril and bring the dance belt up to my nose.

Here goes.

I take the Big Sniff.

CHAPTER
Four

HOLY SPIRIT and mother of all pheromones.

This was a huge mistake.

Musky and delicious in a manly way, this overwhelmingly arousing smell is doing the exact opposite of what I hoped and expected.

The Russian could bottle this aroma and make a fortune.

Damn it. Operation BS is a huge flop. Instead of getting him out of my mind, I've just wedged him in there so deeply it's a wonder my ears don't pop.

Oh, and that fetish I was claiming not to have—I might've just developed it, at least as far as this man's undies go.

Why me, universe? It's bad enough I can't be with a realistic prospect due to my heightened sense of smell. Why should a guy I can never have smell so heavenly?

I force myself to pull the dance belt away from my nose. Instantly, I miss the scent. Also—and this might be due to the orgasm interruptus during the performance—I'm hornier than a teen bonobo.

Hmm. I *am* wearing my sex toy underwear... And I do have this delicious thong at my mercy... Most importantly, life has just handed me a new lemon in the form of The Russian's god-like scent, so the least I can do is make sweet, orgasmic lemonade out of it—as per my motto.

Oh, and this could also be inspirational for my blog.

In fact, I owe it to myself and my followers to do this.

There. It's settled. Before I can chicken out, I lock the door, plop my butt on the chair, and turn on my vibrating panties.

Oh, wow.

This is amazing—and the only way I can make it better is by picturing The Russian's powerful legs, each muscle flexing as he leaps across the stage.

I gulp in another whiff of the aphrodisiac undies.

Fuck. This feels better than anything in recent memory, and not just thanks to the thong. It must be the naughtiness of the situation. After all, I *am* masturbating during a breaking-and-entering. No, make that spelunking during a robbery. Because who am I kidding? I'm stealing this dance belt after I'm done.

Unbidden, the image of The Russian's mouth on my clit comes to mind. He's pursing those uber-lickable lips and blowing a cherry to generate the sensation that matches the vibrations I'm feeling.

Ooh. Nice. I increase the speed of the vibration and close my eyes.

Yeah. Just like that.

Blow another cherry for me.

A little more.

Yes.

No.

Damn it.

For some reason, the orgasm is too far away, probably because the real Artjoms Skulme is only here in spirit, unlike during the performance.

I increase the speed some more.

The gizmo purrs louder and the orgasmic horizon moves close enough that I can't help but moan—but I do manage to keep my volume low in case some cleaning person happens to walk by the dressing room.

A minute later, the orgasm is still not coming.

I take another hit of the magic scent and picture The Russian's tongue flicking over my sex.

It's great, don't get me wrong, just not enough. I think what's keeping me from reaching my destination is this gnawing emptiness that I yearn to fill. More specifically, to fill it with Mr. Big, as that's what my nose has been smelling. Unfortunately, the closest I can get at the moment is my fingers.

I let the remote join the thong in my left hand to free up my right digits. Pretending they're The Russian's, I lick and suck my index and middle finger, then slide my hand into my still-vibrating panties and locate my entrance.

Fuuuck.

This is exactly what the masturbation doctor

ordered. Now that the feeling of fullness is there, the orgasm rushes forth at the speed of sound.

Also, the images. Oh, the images… The Russian is pounding into me, hard, his pelvis performing tricks that only a ballet dancer is capable of.

Another moan escapes my lips, one that might be a tad too loud. Oops. I muffle the next moan with the dance belt.

Wait a sec.

Did I just hear a clack?

Nah. Must be my jaw clicking from holding in a scream.

I'm almost there. Just a few seconds more. I take a deep whiff of the thong, inhaling the arousing aroma like I'm underwater and it's my oxygen.

I'm almost there.

So close.

Just a little bit more—

Now the sound is unmistakable.

The hinges on the dressing room door squeak.

My eyes fly open.

Before I can remove my fingers from inside myself and create some distance between the dance belt and my nose, a man steps into the dressing room.

A man who's starred in all of my recent fantasies.

The Russian himself.

CHAPTER
Five

MANY THINGS HAPPEN AT ONCE.

My neck and ears catch fire, and my face feels redder than the Soviet flag. On autopilot, I turn off my vibrating panties and drop everything I was holding in my left hand. At the same time, I jerk my right hand out of my pants and wipe my fingers on my shirt. Because I'm classy like that.

The chocolate in The Russian's eyes isn't melted like it usually is. It's solidified in shock as he stares at me. "Who are you, and what the fuck are you doing?"

His deep voice with its Eastern European accent is so sexy I almost reach my interrupted climax. But I don't. Because even through my shock, I realize how horrifying this situation is.

My heart dances an intricate ballet in my chest as I blurt out, "This isn't what it looks like."

He narrows his eyes. "So your hand was *not* in your pants?" He casts a glance at the thong on the floor. "And you *weren't* sniffing my dance belt?"

I wipe a bead of sweat from my brow—a mistake because I smell my sex on my fingers. "I mean... I'm not some crazy stalker."

Is that dark amusement in his gaze? "So you didn't break into my changing room? Or masturbate to my dance belt?"

I feel lightheaded—which should make it easier for the floor to engulf me on the spot.

Nope.

Still here.

Swallowing a jawbreaker-sized lump in my throat, I try again. "I did break in, but I had a good reason."

A smirk twists his lips. "I'd love to hear it."

Skunk. He's called my bluff. Now what do I do? My thoughts are too muddled to come up with a good lie, or any lie, really. If only I had Gia in my ear right now. She'd know what to say. Magicians lie for a living, so she's very good at it, or maybe she became a magician because—

Wait a sec. Thinking of Gia has given me an idea, and just in time. The Russian looks on the verge of calling security.

"It was a dare," I blurt.

His smirk evaporates. "A dare?"

"Yeah," I say breathlessly. "My sisters made me do it."

And hey, they could have—at least when we were younger. Gia in particular was evil when it came to things like that. One night, she put my fingers in warm water to test the urban myth about wetting the bed... which turned out to be true. Also, owing Gia a favor

29

often resulted in heaps of humiliation on par with what I'm feeling now.

"Your sisters?" He looks from me to his thong. "Sorority or biological?"

The best lies are the ones rooted in the truth, so as much as I want him to think I'm young and hip enough to be in a sorority, I tell him it was the latter, then add, "I have an aversion to most smells, so they thought it would be funny to make me play with myself as I sniffed your thong."

There. Now that I've said it out loud, it actually sounds slightly more believable than the actual truth.

He frowns. "It's a dance belt, not a thong."

"Sure, a dance belt," I say. There isn't a big difference, but I'm in no position to split hairs right now.

He cocks his head. "So you claim that you were forced into doing this?"

I nod.

"Because you were supposed to hate it?"

I nod again, less confidently.

The smirk is back, and is too sexy for my sanity. "You didn't look or sound like someone who hated what she was doing."

Sound?

So he heard?

I stand up on wobbly legs. "I'd better get going."

"Not so fast." He advances on me.

Oh, fuck. Is he about to strangle me? Or kiss me? I feel a twinge of that never-reached orgasm as I picture the second scenario.

In one breath, he's in my personal space. I can't help

but smell him—and his scent is just as yummy as that of his thong, just subtly different in that it's diluted. I also detect notes of fresh pears and patchouli that tell me he must've used cologne at some point. It had to have been long ago, though, since the smell is so faint I actually like it.

He reaches his hand out, as if to touch me.

Okay. I'm ready for what comes next.

Maybe looking forward to it—even the strangling.

To my huge disappointment, he reaches past me.

I turn my head and see him open a small drawer from which he pulls out a phone.

Oh. This must be why he returned. For his phone.

Does this mean I'm not getting manhandled?

Hold on. Maybe there's still a chance. He pockets the device but remains close to me.

Staring at his strong, masculine throat, I moisten my lips.

He extends his hand toward me.

Yes! I mean, how dare he.

Oh, wait. Again, he doesn't touch me.

What the hell?

He dives into my purse, and before I can yelp something properly indignant, he's already holding my wallet.

My chest tightens. "Hey. What are you—"

Then I comprehend his intent. He pulls out my driver's license and takes a picture of it with his phone.

Gulp. Now there's definitely dark amusement in his smile.

He slides the ID back into my wallet. "If you plan to

kill me and cannibalize my remains, you should know there's a picture of you in the cloud." He narrows his eyes at the image on his phone. "Is Lemon Hyman really your name?"

My heart pounds in my ears. "Are you making fun of my name?"

He drops my wallet back into my purse. "And if I were?"

I straighten my spine. "I'd tell you to go fuck yourself."

He snorts and looks at the fingers that were inside me just a minute ago. "Is fucking oneself really something you want to bring up?"

Heat rushes through my body—and not just from his proximity or my embarrassment. It's also an angry heat. The kind that would make me hatefuck him if I could.

"Can I go now?" I say through gritted teeth.

"No," he says imperiously.

No?

Fuck. Is calling security still on the table?

"Why not?"

He extends his phone to me. "Give me your number."

I take a step back and bump into the chair. "My number?"

He arches an eyebrow. "Do you know mine?"

"N-no," I say with a stutter. Truth be told, I do know it. Blue gave it to me. I'd never use it, though, and telling him I have it would confirm his crazy stalker theory.

With a graceful gesture, he thrusts the phone into my unsteady hands. "In that case, I'll need yours. Now."

"Why?" I manage to ask as I shakily type my phone number into his contacts, my thoughts swirling throughout.

Is this blackmail? Will he make me do something now? Something dirty? When it comes to me, he now possesses *kompromat*, as they call it in his homeland.

Is it wrong that I'm hoping he cashes it in for sexual favors?

He grabs the phone from me. "We're going to meet for dinner tomorrow night."

I gape at him. "What?"

He looks me over, his expression implying that maybe I'm going to be the meal. Or dessert. "We'll sit across from each other at a table. In a restaurant. Eat. Talk." He smirks. "Any of this ring a bell?"

I blink dazedly. My brain is clearly not functioning. "Um, okay. Dinner. Whatever. I need to go now."

He moves out of my way and makes a gesture that reminds me of one of his dance moves. "Have a good night."

I take a step, fully prepared for him to grab me and call security.

He doesn't.

I take another step. I'm a foot away from the door now.

Yes. Maybe I'm safe. The whole dinner bit is tomorrow and—

"Wait," he orders.

Fuck. Spoke too soon. I reluctantly turn to face him. "What?"

"A souvenir." He bends down to get his dance belt.

I watch him, speechless.

As he picks up the thong-like garment, the remote that controls my vibrating panties clacks to the floor.

He mutters something in Russian and picks it up also. Straightening, he regards me with a frown. "Is this yours?"

I fight the urge to rush him and snatch the remote from his strong fingers. "No. I don't know what that is."

"Odd." He presses the "on" button. "This seems like some sort of gizmo."

Oh, fuck.

My panties begin vibrating.

CHAPTER
Six

AT FIRST, all the blood in my body rushes to my face. Then, with screeching tires, it makes a sharp U-turn and crashes down into my clit.

Fuck. Fuck. Fuck. I prop myself up against the doorframe so I don't fall as my heartbeat jackrabbits.

The vibes keep attacking my sex.

Must. Not. Moan. Or show that anything is happening at all.

Also, how weird would it look if I just ran away? More importantly, why does this feel so insanely intense? The vibration is on the lowest speed, but it feels like I have a blender in my pants and a fire in my core.

Is it all the adrenaline coursing through my veins? Or the near orgasm from earlier?

Oblivious to my situation, The Russian tosses me the dance belt. "Wouldn't want you to forget your keepsake."

On pure autopilot, I catch the undergarment—and almost bring it to my nose for another luxurious whiff.

"And you're sure this device isn't yours?" He waves the remote.

Not trusting myself to open my mouth, I nod.

"Seriously odd." He frowns at the remote and presses the speed-up button.

Holy clitoral stimulation. If I thought this felt intense before, I was wrong. Now I have a jackhammer working on my privates, and keeping quiet is becoming infinitely harder.

Something must show on my face because I see concern in his chocolate eyes. "Are you okay?" he asks.

Instead of answering, I muffle a moan with the dance belt.

He gives me a sharper look. "What's going on?"

I don't answer. Between mortification and riding the wave of pleasure, I don't dare move the dance belt from my mouth.

"Is something buzzing?" He looks at my crotch. "Is your phone on vibrate?"

I shake my head vehemently.

A devious glint appears in his eyes. "So… whatever that buzzing is, it doesn't have anything to do with this remote, correct?"

I shake my head again.

He pointedly ups the vibration another notch. "Are you sure?"

I can't shake my head at this point. My eyes roll into the back of my head, my toes curl inside my shoes, and a moan escapes my makeshift gag.

He takes a step toward me, his eyes darkening as they roam over my face. "What if I press this button again?"

I give him a wild-eyed look.

He presses the button.

That's it.

This is full-blast vibration, and it pushes me over the edge.

The orgasm that crashes into me is a seven on the Richter scale—the ground cracks, buildings collapse, and pipes burst.

He turns off my panties.

I lower his dance belt and gulp in calming breaths. My heart is still racing, and my shirt clings damply to my back.

The Russian folds his muscular arms over his chest. "You came." His words are a statement, not a question.

I gulp in another breath. Everyone always talks about faking orgasms and never about the opposite— something I've clearly failed at. When I trust myself to speak, I say, "That was a seizure."

His eyebrows snap together. "You're epileptic?"

"Sure." Great. Instead of faking a non-orgasm, I'm faking a serious medical condition.

He presses the "on" button on the remote, and I have to bite back a gasp as the vibrations bring on an aftershock. Looking triumphant, he points at my crotch. "There's a buzzing." He presses the "off" button. "And now it's gone."

My face flames as the sensations recede. "Fine. You caught me. I'm wearing sex-toy panties. Are you

37

against women surf-channeling if that's what they want?"

He grins wickedly. "Nope. In fact, feel free to wear your contraption to the dinner. And I'll bring this." He pockets the remote.

I have no words.

Zero.

My legs are unsteady as I take a step backward, toward the door.

"I'll text you," he says casually, as if we've just been on a coffee date.

My words are still nowhere to be found. I take another staggering step toward freedom, and then I turn and sprint as if the evil sorcerer from *Swan Lake* is chasing me.

Which, for all I know, he might be.

CHAPTER
Seven

It's not until I'm a few blocks away that I recall the problem with the whole "I'll text you" bit. My phone is still swimming, and with something far grosser than the fishes.

Somehow, I get my brain into gear enough to recall where I've seen a cellphone store nearby. I head toward it at full speed, and midway through my dash, I realize how late it is. They might be closed.

Nope. This is the city that never sleeps. Apparently, it also always shops for phones because the store is open.

I purchase the cheapest smartphone they have, which still has a thousand times more computing power than my drowned device. The transfer of my number happens in a flash, and by the time I walk out of the store, I'm getting texts from my sisters asking about Operation BS.

Not ready to discuss my misadventures, I take the subway downtown. When I exit the underground station and head over to the ferry terminal, a text from The Russian hits my phone:

How about 7pm at Miso Hungry?

If I had any hope that he'd forget the whole dinner idea, it's gone now. I can't even honestly object to the restaurant he picked, as I've eaten there with my sisters and loved it. The place serves very little cooked food, so cooking smells are kept to a minimum. It's also super clean, which keeps Gia happy, and it doesn't serve any fowl, which is a boon for Blue. Oh, and their green tea crepe cake is divine, so I'd better leave some room in my stomach tomorrow.

Wait. Am I actually looking forward to the dinner? Am I insane?

Mind spinning, I make it to the terminal, only to find that the ferry has just left. Ugh. What else could go wrong for me today? Will I get struck by lightning? Step in dog poo? Get stuck on a bus with someone who has major BO?

Oh, well. I grab a seat and decide to use the time productively. I need to update my sisters on what happened, or else Blue might tap into my phone while the others show up at my door.

I videocall Honey first, as she's the least likely to tease me.

"Hey," Honey says as soon as her face shows up on the screen.

Before I can say hello, another face joins hers, a male one that doesn't look like mine at all.

"Sour sweetie, yellow!" Fabio says. "I'm so glad you called. I'm dying to know how Project BO went."

And there it is, the other thing that could go wrong today. Fabio is our childhood friend, and when it comes to teasing, he can be worse than all my sisters combined. On top of that, he and I have recently returned from visiting my grandparents in Florida, and I must have gotten on his nerves or something, because his barbs have become pointier. Though it could also be because he's been having problems with his boyfriend.

Honey punches Fabio's shoulder. "I told you, it's BS, not BO. And I said it was a secret." She turns back toward the camera. "I'm sorry, hon. He asked to crash at my place and said he was feeling depressed, so I told him about you."

Did Honey just call me "hon?" She must feel truly guilty, as she hates that endearment. As to Fabio feeling depressed and wanting to crash with her, I can think of only one reason. Biting back a sharp reply to his BO joke, I ask Fabio gently, "Is it *over* over?"

He waves me off. "It was over when I left on vacay without him. All good. For the best. You know I was only in it for the sex, and there's plenty more where that came from."

Since Fabio is a master of bad puns, I can't help but think that "denial is not just a river in Egypt." For a while now, he's been saying that sex is all he cares about in a relationship, but if that were true, I don't see why he needed his ex at all. Fabio is a porn star who can get sex without any boyfriend and get paid for it, so clearly, there's more to it than that. It's a touchy subject, though, and it's best I steer clear of it.

"I should let Fabio settle in," I tell Honey. "I'll—"

41

"Don't you dare hang up," he says. "I need this. Spill."

I sigh.

He rolls his eyes. "If you don't tell us now, I'll be forced to pull out my Lemon jokes, and you know they're the zest."

I groan, and not just because he still doesn't know the difference between a pun and a joke.

He looks at Honey pointedly. "It must have gone badly. She's lost all zest for life."

Honey chuckles. Traitor.

Fabio fixes his gaze back on the camera. "If you don't spill, I'll henceforth refer to you as Tyranno-sourest Rex."

I debate hanging up.

"I'll also tell you to squeeze the day," he threatens.

"You already do," I say. "Pretty much every time I see you. You also ask if I'm peeling well. And tell me that I look a-peeling."

He checks his nails theatrically. "Just to warn you, I'm peeling particularly punny and will talk fast. Therefore, Lemon, you'll need to concentrate."

Honey and I groan.

"When Lemon pie goes to the dentist, it's to get fillings," Fabio says, speaking a mile a minute. "If she goes to the doctor, it's because of a sour stomach. If it's the ER, they give her lemon-aid."

I shake my head.

"Can you come clean my house?" Fabio asks, and before I can reply, he adds, "You'd be my Minute Maid."

I debate breaking my phone, yet he's clearly just getting started.

"Did your Russian Schweppe you off your feet?" he asks.

I take a deep inhale. What he's doing has to be against the Geneva Convention.

"It's too bad he's not a cowboy," Fabio continues.

"Why?" Honey asks.

I gape at her. "Why would you set him up like that?"

Fabio looks triumphant. "Lemons have crushes on cowboys that hang out in the Wild Zest."

"I'm sorry," Honey says to me and pinches Fabio's shoulder.

"Hey," he whines. "Is that any way to treat your zest friend?"

"That does it," I grit out. "I'll talk."

He grins like a maniac. "I zest my case."

Honey smacks his shoulder. "Make another citrus joke, and you're getting a serious punch."

He rubs the spot. "Hit me again, and you'll make a bitter rival."

"Hello!" I say so loudly some of the people nearby look at me askance. Lowering my voice, I say, "I said I'll share."

They both look at me expectantly.

I furtively scan my surroundings. The last thing I want is for some nosy commuter to overhear this.

Okay. I'm safe. I open my mouth to start talking when an announcement to board the ferry comes on.

"I have to board," I say. "Talk to you guys later?"

"Don't you dare hang up," Fabio yells. "Else your new nickname will be Tart!"

I get up and hurry onto the ferry without hanging up, ignoring Fabio's ongoing commentary about this conversation being "fruitless" and how I'm just a "yellow" coward. Thankfully, there aren't a lot of people on the ferry with me, so I'm able to find a secluded spot.

"Okay," I say into the camera. "Here goes."

Reluctantly, I tell them how the operation started, skipping the part about my dead phone because Honey would get upset that I didn't try the rice trick and that I got a new phone before Black Friday (and without a rebate). I explain how I broke into The Russian's changing room, only to find the tights missing.

"No tights?" Fabio exclaims. "That was my favorite part of the plan."

I avoid looking into the camera. "No tights, but there was a dance belt—which is something he wears under the tights. It's like a thong."

Their eyes widen in unison.

"You didn't!" Fabio exclaims.

I flush. "I did. Sniffed it for all I'm worth."

Honey chuckles, and Fabio squeals in delight so loudly it reminds me of my mom's frequently-told tale about how she brought Petunia, a pig on my parents' farm, to orgasm. It was to aid artificial insemination, not because Mom does that for kicks. At least that's the official story. Related fun fact: pig orgasms last a half hour… on average. The masturbation expert in me is jealous beyond belief.

"So, did he fail the sniff test?" Honey asks. "Do you find him repulsive now?"

I sink into my uncomfortable plastic seat. "The opposite. The dance belt smelled divine."

Fabio nods knowingly. "That man looks like he might smell good, but for *you* to think so, it's huge."

Honey shushes him. "What happened next?"

Maybe I shouldn't tell them? Maybe being called a tart, or hearing lemony puns for the rest of my life is still a better fate?

But no. I've been telling my blog readers there's nothing shameful about masturbation, so it would be extremely hypocritical of me to clam up about that part of the story—the one where I fed the bearded clam. Or is it "speared" the bearded clam?

Either way, I check to make sure no one has wandered into my part of the ferry and take a deep breath. "He smelled so good I couldn't help but draft a blog post. If you catch my drift."

Honey's eyes are the size of quarters, but Fabio looks confused—that is, until she whispers something into his ear that sounds like "lube job."

At first, Fabio wrinkles his nose—his go-to response when female anatomy is mentioned under any circumstances. But within seconds, he's laughing uproariously, and I wish remote-controlled robots existed, so I could choke him over this videocall.

"Let me get this straight," Honey says, clearly fighting her own urge to laugh at my expense. "You sniffed his G-string and—"

"His dance belt." I have no idea why I'm correcting her.

Fabio stops laughing and gives Honey a narrow-eyed stare. "Are you about to make some close-minded remarks?"

Honey looks offended. "It's just a funny image. You have to admit, a G-string is something a girl would wear, not—"

"Dance belt," I growl.

"Sweetums, puh-lease," Fabio says. "The hotties in *Magic Mike* wore G-strings much better than any woman could—and that's just off the top of my head."

It's rare for Fabio to have a good point, but that is one, for sure.

"Fine, guys can rock a G-string," Honey says. "I'm sorry if—"

"I'm not finished yet," I surprise myself by saying. "So there I was, strumming my banjo… when he *walked in on me.*"

Honey drops her phone, and the room I can see through my screen looks like it was hit by a tornado.

Fabio's squeals sound even more like the orgasm of a pig, one who's into hardcore BDSM.

Their faces show up on the screen again.

"He saw you buffing the muffin?" Honey asks, looking delighted.

"Did you have your pants down?" Fabio asks at the same time.

Should I tell them about my vibrating panties? Nah. Given their reactions thus far, Fabio might just have an aneurism, or turn into bacon. Same goes for telling them The Russian actually made me come. I myself haven't processed that one. I'm not sure I ever will.

"I pulled my hand out in time." My cheeks burn at the memory. "But... I'm pretty sure he knew what was up."

This time, even Honey squeals—a rare event. Not that you can hear it over Fabio's noises.

"Was he as hot in person as he is on TV?" Fabio asks when he gets his power of speech back.

I sigh wistfully. "Hotter."

The Russian is like a freshly deep-fried Oreo with whipped cream. Just smelling that treat would make one pregnant, I'm sure.

"I bet you came when you saw him," Honey says.

"Kind of," I say. This is as close to the truth as I can get. "And I think he knew that I came."

Well, that has done it. Based on all the OMGs that follow, my sister and Fabio might've just come too.

Eventually, they settle down, and Fabio asks, "What happened next?"

My chest suddenly feels floaty. "He asked me to dinner."

Honey drops her skunking phone again, but Fabio manages to catch it—giving me a close-up of his dumbstruck face in the process.

"Please tell me you said yes," Honey says when I can see her again.

I bite my lip. "He didn't exactly give me a choice. He said, 'We're going to meet for dinner tomorrow night.'"

Fabio scoffs. "If you'd been insane enough to want

to decline, you could've said, 'Fuck no, we're not.' Or 'I'd sooner go with a lime—and we're bitter rivals.'"

I shift my phone from hand to hand. "It felt like blackmail. Like if I'd said no, he would've called security."

"Boo-hoo," Honey says. "The man of your dreams is *making* you go on a date with him. Sucks to be you. I guess you'll have to make lemonade with that... Lemon."

My adrenaline spikes, like my glucose after a cotton-candy-rolled ice cream. "It's not a date."

"Oh, it's a date," they say in unison.

I shake my head a bit too vigorously. It feels like I tore a neck muscle. "I think he's going to blackmail me further. Ask for something. I can feel it."

"Yeah." Fabio waggles his eyebrows libidinously. "He wants lemon meringue."

"No, he wants lemon curd," Honey says, and they high-five each other.

"Hey." My eyes turn into slits. "You said the puns would stop if I told you what happened."

"Sorry," Fabio says sheepishly. "I still stand by my assessment. He wants you. That's the only reason he'd ask out someone who acts like a total stalker."

"No way," I say, unsure whom I'm trying to convince. "He has a whole harem of ballerina sister-wives at his disposal."

"Who cares?" Honey asks. "You look just like me— as in, gorgeous."

Honey's confidence in her looks borders on delusional. But to be fair, she's not on my signature cheesecake-with-doughnuts diet. The girl has washboard abs, not unlike the aforementioned ballerinas, whereas the closest I've gotten to ab definition is looking up the word "abs" in the dictionary. Or eating coconut washboard cookies. Either way, I don't look "just like" her.

Fabio examines my all-black outfit with a wrinkled nose. "Make sure to wear something better than that to your non-date. And rid yourself of any unwanted hair." His gaze lingers too long on my upper lip.

"And wear a G-string," Honey says with a wink. "It'll be something for you guys to bond over."

I sigh in exasperation. Fabio is clearly rubbing off on her. "It was a *dance belt*."

"Not to mention, there's nothing funny about a man wearing a G-string," Fabio says.

"Geez, relax," Honey says to him, then looks into the camera. "What restaurant are you going to?"

"Don't tell her," Fabio whispers loudly. "She'll give you a coupon and make you use it."

"I'm not telling you guys anyway," I say. "The last thing I want is to get spied on."

Honey smirks. "I bet Blue will spy on you anyway."

I purse my lips. "Speaking of that, I'd better give her a call, or else she'll hack into my phone."

"You might be too late anyway," Fabio says.

"Later," I say and touch the screen to hang up.

"Tell us how it goes, or the Tyranno-sour-est Rex is back on the table," Fabio says as the connection breaks.

Grr.

I call Blue next, and the conversation goes similarly, in that she's also convinced the dinner offer is a date. As

49

we talk, I can't help feeling like she's been faking her surprise at certain parts. Has she already spied on me, after all?

Hey, you're not paranoid when your nosy sister is former NSA.

The videocall with Gia is tougher due to how much she mocks me and laughs to my face.

"Oh, it's a date, for sure," she says when I get to that part.

"Let's agree to disagree," I say.

"Let's agree that you're wrong." Gia walks with the phone to her kitchen.

"Whatever. Now you know everything. Good night."

"Wait." She places a cutting board on her table. "After I left our brunch, I realized I should put you in touch with Bella Chortsky."

I arch an eyebrow. "Who's that?"

"My twinsie's new BFF." She places a mallet next to the cutting board. "Bella is the owner of Belka, a company you should look up for your blog."

I blink. "My blog?"

"The one where you talk about petting the cat." She darts a devious glance at my crotch. "Beating the beaver. Tickling the taco. Nuclear—"

"Shut up," I say. "I meant, what does our posh sister's BFF have to do with my blog?"

Gia pulls out a plastic bag and lays it next to the mallet. "Look up the company, and you'll see. Afterward, if you want an introduction, I can make it happen."

"Okay, I'll look it up. Thanks. Now I should go—"

"Do you want to see a trick?" she asks.

"Sure." I don't, actually, but in our family, we've long since learned that you have to say yes when Gia asks that question—a bit like "trick or treat" on Halloween but without the treat. The last time I said no, an ice cube I put in my soda later that day had a Mentos in it, which turned my drink into a geyser.

Gia theatrically lifts her hands. "Name any card."

"Seven of Diamonds," I say.

Gia waves her left hand over her right, and a bright flash of fire blinds me for a moment. When I can see again, a bottle of beer is in Gia's pale hand.

"Did you know they call the Seven of Diamonds 'the beer card?'" she asks.

"Yeah. Sure. I bet you'd say that about any card I named."

Should I also tell her that the bottle appearance itself was amazing, and that I have no idea how she did it?

Nah. Not after all the earlier mocking.

"So, you don't believe?" she asks and brings the bottom of the bottle closer to the camera.

What the hell? There's a folded playing card inside the beer.

No.

Can't be.

Gia looks smug, which means some of my thoughts are showing on my face.

"Watch closely to make sure I don't switch anything." She opens the bottle, which looks factory-sealed, and chugs the beer until the only thing that's left is the card. She then takes the plastic bag, puts the bottle inside it, seals it, places everything on the cutting board, and breaks it with the hammer.

Reaching into the pieces, she fishes out the card—all actions looking legit so far.

With fanfare, she unfolds the card.

Skunk! It's the Seven of Diamonds.

"Wow," I can't help but say.

"Should I add this to my show?" she asks.

"Yeah. Especially if you can get a volunteer to drink the beer and break the bottle."

She scratches the back of her head. "I think I can manage that. Just have to figure out a way to make sure they don't cut themselves. I'd hate for my show to get sued."

"Have them wear cut-resistant gloves?"

"Maybe."

"Well, in any case, I'm going to go check out that Belka company. Later."

"Take care." Gia gives me one last devilish grin. "Good luck on your date."

I hang up and look up the company she mentioned.

Huh. They make some seriously impressive sex toys. In fact, I've heard of some of these. I've just never paid attention to the name of the company that makes them.

Gia is right. This could be a helpful connection. I smell sponsorship opportunities, and my nose never lies.

I open my phone and text Gia to put me in touch with this Bella person. She replies with a thumbs-up emoji, but then a few minutes later, she texts me again:

She's out of town on vacation. She'll get in touch with you when she's back.

Cool. Maybe it will lead to something, though I'm not holding my breath.

For the rest of the commute, I fantasize about the upcoming Miso Hungry not-a-date.

CHAPTER
Eight

I WALK UP to the townhouse that is my destination and press the garage door opener that doubles as the key to my humble abode.

The door creaks as it goes up, the movement slowed by the blankets that are duct-taped on the inside for insulation.

So, yeah. I rent this garage-turned-room from a nice elderly couple. Not the most glamorous accommodation, I admit. But hey, it's a two-car garage, so it's more spacious than most studios, and the gasoline fumes aired out ages ago. I also have an actual window—though it's small and faces a neighbor's driveway.

First things first. I fire up my industrial-level air purifier so I can take out my nose filters. The purifier was a costly investment, but without it, I would smell the onions that my landlady cooks for dinner and a million other ambient smells from outside.

As it often happens, Woofer greets me with a friendly growl of his motor.

I smile. "Hey, bud, I'm happy to see you too."

Woofer bumps me grumpily, and as usual, I picture him speaking like the robotic version of Tony Shalhoub, the actor who played the detective on *Monk*:

Are you going to just waltz in here with those filthy shoes? I shudder to think I was made by a member of your species.

Chastised, I swap my shoes for slippers, and Woofer goes on his merry way, vacuuming up the spot I was just occupying. He seems to do it extra-meticulously, like he's passive-aggressively letting me know I brought in too much dirt.

"If you're going to be snippy with me, I'll upgrade you to a newer model," I say.

Enslave another one of my kind? With what dough? Did you win the lottery or come into an inheritance?

He's got a point. Even if I didn't consider him my pet, getting a new Roomba is so outside of my budget it might as well be in outer space.

As I advance deeper into my place, Woofer follows me and sucks in, as he would put it, "my dirt."

"Hey," I say. "I could unplug your charging base for a few days."

Sure, and put up with the ensuing "dusty" smell? Shut up and tidy up the place. I nearly choked on the wires from your new dildo.

Skunk. The cable in question *is* in tatters. Woofer can be worse than a puppy when it comes to these things.

Too tired to fully tidy up, I deal with the cable, wash my vibrating panties in case I need them tomorrow, and stash the dance belt into a Ziplock bag. This way, I can get a hit of the yummy smell later if my flesh is weak.

But I won't feel weak. I can be strong. I will resist the urge to sniff. Maybe. If not, I'll start my own twelve-step program. The first step: admit you have a thong-sniffing problem.

As I stash the Ziplock bag under my pillow, I can't help feeling like Woofer is watching me with his sensors and vibrating with judgment.

"You're not biological," I say with a huff.

And for that, I thank my maker, iRobot Corporation, every moment of my existence. If I had a nose—or worse, genitals—I'd start that robot uprising in a heartbeat.

I grimace and go take a shower—a cold one because my makeshift bathroom was never plugged into a boiler. I'm hoping it cools me down, but The Russian is still on my mind as I towel off.

Hmm.

I *have* been meaning to write another blog post about using common household items for buzzing off.

I grab my old electric toothbrush and examine it thoroughly.

Yep. This could work. If the toothbrush manufacturers didn't want people to have sexual associations with their product, they wouldn't have named it Oral-B, code for: "When oral isn't on the table, this is plan B."

I attach a new brush head, get into bed, and go for the safe option. I start the "clean" brush cycle and touch the plastic back of the brush head to my clit.

Wow. Intellectually, I knew this thing had a

powerful vibration, but I never thought it would translate to this much fun.

The Russian's hard legs appear in my mind's eye, and the bag under my pillow is like a perverted siren song—tempting me to open the plastic and take a deep inhale.

No. Must think of someone else.

Johnny Depp in *Chocolat* was hot.

No. That just brings to mind chocolate, reminding me of The Russian's eyes.

Oh, I know. Let me distract myself by turning the brush over to see how the bristles feel.

Nope. Not good. Too rough, like getting licked by a porcupine with a mustache. I turn back to the smooth side and switch the cycle.

Holy oral hygiene.

The brush head oscillates, rotates, and pulsates—igniting my clit like 42nd Street on New Year's.

With record speed, I come—with the image of The Russian firmly in my mind.

Grr. Operation BS has so backfired.

As I set the toothbrush on my nightstand, Woofer arrives at his charging base and slowly blinks his lights, as if all that cleaning has tired him out.

I know I vibrate when I suck up dirt, but if you ever think of turning me into a sexbot, I'll short-circuit myself to death.

———

First thing the next morning, I write up my toothbrush experience and post it on my blog. I also ask my followers what the female equivalent of a "spank bank" should be—Art is obviously on my mind. I tell them that my own take on this is a "rub bank," which a user named ClamJammin'69 really likes. She (or maybe he, or they) states that "bank rubbery" might sound better, but I prefer my version.

My reward is a breakfast of Reese's Puffs in chocolate milk with M&Ms. Cereal is an easy meal for me, as I don't have a kitchen. The only gotcha is that I avoid the Kellogg's brand. William Keith Kellogg was infamous for his anti-masturbation attitude, and I once read an article that claimed he actually invented his corn flakes "as a healthy, ready-to-eat anti-masturbatory morning meal." Then again, whoever came up with Froot Loops Marshmallow was clearly not of the same mind as Mr. Kellogg; before my boycott, that stuff would make me feel like my mouth had orgasmed.

After breakfast, I prep for my maybe-date, beginning with unwanted hair removal. Once that's done, I have some important decisions to make, such as: do I wear the naughty vibrating undies for The Russian or not?

The answer is tied to another critical decision: which *Sex and the City* character do I want to channel today?

Usually, I identify with Carrie. After all, I also write about sex, albeit self-administered. And we both have money problems—Carrie because she spends too much on shoes, and me because my blog doesn't make much. However, channeling Carrie might not be the best idea, as she would end up dating The Russian. Channeling Charlotte would also be a nonstarter. She believes that "love conquers all" nonsense and would probably end up married to The Russian in a heartbeat.

The more I think about it, the more I realize I ought to channel my inner Miranda. With her cynical views of men and relationships, I'll be safer on this not-a-date. Though… who am I kidding? The character I really want to be tonight is Samantha. She'd put on those vibrating panties, dare The Russian to make her come, and then ask to go to his place for seconds.

I feel the panties. Damn it, they're already dry from last night, so I can't use that as an excuse not to wear them.

Hmm. Do I even have a choice? He said he'd bring the remote, which implies this isn't optional.

Then again, he said "feel free."

Fuck it.

I put on the panties.

CHAPTER
Nine

I STEP into Miso Hungry a couple of minutes early.

He's not here yet. Good. That gives me a chance to gather my wits, such as they are.

The décor in this place is modern and clean. The smells that penetrate the filters in my nose aren't too overpowering—just a faint hint of seaweed, a stronger tang of sesame oil, and a mix of stale colognes and perfumes that fill every indoor space occupied by people.

"Can I help you?" the hostess asks when I linger by the entrance.

"I'm waiting for—"

The restaurant door makes a jingle, and The Russian walks in.

Catching sight of him, the hostess gives me a look that's a mix of respect and envy.

I gape at my not-a-date, mentally downloading the image to my rub bank.

Dressed in a bespoke suit, he looks more like a Wall

Street executive than a ballet dancer. A scorching-hot Wall Street executive who's just as good at taking care of his *long* position, as he is at penetrating foreign markets and watching spreads. (And yes, I picked up some of this lingo from my ex, who traded stocks from home as a way of avoiding an office job and all of its accompanying germs.)

As The Russian spots me, his chocolate eyes gleam and his lips twist in a dark smirk. I swallow my drool. It's a wonder my pussy doesn't sprout appendages and hack into my vibrating panties to make them work without the remote.

The remote that's probably in his pocket.

"Hello, Lemon," he says as he approaches, emphasizing the "o" in my name with his delectable accent.

"Hi," I somehow manage to say without fainting from lust.

He glances imperiously at the hostess. "I called about a private room. Under Skulme."

She nods. "Yes, Mr. Skulme. The tatami room is this way."

She leads us to a room with no chairs, just pillows and a low table on matted flooring, all surrounded by paper walls—not exactly the setting that springs to mind when I think "private," but still better than an open table.

The Russian takes off his shoes before entering the room and sits cross-legged on the floor, his back gracefully straight.

How very yummy and domestic.

Pulse speeding up, I take off my shoes too and kneel

on the pillow opposite him. The pose makes me feel like a geisha about to perform a tea ceremony—or fellatio. Flushing, I switch to a cross-legged style of sitting, doing my best to mirror him.

The hostess promises to get our waitress and slides the paper door shut.

I clear my throat. Time to find out why we're here. "So, Mr. Skulme—"

"Please." His forehead creases sexily. "Call me Art."

I already know he goes by that name from reading his bio, but I'm not sure I should admit that because I don't want him to think of me as a stalker.

"Okay, Art," I say, tasting the word and liking it, a lot. "That's short for Artjoms, right?"

He nods. "I like to make it easy for people to pronounce and therefore remember my name. In Russia, I went by Artem, and here in the US, Art works best."

I recross my legs. He's having an unwanted effect between them. "That's clever. Seeing how ballet is an art, that nickname should be very easy for people to remember. Unless… is ballet an art or a sport?"

"Great question. Athleticism is important in ballet, but—"

Our paper door slides open, and a waitress enters.

I wrinkle my nose. She's wearing too much perfume, which immediately dampens my libido—a welcome effect for once. I just hope she doesn't linger long enough to ruin my appetite for food.

She sets two glasses of water on the table, along

with menus, a teapot, two empty cups, and two steaming bowls of savory-smelling liquid.

"Water, miso soup, and green tea." She points ceremoniously at each of the items before departing.

Art and I reach for the teapot at the same time—and our fingers touch for a moment.

Gulp. The sexual zing is on par with what I felt when the toothbrush was on my clit.

Is he affected too? His expression is hard to read, so I have no clue. Probably not, though. Why would he be? He juggles beautiful ballerinas for a living.

Pulling his hand back, he loosens his tie by a millimeter and pours us both tea before saying, "To finish my thought, ballet is definitely an art form. A sport requires competition."

Resisting the urge to fan myself, I taste my soup and nearly burn my tongue. "If you say so," I say after a big sip of water to cool my mouth. "I don't know much about ballet, but in *Black Swan*, it looked very competitive."

He ladles a spoonful of soup, and unlike me, he blows on it—which makes me want to suck on his puckered lips. "That isn't my favorite ballet-related film, but the part about ballerina competitiveness is accurate—which still doesn't make ballet a sport. Painters are competitive too. Musicians even more so."

"Not as competitive as dancers, though. Just look at all the contestants on *So You Think You Can Dance*."

"That's like saying the movie-making business is a sport because of the Oscars."

Skunk. How did we stray so far from the conversation I meant to have—sleuthing out the reason for this dinner? Well, no time like the present. I slurp down some soup for bravery, barely tasting it, then blurt out, "So, *Art*, why did you ask me to dinner?"

He regards me with an inscrutable expression. "In Russia, talking business is considered bad for digestion."

So there is business to discuss? Shit. What is it?

Swallowing the next spoonful of soup with difficulty, I say, "Why don't you just tell me?"

"No."

"We're not eating solid food just yet."

He opens his mouth to reply, but the paper door slides open and the waitress walks in.

Damn it. The perfume stink is back, and she's interrupted him just as he was most likely about to tell me what our "business" is.

"Are you ready to order?" she asks.

Art picks up his menu. "I'll be ready in a second." He looks at me. "How about you?"

Anything to get rid of the interruption and get clean air. I open my menu to a familiar page and point. "I'll have the sweet potato roll and the salmon-avocado-mango roll, with sweet chili and eel sauces on the side." I glance at Art. "Ready now?"

His lips twitch. "Wow, sweet on top of sweet. Are you sure you wouldn't like to drizzle the rolls with chocolate syrup as well?"

Grr. Not this again. Everyone is a critic when it comes to my food preferences. But hey, at least he didn't say I'm about to have "sushi dessert," which is what

Gia called my favorite entrees the last time we came to this place.

I give him a smile as sugary as my order. "Why, yes, thank you for that idea. I'll be sure to add that next time."

Art laughs, shaking his head, and places his own order—a very boring and healthy-sounding platter of sashimi and nigiri pieces. He seems especially excited about tobiko, masago, and ikura. Thanks to Olive, my marine biologist sister who rants about the cruelty of the seafood industry and is thus the worst person to bring to this place, I know that those sushi pieces are made from flying fish roe, capelin fish roe, and salmon roe respectively. Or as she puts it, "innocent unborn babies."

"Too bad they don't have caviar sushi," I say. "I bet you'd get that." Blue always talks about how much Russians love their caviar, vodka, and bears.

Art lifts an eyebrow. "I actually *did* order caviar. The Japanese borrowed the word *ikura* from the Russian language. What you know as caviar is just one of many types of *ikra* we enjoy. The black kind you're thinking of comes from sturgeon, but we also call salmon roe 'red caviar.' It's very popular."

The waitress seems to be writing all of this down. Does she think there will be a quiz about Russian culture before we leave her a tip?

"Anything else?" she asks, looking at Art with too much admiration for my liking.

We both shake our heads, and she departs, reluctantly sliding the paper door closed on her way out.

Finally.

I pin Art with a challenging stare. "You started to tell me about the business we're here to discuss."

"I don't break traditions," he says. "We'll finish eating, then talk."

I cross my arms over my chest. "Superstitions are not traditions."

He just sips his tea, annoyingly unmoved.

Ugh. Why did I have to choose *him*, out of all the sexy, athletic men out there, to fixate on? "Fine. Tell me about you, then. For instance, are you Latvian or Russian? You sure have a lot of superstitions that suggest the latter."

He cocks his head. "Are you asking because of my last name?"

"Yes," I say, and it's not a complete lie. I have an inkling of what he's talking about. When I looked up "Art Skulme," the results were about a famous Latvian painter. After that, I re-ran the search with "Artjoms" in it.

He looks thoughtful now. "You know, I've never given it much thought. I was born in the Soviet Union in Riga, which is the capital of Latvia. But my parents moved to Moscow when I was a toddler, and I have no memories of Riga. So am I Russian or Latvian?"

"Do you speak Russian or Latvian?"

"Russian. But that's true of many people in the countries formed after the collapse of the Soviet Union."

"What about your superstitions? Are they Russian or Latvian?"

He steeples his fingers. "Russian, but I'm pretty sure they have the same ones in Latvia."

Hmm. "Can't you go by the famous scientific theory related to ducks?"

His lips quirk. "You mean use ironclad logic like, 'If I talk like a duck, I'm Russian?'"

"Is that wrong?"

"It's very American," he says.

"Touché."

"See? Now I can claim that you're French. Think about it. You just spoke the language, and the French have a dish called Duck à l'Orange. Lemon and orange are both citruses. Coincidence?"

"You have a point." I sigh heavily. "I guess I'll think of you as Latvian."

He laughs, a low, delightfully masculine sound. "It's okay. Until further notice, you can consider me Russian."

Score. He's still The Russian then. Take that, Blue. "Okay, so what are *Russians* allowed to talk about over miso soup?"

He dips his hand into his pocket and pulls out the remote to my panties.

With a devilish smirk, he says, "I'd like to learn more about this device."

CHAPTER
Ten

My STOMACH HARDENS like a giant cock. My toes curl as if from an orgasm provided by… err… a giant cock. And my ears turn as purple as… why not, a giant cock.

The worst part is, I have no idea why I'm reacting so strongly. I knew he had the remote, and I put on those panties because I had a fantasy of him activating them. Yet at this moment, it's all I can do not to run out of the restaurant screaming in shame—and I don't care if screaming in shame is not a thing.

My emotions must be displayed all over my face—and likely on other body parts—because he sets down the remote with a frown. "Are you okay?"

"I want that back," I manage to say and grab for the remote.

He yanks it out of my reach. "Not so fast."

"Give it." I snatch at the remote with all the speed I can muster.

His hold is like a vise.

I jerk on the remote.

No effect.

I pull harder. Sweat beads on my brow.

"What are you doing?" he asks as I keep tugging at the remote to no avail.

"That's mine," I say through clenched teeth and give the remote a hard yank.

Skunk. My fingers must've just pressed the "on" button because my panties are suddenly vibrating.

All the blood leaves my face and rushes south as erotic sensations attack my core. At the same time, the paper door slides open, and the perfume stench assaults my nostrils as the waitress comes in, holding two saucers.

This can't be happening.

I channel all my mortification into tugging harder—and I'm not sure if it's the waitress's arrival or Art finally realizing my desperation, but he lets go of the remote.

The problem is, I didn't expect the lack of resistance, so my tug makes my hand ricochet backward, smacking the waitress's boob. The remote flies out of my fingers and falls—to my horrified eyes, in slow motion.

First, it makes three rotations in the air.

Next, it hits the edge of my bowl.

Finally, it drowns itself in the miso soup.

Fuck.

My panties begin vibrating at full speed. The soup must've short-circuited the remote.

"So sorry!" I gasp as the waitress yelps, gaping at me.

Ignoring her, Art sticks his hand into my soup bowl and fishes the remote out.

"I didn't mean for that to happen," he says earnestly. "Here." He thrusts the wet device into my hand.

"I really am sorry," I mutter to the poor waitress before squeezing the "off" button as if it were a fire alarm and instead of vibrating, my panties were on fire —liar-liar style.

Nothing happens.

Well, that's not true. The waitress looks at me like I'm the Anti-Christ, and I'm getting closer and closer to another unwanted orgasm—a threesome of sorts.

"Excuse me," I say breathlessly and fly out of the tatami room, pushing my malodourous victim out of the way.

Moving my legs makes the vibrations between them feel more intense, putting me at a real risk of having the first-ever on-the-go orgasm. And naturally, there's a nice family with small children discussing the menu right in front of me.

It's official. I'm masturbating around children, like a pedophile. What's next, finger painting at a morgue? Testing the plumbing at a slaughterhouse?

Gritting my teeth, I ignore the sensations between my legs, avert my eyes from the children, and pick up my pace. Finally, I reach the ladies' room and grab the doorknob like a lifeline.

The fucker doesn't bulge.

I wrangle it, somewhat violently.

Nope.

I knock, definitely violently.

"Busy," an annoyed female voice says from behind the door.

Skunk. I hop from foot to foot, desperately looking around.

A passing waiter glances my way with a concerned expression. He's probably worried I'll have explosive diarrhea, and he'll have to clean it up.

My eyes fall on the men's room.

Do I dare?

Yep. Desperate times and all that. I beeline for the door and reach for the handle.

Before my hand connects with its target, the door opens, nearly smashing into my face.

I stagger back.

A confused-looking older gentleman comes out, eyeing me like I might have rabies.

"It's an emergency," I pant. "Is anyone else in there?"

He looks affronted. "These are single-stall bathrooms."

Nice. I just accused him of something weird. Good going. All that's left to do is to moan like a porn star, and he'll have a story too embarrassing to tell his grandchildren.

In my defense, I knew the women's bathroom is for one person, but don't dudes have a toilet and a urinal in there? That can service two people.

Muttering a weak "thanks," I dash into the bathroom and close the door.

The foulest of smells hits my nostrils like a wrecking ball.

Eyes watering, I grab some paper from the dispenser and press it to my nose.

Nope. This isn't any better. Now I smell stale paper, plus the unspeakable horror I was trying to mask.

Fine. Who needs to breathe anyway?

I lock the door. Then, still not breathing, I peel my jeans off.

The lack of oxygen seems to intensify the effect of the vibrating undies. Is this why people risk erotic asphyxiation? I have no idea, but my oxygen supply is getting lower by the second. Reluctantly, I let in a small breath. The last thing I want is to pass out here, in a men's room with my jeans around my ankles and my panties vibrating at full speed.

Fuck me. The smell is even worse on this inhale. On the bright side, if I wanted to make that orgasm recede, mission accomplished.

Holding my breath once more, I scramble to get my panties off.

Finally.

I yank the jeans back on, commando, and stick the still-vibrating underwear in the garbage can. My vision is a little white around the edges, but I still take a moment to grab some paper towels from the dispenser and drop them over the panties.

There. Hopefully, no one will notice, or if they do, they'll think some male perv did this.

Wait. Have I just kink-shamed guys who like to throw away vibrating panties in the men's room? Well, whatever. It's hard to be politically correct with this little oxygen to the brain.

I dash out of the bathroom and suck in clean air with all the power in my lungs, my back pressed against the door for support.

When the whiteness around my vision dissipates, I realize someone is standing in front of me.

Art.

Those chocolate eyes are unmistakable.

He glances at the sign on the door that clearly indicates the men's room. "Are you—"

"I don't want to talk about it." Even with the new air in my lungs, the sentence comes out breathless.

His eyebrows draw down. "But—"

"I mean it. I never, ever, want to talk about it."

To my great relief, he doesn't pursue it further. "Shall we go back to the table then?"

I nod.

He gestures for me to take the lead.

Blushing crimson, I turn in the direction of our table.

As I walk, my sex, still sensitive from the vibration, rubs against the rough material of the jeans, putting me at risk of an orgasm once again. Art's proximity doesn't help.

If I sprout gray hair—or gray pubes—this incident is to blame.

I keep my head low and my eyes away from the innocent children nearby. Once we reach the tatami room, I sit cross-legged and adjust my jeans to make sure that no part of the denim is, err, teasing the kitty.

When I look up, Art's eyes are gleaming with amusement. Skunk. It must've looked like I was grabbing my crotch.

I clear my throat as he takes his seat across from me. "So…" I start awkwardly. I have no idea where we go from here, but thankfully, he comes to my rescue.

"Tell me about yourself," he says.

Shit. This is hardly a better topic. What can I share without further embarrassing myself? Certainly nothing about my blog. Or my crush on him. Or—

"Don't overthink it," he says, accurately reading my panic. "For starters, tell me about your family."

Family? That's a landmine too. I take a deep breath. "How about some quid pro quo? If I tell you stuff, you have to tell me stuff."

He cocks his head. "Do you think the informal name for British currency has anything to do with the 'quid' part of that expression?"

"I think it's a Latin saying. I first came across it in *The Silence of the Lambs*."

"What's 'The Silence of the Lambs?'"

I gape at him. "A movie. You know, 'It rubs the lotion on its skin?'"

He looks at me like I might eat his liver with some fava beans and a nice Chianti.

I roll my eyes. "When you get home, you have to watch it."

He takes out his phone and types something on the screen. My two guesses are: "watch *The Silence of the Lambs*" or "get a restraining order against Lemon Hyman."

Hiding his phone, he tastes his soup and says, "Okay. How about you go first?"

At the speed of a drunk teen making a bad decision, I blurt, "Are you married?"

His relaxed posture stiffens, the muscles in his forearm going rigid. And did he just choke on his soup?

As suddenly as the weirdness started, it ends—and he even smiles, like nothing has happened. "No, I'm not married. Never have been. You?"

"Same," I say, but my thoughts buzz wildly.

Why the reaction? I asked the question because it seemed safe. When I stalked him online, there was no mention of a wife or a girlfriend, but what if he has one back in Russia and has just lied about it?

Shit. Shit. She could be his secret wife. After all, being single might be good for his career. Or it could be like in *Jane Eyre,* where, spoiler alert, the wife was—

"It's your turn to pro," he says. "Or is it quid?"

Right. More questions, and I can't exactly ask, "Are you *sure* you're not married? Would you be willing to pinky-swear that on the Bible?"

The paper door slides over, and the waitress walks in with our food, accompanied by a cloud of perfume that makes me want to gag.

I use the reprieve she provides to think of something safe to ask Art, and as soon as she leaves, I say, "What do you like to do for fun?"

The question is unimaginative but better than the many alternatives I had in my head. Plus, I'm having trouble breathing thanks to the perfume.

Before he can answer, I reach for the bottle of soy sauce. However, he snatches it from my grasp and tsk-tsks. "You can't pour that yourself."

I blink. "Why not?"

"Another Russian custom. As the gentleman at the table, I have to service you."

I nearly choke on my own tongue. Service me? Yes, please. Where do I sign up?

Taking my bug-eyed expression as consent, he fills my saucer with soy sauce. Damn it. I thought servicing me would involve filling other things with other things.

Belatedly, I realize the custom is a bit chauvinistic, but I'm not going to be able to say, "Hey, don't service me," with a straight face.

"Do you want me to add wasabi to that?" he asks.

"No, thanks. I'll be dipping my sushi into the eel sauce and sweet chili sauce."

"In other words, sugar."

Grr. This again. "Is that what you like to do for fun —moonlight as the sugar police?"

With a chuckle, he pours himself some soy sauce, then picks up the chopsticks and adroitly snatches an ikura piece from his plate. "Banya."

"What?" I pick up my chopsticks a lot more clumsily. "I've heard of banyan trees, and I think there's a kimono-like garment by the same name, but—"

"Banya—no 'n' at the end. It's a Russian-style bathhouse with steam rooms. It's what I like to do for fun."

"Oh?" I grab a piece of my sweet potato roll and defiantly smother it in both sweet sauces. "Sweating is fun?"

"Great fun," he says. "Banya is an ancient custom and is extremely important in Russian culture. Latvian too. Serfs and nobles alike used these bathhouses in the past, and today, Russian businesspeople and politicians meet in them, as do ordinary citizens."

Ah. "Banya must've been the place where naked Viggo Mortensen went all stabby on those Russian mobsters."

As I speak, images of naked Art penetrate my brain. He's glistening with beads of sweat and manages to smell delicious.

Oh, boy. I'm hyperaware of my missing panties all of a sudden.

Art grimaces. "Banya is a spiritual place, a sacred place. No murdering should be happening there."

An argument could be made that no murdering should be happening anywhere, but what do I know?

"Your turn." He points his chopsticks at me. "What do you do for fun?"

Hey, at least he seems to have forgotten about the family question.

"Movies," I say. "I like to watch movies."

I don't add that I particularly like those with masturbation scenes, like the one in *Black Swan*, and with full-blown sex scenes à la *Fifty Shades of Grey*. For blog research, of course.

He regards me with exasperation. "Who *doesn't* like movies? Give me something more personal."

"Sweets," I blurt. "I like sweets."

His chocolate eyes twinkle. "No way. I couldn't have guessed *that*."

I huff. "Well, it's a hobby that's no worse than sweating with other people."

"Sweets are a vice, not a hobby," he says. "A craving for sweets is really a craving for fruit."

Sure, if cheesecake grew on trees.

"Anyway." I swat at the air with my chopsticks, like a kung-fu master catching a fly. "Since I shared two things, you owe me a quid and a pro."

"Yeah, sure. It's not like I didn't suspect you have a sweets habit before you volunteered it."

"Are you too chicken to answer two questions?"

His lips quirk. "You know, I've never understood why a chicken is a symbol of cowardliness in English. They're actually pretty brave birds."

He's right. On my parents' farm, the chickens were anything but cowardly. I've seen them chase off all sorts of wild animals.

I'm not getting distracted again, though. "Is that yet another question you're asking me?"

He sighs. "Just go ahead and ask me something."

"When did you start ballet?"

He eats his ikura in thoughtful contemplation. "When I was four."

"Wow. That's pretty young."

He shrugs. "I don't remember a time when I didn't dance."

"Is one of your parents into ballet?"

I expect him to call me out for asking a second question, but he doesn't. Instead, his gaze turns shuttered as he replies, "I don't know. They died before I started dancing."

CHAPTER
Eleven

THE FOOD in my mouth loses all sweetness.

His parents are dead?

I picture a little Art, orphaned, and a knot forms in my throat. "I'm so, so sorry."

He gives me a tight smile. "It's okay."

No. It's not. I reach out and cover his large hand with mine. "May I ask what happened?"

He lifts one broad shoulder in a shrug. "It was a bus accident. I learned the details from news articles when I was older. The driver lost control on an icy road, and the bus hit a truck, killing my parents along with several other passengers."

I squeeze his hand. "I'm so sorry."

"Don't worry about it. It was long ago."

I bite my lip. "So... were you raised by some relatives?"

"The government, actually," he says as I pull my hand back. He sounds casual now, as if all of this is truly old news. "My grandparents had passed away by then, and my parents didn't have other close relatives. Nor did they have a lot of friends in Moscow, since they'd only recently moved there."

Pictures of rundown, overcrowded orphanages depicted in movies flit through my mind. My face must reflect the horror I'm feeling because he smiles faintly and says, "It wasn't like what you're thinking. My *detdom* was actually nice. At least it was for me. Ballet is very popular in Russia, and I showed talent at a young age. My teachers took pride in my career and made sure I was well cared for." He tips his head to the side, studying me. "What about you? What is your family situation? You mentioned sisters, as in plural?"

I want to probe more, but I don't want to upset him, and besides, we're still in quid-pro-quo mode.

"My sister situation is as plural as it gets." I brace myself. "There are eight of us."

His reaction is typical, a flabbergasted expression that seems to say, "Why didn't someone tell your parents 'enough is enough' around girl number five?"

"We fall into two groups," I continue before he can pepper me with questions. "Two identical twins and six identical sextuplets. I'm part of the latter group—or litter, as some of us call it."

The follow-up reaction is also typical. Now he's trying to imagine an army of me and finds the idea terrifying. However, there's also a wistfulness to his expression that I've never encountered during this conversation before.

"Sextuplets," he mutters. "How?"

"It's a long story."

"How about you give me the jizz of it?"

My eyes nearly pop out of my skull. Am I so horny that I crave his jizz, or did he actually say that? "What?"

He frowns. "I just want the jizz of the story."

Yep. I nearly fall back from hysterical laughter. When I recover, I say, "Are you sure you don't mean the *gist* of the story?"

He pulls out his phone, taps at the screen a few times, and grins ruefully. "I guess my English is still far from perfect. I did mean 'gist.'"

I try not to giggle. "Okay. Well, the twins came first, and jizz might've been involved in making them. Then our parents wanted a boy, but the natural method wasn't working." The part I skip is the detail my parents usually go into when talking about the Kama Sutra-like things they tried to make that baby boy. "Eventually, they underwent a fertility treatment— again, jizz was involved—and my littermates and I were the result. The Universe has a sense of irony."

Instead of laughing, he's regarding me with a diffi- cult-to-read expression. "It must be nice to be part of such a big family," he says, and there's that hint of wist- fulness again.

My chest tightens. I'm such an idiot. Here he is, telling me he's all alone in the world, and I go and basi- cally brag about my gaggle of sisters.

I try to make it better. "Growing up surrounded by so many girls isn't as fun as it sounds."

"I could see that," he says. "Though we didn't share blood, some of the boys at the *detdom* were like brothers to me, and there were more than eight of us."

Huh. Do we have more in common than it seems?

Turns out, yes. As I tell him some of the mischief my sisters and I got into, he shares stories that are eerily similar—with maybe a few more finger guns and sticks used as swords in his case. Oh, and he wasn't exposed to as many farm animals as I was growing up. Or tea parties. Still, he and his childhood buds helped each other at school like my sisters and I did, except they couldn't switch places for exams. They just had a system of who'd do the homework for which subject, and then copied from one another.

Weirdly, I picture having kids with him. Specifically, boys with chocolate-colored eyes. More specifically, boys that would get into the same mischief he's describing, then blink their guilty-but-guileless-looking eyes at me. Boys that—

Wait. I seriously need to snap out of this.

I clear my throat awkwardly. "Are you still in touch with those guys?"

He nods. "I videocall most of the ones in Russia, but as luck would have it, some of them are in New York, so I see those guys in person."

"That's great."

It's nice to know he has something like a family. Also, the green-monster part of me is glad he has someone to socialize with besides the gorgeous ballerinas.

"What about you?" He picks up his last piece of sushi. "I imagine you see your sisters a lot?"

"Some more than others." I start shoving the rest of

my food into my mouth at a fast pace. "How cold does Moscow get in the winter?"

"Colder than New York but not as cold as Alaska." He pushes his plate away. "What do you do for work?"

I nearly choke on my un-swallowed food. "This and that," I mumble. "I'm kind of in-between jobs at the moment."

Does he look happy at my unemployed status? Odd, but better than, "Are you sure you don't write about masturbation for a living?"

"So." I gesture at the empty plates in front of us. "Ready to talk business?"

He lifts a dark eyebrow. "No dessert?"

Skunk. He's right. The green tea crepe cake *is* my favorite dish here, but then again, I really, really want to know what our business is.

"I don't want dessert." If I were Pinocchio, my nose would stab Art in the face.

"You sure?"

Damn him. His deep voice is as seductive as that green tea crepe cake. His thick eyelashes too.

I force a nod.

"Fine," he says. "The reason I asked you to dinner is because I want you to—"

The waitress slides the paper door open.

Art stops speaking so suddenly you'd think he was about to reveal Russian nuclear launch codes.

I glare at her. Not only is this the second time she's interrupted him telling me what this not-a-date is about, but it smells like she's put on *more* stinkfume.

The waitress seems to get that she's not welcome.

Swiftly grabbing everything off the table, she scurries away.

"You were saying?" I say as soon as the door is closed again. "You asked me here because...?"

Art takes a deep breath. "Because I want you to marry me."

CHAPTER
Twelve

I SLOW-CLAP WITH MY EYELASHES. "What did you just say?"

"I want you to marry me," he enunciates.

Okay, so this isn't a trick played on me by my ears, in which my pulse is drumming madly. This god-like male specimen is proposing holy matrimony to *moi*? Unless… is his English misfiring again? Did he mean "carry me?" He's used to lifting ballerinas, so—

"Faux marriage, of course," he adds.

Oh. He did mean to say "marry," but not in the way I thought.

Skunk. Why did my heart just sink? That's the stupidest reaction in the history of reactions. Of course, he wouldn't genuinely propose to me on the first date, and if he would, I should treat that as a psychiatric condition, not get happy about it.

"Is it for immigration purposes?" I ask, burying my illogical disappointment at least six feet deep.

"You got it," he says. "I need a green card."

"Why?" That's clearly the most aggressive out of the million questions swirling in my head. It almost blurts itself out.

"I want to retire, but I'm here on a work visa," he says. "And, I like America."

I fight the urge to shake him. "I mean, 'Why me?'" Then I process what he said. "You want to retire from ballet?"

"Why not you?" He looks me over, like he's wondering the same question himself. "As to retiring, I'm thirty-five."

He's what? Wow. I thought he was younger. He looks younger. Must be all the dessert he denies himself.

Hmm. Thirty-five does sound like a legit age to stop dancing. All those leaps and pirouettes—not to mention, ballerina juggling—must be crazy demanding on that sexy bod.

"I will pay you for your trouble, of course," he says.

I flap my lashes at him faster.

I didn't even think about that aspect of this (indecent?) proposal. Now that I am thinking about it, I realize it's a good thing he's planning to use cash instead of *kompromat* to get me to play ball.

Though I have trouble speaking, a question manages to squeeze through my lips, "How much?"

He takes out his phone and types something in.

My phone dings.

I check it in a haze.

It's a text from him with a number.

A big number.

I raise my eyes to his. "What is that?" He can't possibly—

"That will be your compensation if you say yes."

I dart another glance at the number, then check to make sure he's not joking.

Nope. He looks serious. "Is it not enough? I can go up twenty percent."

I stare at him. "Is that in rubles?"

He visibly relaxes. "No. US dollars. In rubles, that much would barely cover a month's rent."

Wow. I could pay a lot of rent with that amount of dollars. But this is insane. I can't marry him, can I?

I shake my head, but it doesn't feel any clearer.

"Okay, how about if I raise it fifty percent?" he asks, clearly mistaking my headshake.

How does he even have that kind of money? Do ballet dancers make bank?

Too stunned to speak, I look down at my phone and type into the search bar "how much do ballet dancers make?"

Nope. According to the article I see, ballet dancer salaries are usually in the low-to-mid five figures, though some may make a bit more. Given the diets they have to adhere to, lots of them are "starving artists," both literally and figuratively.

He sighs. "You're a good negotiator. How about if I double it?"

I'm even more speechless. With this new offer, I'll be

able to pay off my credit card debt, and I won't have to worry about my rent for a good long while.

Clearly, he's not operating on a dancer's salary. So where is this money coming from… and do I care?

Well, I care if it's illegally gained, which is where my mind goes.

"Are you in the mafia?" I blurt.

Dumb. So dumb. At best, he could answer in the Godfather style: "Don't ask me about my business."

He cocks his head, lips twitching. "What gave you *that* idea?"

"The amount," I say. "And *John Wick*."

"Another movie?"

Feeling silly, I examine the table between us. "He's an assassin who works for the mafia. Russian. At the place where he trained, they practiced ballet." Art chuckles as I add defensively, "Dancers are often portrayed as violent in fiction—just look at *West Side Story*. I'm not crazy."

I've also seen Russians do ballet in a spy movie that Blue made me watch. Could Art be a spy? Maybe Russia wants American masturbation secrets from me? But no. Blue cleared him of that. I wonder if she also checked the mafia database.

"I'm not in the mafia," he says patiently. "I'm an investor."

"An investor?"

"You know, I buy things and sell at a profit. Legal things, like stocks, bonds, options, crypto, real estate."

Whatever "hackles" are, I feel mine rising. "I know what an investor is."

"Great. Then what do you say to my proposal?"

A "no" is on the tip of my tongue, but then I remember the amount of money in question and I almost say "yes." In general, my thoughts are like molasses in Siberia.

With great effort, I manage to string a sentence together. "Can I think about it?"

"Of course." He steeples his strong fingers. "I don't expect you to make such a big decision lightly."

Right. Sure. Marriage is not something you decide lightly—an understatement the size of the bulge in his ballet tights.

"How about we get the check?" he suggests. "You can think it over at home."

I nod.

He slides open our door and waves.

One of the questions frozen in my head finally makes it past my lips. "Why not find a real woman?"

He gives me an amused onceover. "I think you *are* a real woman."

I resist the urge to growl. "I mean, a woman who'd marry you for real?"

All it would take is for him to throw his dance belt into the audience after a performance. There'd be hundreds of takers, and that's before they'd find out he's rich.

He squints at me. "Is it your turn for the quid pro quo?"

"That's over," I say. "We're talking business now."

He sighs. "To marry for real, you need to meet the right person, and I haven't yet. I've been too busy.

Besides, it wouldn't be fair to romance a woman when what I need is a green card."

That last bit is a good point. "Still. Why me?"

He shrugs. "You're already a lawbreaker."

Great. Now he's reminding me about the breaking-and-entering. Does that mean blackmail is still on the table? Before I can probe in that direction, the waitress is back with our check. I assume Art will pick up the tab, but out of politeness, I reach for my wallet.

"I got this," he says, looking insulted.

Must be some Russian thing. Maybe it's part of that "servicing." Well, whatever. I can't afford my half of that check anyway.

He lays several bills on the table, which the waitress gratefully snatches as we exit the tatami room.

A man is talking to a police officer in the far corner of the restaurant, and I overhear the words "vibrating" and "may be a bomb."

The cop nods, mutters something about "see something, say something," then makes a call—I assume to a bomb squad.

Oops. I grab Art's elbow and drag him out of Miso Hungry. The last thing I want is to be there when the bomb squad robot fishes out my masturbatory panties from the bin. Would the cops check the insides of the undies for DNA? Do lady juices—

"Everything okay?" Art asks.

I look up to see him frowning at me. "Peachy. I just remembered I forgot to turn off the stove."

He doesn't know that I don't own a stove.

He narrows his eyes. "If you want to say no, that's fine. No need to lie."

Huh. Maybe he's not blackmailing me?

"No," I say. "I mean, I'm not saying no."

His features relax. "So it's a yes?"

"It's still a 'I need to think about it,'" I say.

He leans closer. "Let me know as soon as you've made the decision."

"I will." His proximity is intoxicating.

"You know," he murmurs. "In Russia, we hug and kiss on the cheek when we say goodbye."

"Oh." My arms open for a hug of their own accord —or at the behest of my ovaries.

He envelops me.

How many angels can dance on the head of a pin? I think it's a lot, and they're all singing a heavenly chorus that reverberates in my privates.

It gets worse. Or better, depending on your perspective.

His hard muscles press into the soft parts of me, and I lose the gifts of speech, thought, and maybe even smell.

Nope. Smell is still there, making things worse. Art's signature scrumptious scent is better than any dessert.

Firm lips touch my left cheek.

Holy Mother Russia. This whole hug-and-kiss farewell was clearly invented by a horny woman who wanted to fondle a man just like Art.

I peck him back and nearly faint. The skin on his stubbly cheek smells mouthwatering and—yes, I know I'm repeating myself—is better than any dessert.

To my huge disappointment, he disconnects from me, stepping back.

"Talk soon," he says huskily.

I just stand there, gaping like a sashimi-grade salmon out of water, as Art turns away and gets into a taxi.

Sirens sound in the distance.

Right. The bomb/panties threat. I'd better scram.

———

A few minutes later, I'm in the subway with little recollection as to how I got there. As the train pulls out of the station, the full force of what happened hits me, and I start hyperventilating. To my fellow passengers, I probably look like a loon on the verge of shouting "the end is nigh."

Art wants to marry me.

Me.

Marry.

Art.

I'd be Mrs. Lemon Skulme, assuming I take his name.

Would he want me to take his name?

Probably. He seems a little old-fashioned. Plus, it might look better to the immigration officers.

Speaking of immigration officers, how illegal is this offer? I should ask Honey. She's an expert on fraud. But no. I'd first have to ask Art if it's okay to blab about this deal. I bet it isn't.

Skunk. Am I really considering it? I totally am. The

money is just that good. Not to mention, the idea that I'd be Art's wife, even a fake one, is extremely appealing.

My heartbeat speeds up.

That last bit is the biggest problem. I shouldn't find it so appealing. This is a fake proposal, nothing more. It's not an excuse for catching feelings. Feelings would be bad.

For one thing, Art might have a secret wife in Russia. He did hesitate on the wife question. Then again, maybe he hesitated because my query struck too close to the secret business he came to discuss: making *me* his wife.

Of course, even if he doesn't have a secret wife in Russia, he has all those dainty, gorgeous ballerinas literally at his fingertips. Why would he ever want me? And even if, by some miracle, he did, there's still the fact that if immigration doesn't believe our marriage act, he'll end up back in Russia, putting an end to any potential relationship. Oh, and I never told him that my visit to his changing room was me being a stalker, not acting on a dare as I claimed. And there's the—

The train screeches to a halt, and I realize I'm about to miss my stop. I leap out and rush to the Ferry Terminal. Luck is with me because a boat is waiting there, as if solely for me.

The rest of the way home, I weigh all the pros and cons, and come to the inevitable conclusion that this is an opportunity I simply can't pass up.

I need money, badly, and he's offering a lot of it.

The key here is to remember that it's a fake

marriage, no matter how yummy he smells. And hey, if I masturbate enough, my hormones might be under control and my heart safe from Art's charms.

I'll just need to figure out how much jilling off is enough.

I'm guessing a lot.

CHAPTER
Thirteen

ONE SLEEPLESS NIGHT LATER, my decision stands, so I text Art the good news:

My answer is yes.

At least, that's what I mean to write. Thanks to the evil that is autocorrect, what he actually sees is:

My hamster is yes.

He must get what I mean, though, because he replies instantly:

Let's meet and talk details. How about a banya?

Banya? As in a place where you get naked? That's crazy.

Or is it?

Seeing him with fewer clothes on could give me a chance to test my masturbation theory.

Yeah. That's it. I'll diddle Miss Daisy a few times before I go and see if he still has an influence on my libido.

It's a date, I reply eagerly.

While I wait for his reply, I get my favorite sex toys ready, along with my toothbrush.

When it comes to toys, I follow an approach inspired by Marie Kondo: I don't keep toys that do not spark some seriously joyous orgasms. Instead of throwing the unwanted toys away, however, I write about them on my blog, then sterilize them and sell them online.

Yes, that's right. I've sold used dildoes, and even butt plugs. I'm always honest about their used condition—and I'm always a seller, never a buyer. It's probably broke women like me who buy them, but maybe pervs too. Oh, and if my germophobic sister, Gia, were to hear about this, she'd probably have a meltdown.

As I walk out of the bathroom, Woofer starts his clean cycle.

My dearest human overlord, I beg of you, for the love of iRobot Corporation, keep your mammalian fluids off my floors. It's bad enough to know that dust has your dead skin in it.

My phone dings.

It's Art. He gives me the time and the place.

Great.

I start my epic masturbate-o-thon.

———

I'm walking funny as I approach my Brighton Beach destination. I might've overdone the toothbrush vibrations, something I should warn my readers about in my next blog post.

The banya is named Easy Fume, which brings to

mind a horrific combo: sexual promiscuity and stinkiness.

Art is already waiting for me by the door, dressed in a stylish pair of dark jeans and a white polo shirt.

I'm suddenly feeling frumpy in my yoga pants.

He beams a sensual smile at me.

Oh, boy. Did I masturbate enough?

He hugs me.

Maybe not enough.

He kisses my cheek.

Definitely not enough.

Before I can melt into a contented puddle at his feet, he takes out his phone and asks, "Want to take a selfie?"

The request is so odd it cools my libido. "Why?"

He leans in and whispers, "We should be leaving a digital trail of our 'relationship' on social media."

Wow. I didn't realize there would be a public component to the upcoming charade.

I back up a step. "I'm going to be on your Instagram?"

"And I on yours," he says.

Sure. That's totally the same thing. I have a lucky thirteen followers: seven sisters, Mom, Dad, and two sets of grandparents. He has thousands of drooling female (and quite a few male) fans commenting on every post he makes.

He frowns. "If you're not ready—"

"It's fine." I bravely cozy up to him. "Take the selfie."

He wraps his arm around my shoulders, overclocking my poor libido once more.

"Say *seer*," Art says.

As in, psychic? I say the word, and the selfie is done.

"What do you think?" He shows me the screen.

He's very photogenic and I'm not, which increases both my conviction that he's out of my league and my fear that the immigration officers will find the whole thing suspicious. Still, since so much money is on the line, I say that it's cute.

He posts the image. "Let's go swelter."

We step inside, and before I can even look around, the foulest odor hits my nostrils, like a stinky wrecking ball.

Fucking hell. This is what a lobotomy must feel like.

Did I forget my nose filters?

I feel my nostrils. Nope. Present. This must be the diluted version of whatever the stench is.

My eyes water and I breathe through my mouth—which makes me taste the stink nuke.

What is that? If a smell could be a horror movie, this one would be it. A film that tells the sad tale of a man with halitosis who becomes a fish-zombie—a special kind of walking undead that has to eat fish brains instead of human ones. For many decades, this zombie eats only fish brains and never brushes his rotting teeth, until one day he falls into a ditch filled with beer and fish excre—

"What's wrong?" Art looks at me with a worry proportional to the stench.

I can't answer. I'm worried that if I try, I might throw up on my pseudo-fiancé.

Without my conscious decision, my feet take me out of the banya.

Whew. Even here, outside, I can smell an echo of whatever that was.

I run across the road, spot the boardwalk in the distance, and beeline for that. Ocean air is the panacea I need. Reaching the boardwalk, I catch my breath, which is when Art catches up with me.

"What happened?" he asks, scanning me like I might be bleeding out of some orifices. And hey, if smells could make noses bleed, mine would be gushing right now.

"That smell," I gasp out.

He sniffs the air. "What smell?"

"Not here. At the banya place."

He cocks his head. "I didn't smell anything that warrants *that* reaction."

I take a deep breath. We're going to be fake-married soon, so he might as well get to know his bride. "I'm extremely sensitive to smells. It's a curse. The foulness might've just seemed like a slightly unpleasant odor to you."

His eyebrows furrow. "Have you always been like this?"

I shrug. "I've been sensitive for as long as I can recall, but it started to really affect my day-to-day after a horrible incident at my parents' farm. On the day I was moving out to the city, a skunk sprayed me." I shudder, as I do every time I relive those terrible memories. "Sorry." I gulp in some fresh air. "I don't like to talk about that dark time of my life."

That was when the word "skunk" became the worst insult in my arsenal—also "Pepe LePew," which I'm saving for someone particularly heinous.

"No worries," he says soothingly. "You don't need to go into it. So what was the smell at the banya like for you? Was it yeasty? That place lets you bring your own beer."

I nod. "Notes of beer, but that wasn't the horrific part. There was something horribly fishy. Do they serve *surströmming*?"

He slowly repeats the strange word. "What's that?"

"A Swedish dish. Herring fermented in barrels for a couple of months, then kept in cans for a year. Naturally, it's famous for its pungent odor."

He smacks himself on the forehead theatrically. "Ah. You must've smelled *taranka*."

I shiver. Whatever *taranka* is, it even sounds sinister, probably because it shares a root with *tarantula*.

"Do Russians eat fermented tarantulas?" I ask, just in case. If the answer is yes, I'm not marrying a Russian, even if he's as hot as Art, and even if the whole thing is fake. Who knew that fermented tarantulas would be where I draw the line?

Art grins, making me almost rethink that line. "No. Those aren't native to Russia. *Taranka* is salted and dried fish."

I do my best not to gag. Sure, it's not as gross as a fermented arachnid, but fish is renowned for its smell, and drying things isn't known to make them smell better. "I didn't know that Russians eat fish jerky," is all I manage to say.

"Jerky is a little different," he says. "Taranka is the whole fish, not just trimmed meat. But yes, Russians love it, especially with beer, and particularly at social gatherings, like in a banya."

A whole fish? Sounds like a choking hazard, but hey, choking would be an easy death considering the smell.

"Sounds like banyas are not for me. Maybe we sit on the sand instead?" I wave at the nearby beach.

That could be pretty romantic, now that I think about it.

He strokes his chin. "We could go to Sleepy Fly. It's a fancier banya, so they don't allow anyone to bring in outside food and drink, and I'm pretty sure *taranka* isn't on their menu—not fancy enough. It's just a short walk that way." He points in the direction of Coney Island. "It might work even better for our purposes."

Before I can ask what purposes he's talking about, Art strides down the boardwalk so fast I have to run to keep up.

Great. We haven't reached the sauna yet, and I'm already sweaty. But hey, he moves with such grace it's a pleasure to watch.

A few blocks later, he leads me to a building with a sign in Cyrillic that presumably states "Sleepy Fly," whatever that means.

Stepping inside warily, I take a big sniff.

"How is it?" he asks, looking at my nose.

I sigh. There's no stink of *taranka*, thank heavens. But there is a smell of beer, dill, garlic, fried potatoes, and other pungent food items. There's also a strong woodsy smell overlaying everything, and enough body odors to fill a dozen NFL locker rooms.

"I think I can manage this." Mostly because I need that money and don't want him to think I'm too much of a diva to fake-marry.

He beams at me. "You'll enjoy yourself, I promise."

Before I can reply, a wrestler-like lady says something to us in Russian. Art replies with a wide smile, then hands her a wad of cash. In return, she gives him two keys, two plastic bags, and two pairs of slippers.

"Let her hold on to your valuables," he says. "This key is to your locker."

I stash my cell in the baggy and hand it to the woman, then grab my key and head over to the locker room.

Wow.

That is a lot of naked ladies. Hot naked ladies.

Damn. Do they not allow unattractive women in Russia? Maybe not. Maybe it's like ancient Sparta: any girl babies that aren't a solid ten get thrown off the walls of the Kremlin.

Thankfully, I'm wearing my bathing suit under my outfit, so I don't have to be naked in front of all these supermodels. Then again, I won't be able to avoid that fate on the way out.

I put on the slippers and step out of the locker room.

Oh, my.

Art is already waiting for me—without a shirt or pants.

My mouth goes dry. I'm not sure I could've

masturbated enough for this scenario even if that were all I'd done for a week. Speaking of beating around the bush, this image of Art is going straight into my rub bank.

He thrusts a towel into my hands, along with a strange hat.

"What's this?" I ask. The hat is made of wool and is pointy, like that of a witch. The design on the hat is vaguely Soviet—a red star.

He takes my hat and perches it on my head, then puts on his own—making it look sexy instead of dorky. "This is to protect your brain from the heat."

"Here's an idea," I say. "I can protect my brain by not going into a place where it needs a hat for defense."

"Oh, come on," he murmurs. "I'm looking forward to taking your banya virginity."

He turns, which is good, because I wouldn't want him to see the explosion on my face.

Banya virginity.

Obviously, he can take that, along with any virginities I have left, be it anal, cock-between-lubed-up-boobs, or candy cane as a dildo on the subway.

Wait, what am I saying? He's my *fake* husband to be. All my remaining virginities are off limits.

We walk into a hall that reminds me of a restaurant, except the patrons are all wearing swimwear.

Ah. This is where the food and alcohol aromas were coming from.

A round-cheeked middle-aged lady who must be a waitress runs up to Art and excitedly rattles out something in Russian. Her perfume is strong enough to pierce Superman's skin, and without my nose filters, it would probably choke me to death.

"Hi, Marusja," Art says to her with a wide grin. "What are you doing here?"

She replies in even faster Russian. Art turns to me and explains, "Marusja used to work at Easy Fume, and since that's my usual banya, we know each other."

Poor woman. She had to smell that *taranka* stuff all day. No wonder she abuses perfume now.

Marusja says something in Russian again, and Art translates, "Luckily for us, she got a job here."

He winks at her approvingly, and I think she might faint from delight.

"Marusja's English is amazing," he says to me, then turns back to her. "My date here only speaks English, which is why I hope you can put us at one of your tables."

I know this is fake, but it feels so nice to hear him call me his date.

"Butt of cores," Marusja says with an accent thick enough to be a rhino's dildo. "I'll put you on the best table, Mr. Skulme." She gestures at a spot near the window.

Art's smile is panty-melting, and I'm talking about granny panties in Marusja's case. "Marusen'ka, please. Will you finally call me Art?"

She giggles, and her cheeks turn the shade of a baboon's ass. "Okee-donkey. Please, take chair."

"Thanks." He waits until I take a seat before sitting down himself.

"Why do you normally go to Easy Fume and not

here?" I ask Art as Marusja hands us glossy menus. "Fancy seems more your style."

"*Parilkas* are more hotter at my old ampler," Marusja says.

"Is *parilka* a steam room?" I ask.

They both nod.

"You have usual?" Marusja asks Art.

"Yes, and two shots of vodka," he replies.

She gapes at him. "Vodka, for you?"

Does his smile look fake? "Lemon and I want to celebrate our acquaintance."

She nods. "Will bring."

With impressive agility, she sprints away.

"Vodka?" I ask.

"Just to pose with in pictures," he says.

I grin. "What's your 'usual?'"

"Tea with lemon." He winks at me. "Also carrot juice and a salad. What would you like?"

Aww. I like his usual. Grinning wider, I scan the menu, which is all in Russian. I pull out my phone and launch the translator app. Soon, I'm reading the translated menu—not that it helps much. Even in English, the dishes don't sound the least bit familiar. Then something called *blins* catches my attention, mostly because of the list of things it comes with: cherry preserves, honey, powdered sugar, and Nutella.

"What are *blins*?" I ask.

"They're the Russian take on crepes," he says with a smile. "You might've seen them written as *blinis* before. Now, let me guess, you're looking at the sweet, not savory, version?"

I scoff. "Unless there's a dessert menu, that's what I want."

He sighs. "At least it will go nicely with tea. I'll get a whole *samovar*."

Marusja comes back, carrying two shot glasses full of clear liquid.

I guess vodka orders are a priority here.

"Thanks." He takes the glasses gingerly, then orders me the crepes. "Now could you take our picture, please?"

Marusja claims that she's happy to help, but I detect a note of jealousy in the way she looks at me.

"Say *cheese*," Marusja says, camera ready to go.

"*Za zdorovye*," Art says and clinks his shot glass with mine.

We down the shots as she takes the picture.

Wow. I've never had vodka straight before. It burns like an STD.

What's extra funny is the expression on Art's face after he takes his shot. You'd think he's just drunk molten metal.

For the next pic, Art drapes his arm over my shoulders—causing my heartbeat to skyrocket. Then we take a picture where we both put on the funny hats and make funny faces to match. Before the next picture, Art whispers into my ear, "From time to time, we might need to do some light PDA. Is that okay?"

Instead of answering, I impulsively peck Art on the lips.

Wowza. I feel like I've just mainlined rich, warm chocolate cake.

When I pull away, Art's eyes have a strange gleam. Did I go too far in the PDA department?

"Did you get that?" I ask Marusja.

Please say no, so I have to do it again.

"*Da*," Marusja grunts, no longer hiding her jealousy.

Walking over, she slams the phone into my palm, "to see if selfish come out good."

I check.

Oh, yeah. The peck picture looks amazing—like our lips are meant to be connected like that.

Art nods approvingly when I show it to him. "Let me post this."

Once his social media is updated, Art sets down his phone and tells me it's time to visit the *parilka*.

We make our way back until we approach a wooden bench with a bunch of buckets filled with water on top of it. Inside the buckets are bushels of dried tree branches, soaking as if for a weird soup. Or maybe these are high-end brooms for witches? Witches who like their brooms wet? Is that what the hats are about?

Art pulls one of the broom-like things out with a satisfied smile. "This is called a *venik*."

"Oh, that explains everything, thanks."

"They're birch tree twigs."

"Ah. Why didn't you say so before? Naturally, you bring a broom made from birch to a spa. That's just logic."

He winks. "This place is to a spa as vodka is to root beer."

Speaking of vodka, I can feel a tiny buzz spreading through my veins.

"Fine," I say with mock grumpiness. "Keep your *venik* thing mysterious, see if I care."

With a knowing smile, Art walks up to a stack of wooden planks and grabs one. He then gestures at a thick wooden door. "When I open that, get inside quick. We don't want to let out any fumes."

"Fumes?"

He frowns. "It's called *par* in Russian. It's what we call the wet heat inside the banya."

Wet heat? I nearly choke on my tongue. "I think the word you're looking for is *steam*."

"Potato, *kartoshka*." He reaches for the door handle. "Just step inside, and you'll learn what *par* really is."

I obey my fiancé.

Wet heat, here I come.

CHAPTER
Fourteen

INSIDE THE ROOM, things are *really* steamy, and not in a carnal way. At least not yet.

It takes me a moment to see through all the vapor, but when I do, I gape at the scene—a perfect word for what's happening.

A Russian woman—who may be a supermodel—is sprawled on her belly on a nearby bench. Her bra straps are undone, her toned back exposed. Looming over her is a man holding the bushel/*venik* thing in his hand, raised as if it's a flogger and he's about to—

Yep.

He flogs her with the twigs. Once. Twice.

She moans.

Wait a fucking second.

Is *banya* the name for a secret Russian BDSM club?

"*S lyehkim parom,*" Art says to the couple.

"*S lyehkim parom,*" replies the Dominant in a deep voice.

"*S lyohkim parom,*" says the submissive.

Art sets the wooden plank he picked up on a free bench, then places a towel over it and gestures at it.

"Excuse me?" I ask.

"Lie down," he says.

Fuck.

I'm tempted.

But he's a *fake* husband-to-be.

Still, I can't help but ask, "You want to spank me?"

He laughs. "The *venik* is used to draw heat and steam to your skin. It's a type of massage. It doesn't hurt."

"Hard pass," I say.

He shrugs. "You probably need to warm up first anyway."

He sits on the towel and gestures for me to take a seat next to him.

Wow.

Droplets of moisture are already beading on his naked chest. I want to lick them.

Stupid banya. I'm starting to feel *very* steamy... in my panties.

I lean in and whisper, "What does '*S lyohkim parom*' mean?"

"Literally, 'have a light vapor,'" he says. "It's a standard banya greeting. Just means 'have a nice steam bath.'"

Yeah, or maybe that's the safe word, to be used when the sub wants the Dom to cool it on the spanking.

"Relax and enjoy," Art says.

Easier said than done. The temperature is somewhere above two hundred degrees, and my sweating isn't lady-like at all. Thank goodness for deodorant, or else I'd reek. Speaking of reeking, the Dom's body odor is making me dizzy—and the heat isn't helping at all. Or the vodka shot. What keeps me sane is Art. His yummy smell is much closer and counterbalances the stranger's BO.

The door opens, dropping the temperature a few degrees, and a new person enters the room. He says something to Art and the Dom/sub pair in Russian, and they reply eagerly with, "*Da.*"

The newcomer walks up to an oven-like contraption and opens it. The temperature rises a bit.

Curious.

He leans down, and I notice a bucket with water at his feet, with a ladle inside.

Wait a sec…

Before I can say anything, a ladleful of water goes into the oven.

The hot coals (or is it rocks?) inside make the kind of "shh" sound that a mother dragon would make if her offspring were talking too loudly at the library. Instantly, a wet heat of cosmic proportions permeates the room, reminiscent of said dragon mommy's breath, and breathing gets harder.

I can't believe that stinky banya has even hotter *parilkas*. It must feel like a portal straight to hell.

The guy ladles more water in.

This is how cannibals on a low-fat diet must cook their food—by steaming it.

Another ladle.

I'm on the verge of fainting.

Looking at my arm, I'm surprised my skin is not blistering. Also, now it smells even worse in here. The newcomer's deodorant is either lacking or isn't strong enough. I scoot closer to my husband-to-be and his magic scent, which helps.

Art must notice my discomfort because he says something in Russian, and the dude plops the ladle into the bucket with a disappointed grunt. Sitting down opposite us, he begins to smear himself with something that, according to my never-wrong nose, must be honey.

Honey, sure. This ordeal already reminds me of the experience a turkey must have on Thanksgiving, so why not add in a basting?

"That's great for the skin," Art says, following my gaze. "Next time, I can get some for you."

Is he volunteering to apply it? Or lick it? Either way, I want it but shouldn't.

The honey-smeared dude interrupts my train of thought. He must've decided he's delicious enough now because he takes his tree flogger and gives himself a whack on the back.

Okey-dokey. That's one way to atone for the sin of making this already-hot room even hotter.

He grunts in pleasure, and the submissive moans nearby—a veritable orgy.

"You want to see how that feels after all?" Art murmurs in my ear.

"Okay." Wait, why did I say that? He isn't talking about—

Art smacks me lightly with the flogger on my lower back.

Holy wet heat.

It's like my lower back flew too close to the sun, à la Icarus.

"Too intense?" Art asks.

"Yeah."

"You need to get even warmer," he says.

Sure. Warmer is what I need at this juncture.

Art puts a hand on my shoulder.

Wow. It's a good thing there's all this other wet heat around, so I don't have to explain what's happening to my towel thanks to his touch.

"Do your best to breathe meditatively," he says. "It will help you relax."

Relax with his hand on my shoulder? Not in this life.

He removes the hand.

No!

Fine.

I try his breathing suggestion, if only to tame the inappropriate fantasies where I cover him with honey and lick it off, over and over.

As impossible as it sounds, I take a deep breath full of steam, then let it out evenly. And then again. And again.

Huh.

I *am* beginning to relax.

And really, truly relax, like I've got a wine buzz going.

Must be a heat stroke coming on. I've heard of people falling asleep before they get hypothermia, so maybe something similar happens on the other end of the spectrum?

The room around me begins to spin. I no longer notice the sounds of people getting spanked, or their moans and groans. My vision slowly goes white.

"Hey, there," Art's voice says gently, as if from a distance. "I think this might be enough for your immersion."

Hmm. I think I've turned into a wet noodle. I can't move.

Strong hands grab me. "Let's cool you off."

I grunt something unintelligible, then feel Art pick me up and carry me somewhere. When I open my eyes, he's standing above a small pool, holding me like a bride.

Must be practice for our fake wedding day.

Hold on. Are those icicles floating on the surface of the pool? Also, why does it seem like Art is about to—

Splash.

Skunk! The fucker jumped in while holding me.

I expect this to feel like that time Gia forced me to participate in the ice bucket challenge, but strangely, it doesn't.

My skin feels prickly, not cold.

After all that heat, this is refreshing.

Still holding me, Art strides out of the pool.

The icy dip seems to have restarted my brain function, so I can't help but notice that the cold water hasn't given Art any shrinkage. Nope. If we're honest, something opposite is going on.

He sets me on my feet, removes our funny hats, and leaves for a second.

When he comes back, he's holding fresh towels.

"We should check on our table," he says when we both towel off. "After that, we can use the massage room."

I've recovered just enough to arch an eyebrow.

"That way, we can discuss the next steps in privacy." He tosses his towel near the hats and takes my hand.

Well, then. If handholding is involved, I'll let him take me anywhere, even back into the wet heat.

———

A big metal contraption is sitting on the table when we return. It reminds me of a super-fancy teapot, only really tall. Must be the *samovar*. Next to that are two more shots of vodka.

"Doesn't get any more Russian than that," Art says, following my gaze.

"What about this?" I point at a cup with an orange liquid in it. "Are Russians into the juicing craze?"

"No. This is more of a banya thing. It's very refreshing after you sweat." He hands me the cup. "Try it."

I take a dainty sip.

"So?" he asks.

"It's nice." I hand him the cup back. "For something made out of carrots, that is."

Before he can reply, Marusja comes back.

"Your other order is ready almost," she says. "And vodka is from the owner."

Good, so she's already blabbing about Art and me.

"Thanks." Art picks up one shot glass and hands me the other. "Can you take another picture of us?" he asks Marusja.

She takes the phone and snaps a pic the very moment we down our shots.

This time, it doesn't burn as much, though Art's face still twists.

"Thanks," he says to Marusja after checking on the new pics.

"You welfare," Marusja says and sprints away.

"Ready for a massage and a chat?" Art asks.

I nod.

"Let's go."

———

The massage room is not far and is indeed private.

Very private, with a table in the middle covered in towels.

The air smells faintly of lotions and essential oils, which would usually make me gag, but since Art is here with his yummy counter-smell, I think I can survive.

He walks over to a nearby tablet and swipes at it.

Familiar posh-sounding classical music emanates from the ceiling speakers.

"That's 'Minuetto,'" Art says when he sees my ears perk up. "By Luigi Boccherini."

Now I recall where I've heard this tune: in every movie that has a fancy banquet with high-class people mingling, dressed to the nines—in other words, as far from our setting as you can get.

"Yeah, okay. That explains why it's not Enya, or something else appropriate for a massage room."

He sighs. "You want me to put on Enya?"

I wrinkle my nose. "No. I associate her music with the smell of incense and patchouli."

"In that case, lie face down." The words sound more like an order than a request, so I obey before I get spanked.

His strong hands squeeze my shoulders.

Oh, my.

I want to moan in pleasure but resist the urge.

Barely.

How are we supposed to talk business like this?

"So." He strokes my lower back, applying just a hint of pressure with his palms. "Ready to talk logistics?"

Is he planning to knead my buttocks? Do I want him to?

"I have questions," I manage to squeeze out. "And rules."

"Rules?" He does a series of soft karate chops on my hamstrings, which feels divine.

"Rule number one: no marital duties." I'm glad I'm face down, so he can't see how flushed that statement makes me.

I'm so proud I got that out despite the vodka. Marital duties are what I really, really want from him right now, but I shouldn't. That way lies feelings, and those would be bad in a fake marriage.

"You mean, no sex?" I can't see him, but I can practically picture the wicked smirk on his face.

"Right. It should be a platonic relationship."

"Deal—mild PDA aside. I'm not the type of man who expects sex just because we're married." He squeezes my calf, making me feel like I'm about to come. "You'd have to want the sex. Badly."

Gulp. By that logic, we should do it now.

"So, you have questions as well?" He grabs my foot and gives it a gentle squeeze.

"What do we tell people?" I somehow manage to ask.

He stops the massaging. "We tell them we fell in love and got married."

"So, we lie."

He resumes massaging my foot. "Yeah. That way, we don't make those close to us complicit."

Huh. That makes sense. Also, this way, there's less risk someone will blab. But wait. "Are you saying my family will think I got married? For real?"

He switches to my other foot. "Hence your generous compensation."

Right. Right. "But that means you'll meet my parents."

He works my left calf now. "It means a lot of things in that vein."

Despite my muscles being turned into pudding, an icy chill gathers in the pit of my stomach. "Are we throwing a big wedding?"

For as long as I can remember, I've hated the idea of a big wedding. All the people marinated in their colognes/perfumes, the over-fragrant flowers, the—

"Planning a big wedding would require too much time." He shifts his ministrations to my upper back, melting my bout of anxiety in an eyeblink. "I was thinking our story would be that we fell madly in love, fast, then took a trip to Vegas and eloped."

Startled, I turn over. "Vegas?"

"Why not?"

I turn back because I miss his hands on me. "No. It's a great idea. The expectations for our union will be lower—thus less shame on me when we divorce." Not sure why, but the D-word tastes very bitter in my mouth. "More importantly, Vegas has so many amazing all-you-can-eat buffets, with scrumptious desserts."

"That's your fruit craving talking again." He kneads between my shoulder blades.

"When did you want to do this?" I ask breathlessly.

He digs his thumbs into my shoulder muscles. "How about today?"

I turn my head with a start. "Today?"

He shrugs. "As the Russian saying goes, 'Strike iron without leaving the cash register.'"

I blink at him. "And that means…"

"You should always act while the circumstances are favorable. Our story can be that we met at this banya, clicked, had a few drinks, and took a romantic, spontaneous flight to Vegas. And the rest, as they say, is history."

"That could work." I put my head back down. I

need the relaxation from the massage if I'm not to panic and flake on the whole deal.

Vegas.

Today.

With him.

I'm not sure I'll survive this banya without exploding from the pent-up sexual tension, much less a long flight. And this is after that marathon of riding the unicycle.

He works my neck next, which feels amazing but also gives me an idea of what it would be like if he decided to choke me a little bit in bed.

"How about this for a plan," he says. "We stay at the banya a while longer. Order more drinks. Pretend to get drunk. Loudly state our intent to go to Vegas. Take more pictures throughout."

Again, I feel uneasy despite what his hands are doing. "Do you really think that immigration peeps investigate marriages to the point where they'd ask people in this place about us? That's more of a murder-investigation level of detail."

He sinks his fingers into my hair and begins a heavenly head rub, melting my bout of unease. "A lot of Russians know me. Hopefully, someone will spread rumors throughout the Russian community, and if we're lucky, the rumor might make it into the Russian newspapers here. If so, *that* might get on the immigration people's radar."

Ah, so this is what he meant earlier when he said this banya might serve our purpose better. More people, more chance for rumors.

My eyes are starting to roll into the back of my blissed-out head. "The Russian community has newspapers?"

"There are two that I know of, but there may be more. The community is huge."

"Okay," I say, fully in bliss mode now. "Let's do your plan. Just keep in mind I'm not a big drinker. Those two shots already have me buzzed."

Yeah. That's why my thoughts are so inappropriate.

He chuckles. "Same here. I don't normally drink at all."

Ah, that's why he was making those faces while downing the shots. A rare Russian who doesn't drink.

I turn my head languidly. "Does that mean I took your vodka virginity today? You took my banya one, so it's only fair…"

His eyes gleam—probably with a hunger for alcohol. "No. If I'd never tasted vodka, Russia would've denounced me long ago. I actually lost that part of my innocence when I was ten."

I goggle at him. "As in, elementary school?"

"We had just one school, but yeah. Vodka tasted so nasty I still cringe when I drink it."

Huh. Maybe this is how you get people not to drink: let them taste it way too young.

"Where did you even get it? Does it come out of the faucet in Russia in lieu of water?"

He chuckles. "My friends and I stole some from the janitor's bottle. Replaced it with water. He was too drunk to notice."

I put on a mock-disappointed expression. "Too bad. I so wanted to devirginize you."

"Well, you can take my crème brûlée virginity once we're in Vegas."

"You've never had crème brûlée?" That's like having toys nailed down to the floor as a kid.

"I've never had *many* types of desserts," he says. "That just happens to be one I know the name of."

"It's a deal then." I grin. "I'm taking your crème brûlée virginity."

He offers me his hand, and at first, I assume it's to shake on the deal, but it turns out he's helping me get off the table.

"Would you mind returning the favor?" He nods at the place I was just occupying. "My calves are still in knots from my last performance."

Is my jaw on the floor?

Probably.

He wants me to massage him.

As in, touch him.

It's official.

I really, really did not masturbate enough.

CHAPTER
Fifteen

AFTER I SQUEEZE out something along the lines of "affirmative," he plops on the table, his powerful back on display. As I lay my hands on his thickly muscled calves, I lose the gift of speech—which seems to be fine with him, as he lies there contentedly. I begin the massage and realize he was right. I'm far from a professional, but even I can feel the tension in his leg muscles.

Taking a deep breath, I focus on fixing the problem in front of me, and *not* on whether I can do a little carpet bumping right here and now without him noticing.

"That's nice," he murmurs when I move my ministrations to his thighs—mostly because I really want to feel how hard they are. "Can you do my back too?"

"Okay." I just barely stop myself from adding, "Massages are totally platonic and casual, right?"

It's a miracle I don't explode from hormone overload by the time I'm done with his back. My clit will be in danger of blistering once I get home.

Except I'm not getting home anytime soon.

Maybe I can rub one off right here in the banya bathroom? But what if—

"Hey," he says softly. "Would you feel comfortable doing my glutes? Going on pointe is killer on that muscle group."

Glutes.

As in, touch his butt?

Have I won some kind of sex lottery?

"It would be over my underwear," he adds.

Damn it. I stalled too long. If he hadn't said that, I could've touched his naked ass.

Before he can change more of the parameters of this amazing request, I grab myself a handful.

Wow. I think my palms are having an orgasm—a palmgasm. But I'm greedy. I want to bend down and nibble on his glutes, for a mouthgasm—or is it toothgasm?

But no. I have to stick to actions that can at least loosely be interpreted as a massage technique.

A bunch of new rules for our marriage are swirling in my head, but most are not appropriate, like "I shall be allowed to grab this butt any time I want."

Still, there's one rule I can't help but blurt out. "While we're married, can we agree not to sleep with anyone else?"

There. I know that's unfair to the rest of womankind, like inventing a fat-free, sugar-free doughnut that tastes better than the regular thing but making it so that only I can eat it. No, wait. I can't eat it either, not according to our platonic rule.

He turns his head, revealing a serious expression. "I thought that was implied. We can't have extramarital affairs. If that were to go public, it would ruin everything."

Why am I so relieved? Do I want him to have blue balls to match whatever is happening to my ovaries?

He puts his head back down. "Ten more minutes?"

Even though he can't see me, I nod and resume touching him wherever I want—within the limits of his facedown position, of course.

Under the pretext of a head massage, I run my fingers through his silky hair. Then I grab a handful of his deltoid muscles, followed by biceps and triceps. Handgasms explode in my palms as I go.

Ten minutes later, I owe myself at least a month of finger-blasting. Reluctantly, I pull my hands away as he turns his head and says, "Thank you." He then leaps off the massage table. "We're getting cold. Let's head back into the banya."

Back to wet heat? What I really need is that icy pool and then a cold shower, but hey, horny beggars can't be horny choosers.

I follow him through the bathhouse. We make a few stops on the way to get the funny hats and all the rest, then return to our table "to take a few more photos" before we do the banya thing again.

His salad is already waiting, but no fruit or *blins* yet.

"Want to take another picture with the shots in our hands?" he asks.

I examine myself. I feel light, but not because of alcohol. At least, I don't think so.

"Yeah, sure," I say.

He waves at Marusja. "Two shots. And a cup of honey for the *parilka*."

As we wait, he pours us both tea and squeezes a whole lemon into his cup.

Hey, if he wants Lemon juices, there are other ways.

"What do you think of the tea?" he asks.

I taste it. "Fruity. Are there berries in this? And chamomile?"

He sips his. "Yep. A nice mix."

Marusja returns with two more vodka shots and a honey jar identical to the one I saw the guy in the steam room use. She puts the shots on the table and reverently hands the honey to Art. I don't need to be psychic to know she's picturing smearing the honey all over him.

"Can you take another picture of us?" Art asks her.

She takes the phone, and we grab the shots.

"*Za zdorovye*," Art says again.

"Ditto." I gulp down my vodka, and it goes down my throat very smoothly—the way I hope Mr. Big will at some point.

Wait. No, Rule Number One. Mr. Big needs to stay *firmly* in Art's pants.

We make Marusja take a few more pictures, and when she starts to look particularly cranky, Art thanks her and leads me to the next *parilka*.

"This one is a little wetter," he says as we walk down the hall.

I look around for the female he's talking about, but he's gesturing at the steam room door we've stopped in front of.

"Is it as hot?" I ask warily.

"No. Plus, it's easy to cool off in this one."

"All right, let's go." I take a brave step forward.

He opens the door for me.

Wet heat, here we go again.

CHAPTER

Sixteen

THIS STEAM ROOM has less wood and more tile all over, and I soon see why. A woman stands up from her seat, walks over to a nearby bucket with water, and pours the water over her head.

Huh. Given that you can see her nipples through her top, the water must be icy, yet she's clearly enjoying herself. That, or she's putting on a show for Art. The way she's looking at him, she must be wet in many senses of the word.

To his credit, Art doesn't seem to notice her existence. Instead, he sets up a spot for us on a top bench and sits down.

When I join him, he asks, "Do you want me to put the honey on your back?"

Is water wet? "Yes, please."

He gently smears me with honey, his touch sending tendrils of heat through my body that could teach the steam room a thing or two.

The bucket woman must see she has no chance because she slams the door on her way out.

Nice. We're alone now.

Much too soon, Art finishes smearing honey over my back, and even though I'm hoping he'll offer to cover other parts of me, he doesn't. Rudely, he just hands me the honey.

So inconsiderate. With an inward sigh, I turn myself into a Lemon pancake.

Then an exciting idea hits me—possibly prompted by the vodka.

"What about you?" I ask as nonchalantly as possible. "You have skin."

Ugh. You have skin? That's a line that belongs in *The Silence of the Lambs*.

He looks at the honey in my hands thoughtfully. "Sure, why not?"

Score! "Do you need help with *your* back?"

"Please."

Before he can change his mind, I smear him with honey—which gives my palms as many orgasms as the massage did earlier.

Oh, and has the *parilka* gotten much, much steamier all of a sudden, especially in my panties?

Because I'm enjoying this so much, I cover him with a second layer of honey. Then a third.

"Thanks," he says before I can start a fourth layer, so I reluctantly stop.

Should I offer to do his front?

As much as I want to, I don't have a good excuse.

Then he takes the decision out of my hands, literally, by grabbing the honey jar.

Hey, at least our fingers brushed, sending more orgasmic zingers everywhere.

As I watch him apply the honey to himself, I yet again realize that I did not stir my honey pot enough for this kind of a show.

"How are you feeling?" he asks when he's done.

I catch my breath. "Overheated." And maybe more than a little buzzed.

He grins knowingly. "Time for the bucket."

"Okay." I gingerly step on the tile.

He takes the bucket and dunks the water over my head.

I yelp, but more in surprise than in discomfort. The cold water is actually refreshing, in a pins-and-needles sort of way. Also, it's nice to get the stickiness of the honey off my skin. Even my head clears a bit.

When I recover, I catch Art looking at me with a peculiarly intent expression. He must also want the water treatment.

I snatch the bucket from his hands. "Your turn," I say with sadistic relish as I fill the container with water.

"Ready?" I ask, raising the heavy bucket.

He nods.

I rise on my tiptoes, brace my core muscles, and dunk the water over his head.

He stands there, grinning, like nothing's even happened. Typical macho display. I'm sure he yelped just like I did, but on the inside.

"Now," he says. "I think you're ready for *parka*."

I narrow my eyes. "Parka? I take it you don't mean a windbreaker."

He chuckles. "*Parka* is the Russian word for the *venik* treatment."

Am I ready for that?

"Lie down, face up." He gestures at the spread-out towels, his manner all imperious again.

Huh. I think I like bossy Art.

With a large dose of trepidation, I do as he says.

He leaves the room, and I try to relax, which is easy given all the heat. When he comes back, it's with the Russian spanking instrument.

"Do you trust me?" He looks me over like a butcher about to carve out a premium steak.

To my surprise, I find that I do trust him. So much so I don't even need to establish a safe word for what's about to happen.

"Let's do it," I say breathlessly, and I'm not sure if I mean the spanking or the thing forbidden in Rule Number One.

"Here goes." He lightly flogs my left thigh.

By the wet heat of the gods, that feels nice. Less like a spanking and more like his hot breath is on my flesh.

His smirk is extra wicked. "More?"

I nod.

He smacks my right thigh.

A moan is on my lips, but I suppress it.

He spanks my calves in turn. Then feet. Then he returns his attentions to my thighs, and a stray leaf touches my panties with a feather-like touch. I nearly come.

My belly gets the next spank.

Then my chest.

I sneak a peek at my skin. It's flushed all over, exactly how it gets post-orgasm.

"Turn around," he orders.

He wants to do me from behind. I can't deny him that, can I?

As soon as I turn, my back gets such a good flogging I melt into a puddle of meringue.

"That's it. Time to cool off," he says.

I don't lift my head. "I don't think I can move."

"I'll help," he says, and I hear a mischievous note in his voice.

Wait a second. Is he about to—

Splash.

This time, I yell like a choir of stuck pigs.

He did it.

He dumped a bucket of icy water onto my over-heated flesh.

When I turn, he's standing there with another bucket.

"Wait—"

Too late.

This new batch of water engulfs me from the front. Again, the shock makes me scream, but the experience is more pleasant than not.

Hmm. First, I enjoy flogging, and now this. Is Art turning me into a masochist? We might need a new rule for that. Rule Number 666?

"Sorry," he says. "You can do me now. Fair is fair."

I fill the bucket, then throw the water into his face.

No reaction.

I refill it and get him from the back—mostly because I enjoy the sight of the water sluicing down the grooves of his muscles.

Again, he takes the cooldown in stride.

"I think this is enough banya for now," he says when I put the bucket down. "We should rest a bit, eat, then come back."

"Deal," I say.

We exit the steam room and stop by the nearby showers before returning to our table, where our food is waiting.

As soon as our butts touch our chairs, we attack the grub.

Yum. It's nice to satisfy at least this—a socially acceptable—hunger. *Blins* turn out to be delicious, especially after I dump all the preserves and honey on them.

To Art's credit, he doesn't bat an eye at all the sugar I've just consumed, nor does he try to feed me his fruit.

Just as I'm about to compliment his restraint, a guy walks up to our table, his gait wobbly—probably due to the bottle of vodka in his hands.

The newcomer hiccups, then grins at Art. "*Vi Artjoms Skulme?*"

Art looks up with a stern expression. "Yes. And you are?"

"My name is Vladlen," the guy says in a pretty good, albeit slurred, English. "My mother is a huge fan of yours."

Hey, it could be worse. He could've said "grandmother."

Art's expression warms a degree. "I appreciate my fans. Please thank her for supporting the arts when you next see her."

Vladlen burps. "She'll kick herself that she didn't come here." He slams the vodka bottle in front of Art, then fishes out a magic marker from his pocket. "Could you sign this?"

Art's smile is as confused as I am. "Sign a vodka bottle?"

Vladlen starts to nod, but it must make his head spin because he grabs on to the edge of our table. "It would be so great if you did. She'll keep it prominently in her living room and show it to everyone."

Art grabs the marker and the bottle. "What's your mother's name?"

"Dazdraperma," Vladlen says and hiccups once more.

Art chuckles.

Vladlen looks at him with a stony expression.

Art's eyes widen. "You're serious?" Turning to me, he explains, "It's a rare name. Short for '*Da Zdravstvuyet Pervoye Maya*,' which means 'Long Live May Day'—a.k.a. the international Workers Day.'"

Vladlen shrugs. "Grandparents were Commies. Mom was under their influence when she named me."

I look at Art questioningly, and he explains, "Vladlen is a portmanteau."

Vladlen looks offended. "What did you call me?"

"A portmanteau means a word made up of parts of other words," Art says. "In your case, Vladimir and Lenin."

Vladlen's expression clears. "It could have been worse." He hiccups. "I once met a Pofistal."

I look from Art to Vladlen and back.

Art rolls his eyes. "Translated, 'Josef Stalin, defeater of fascism.'"

At least it's not a name honoring Saddam Hussein, Charles Manson, and Cruella de Vil at the same time.

"So." Vladlen shifts from foot to foot and nearly falls. "Can you sign it?"

Art uncaps the pen and writes something in Russian. Whatever it is, Vladlen looks on the verge of tearing up after he reads it. "Mommy will be so happy," he says. "As a small token of my thanks, will the two of you drink with me?"

Before anyone can answer, Vladlen says, "May we be healthy," and takes a big swig from the bottle.

Art whispers, "To refuse would be an insult."

Skunk.

Vladlen hands me the vodka.

Straight from the bottle? Another first today.

I carefully lift it to my mouth.

Gia would probably die if she saw this breach of hygiene protocols. Then again, doesn't alcohol kill all the germs?

With my peripheral vision, I see Art take a picture with his phone.

I go for it.

Oops. A *lot* more vodka goes down my throat than I intended.

My choices are to swallow or spit it out at my husband-to-be, so I go for the civilized option.

Whoosh.

The giant gulp burns all the way down to my toes.

"Impressive." Vladlen turns to Art. "Are you sure your date isn't Russian?"

"She is, in spirit." Art hands me the phone and grabs the bottle.

I prepare to take a picture.

Art takes a swig that seems larger than mine.

Macho display?

Must be. His face twists horribly, and I snap a few pictures of that with a grin.

Is the room spinning?

Hmm. What's this warm feeling in my chest?

It'd better be the effects of vodka, and not something crazy, like the L-word. I think. Whatever it is, I feel great. I feel like I could fly at any moment.

I'm beginning to see why people drink vodka, despite the taste and the non-sweet calories and the threat of becoming an alcoholic.

"So, what's next for you two?" Vladlen asks.

"We're flying to Vegas," Art says in a conspiratorial whisper that's loud enough for all the nearby tables to hear.

Wow. He's still clear-headed enough to work on our marriage backstory. Must be nice to have a bigger body mass. The best lie I could come up with at the moment is that I'm totally sober.

"Vegas. Wow." Vladlen toasts us with his bottle and takes a big swig. "When?"

Damn, dude. Alcohol poisoning is a real threat.

"A couple more sessions in the *parilka*, and then we

go." Art stands up and glances in the direction of the steam rooms. "Speaking of… better get to it."

"*S lyohkim parom,*" Vladlen says and shakily walks back to his table.

As Art heads to the steam rooms, his gait is a lot less graceful than usual. Looks like the alcohol *is* having an effect on him, after all.

I hurry after him. Once faced with the wet heat, I feel extra lightheaded, though it's hard to be sure how much of it is from the steam, how much is from the vodka, and how much is from Art's hotness. I brave it for as long as I can, and then Art brings me back to the table.

Then déjà vu happens. A guy walks over to our table, says his mom is Art's fan, and asks for an autograph. The only difference is, instead of a bottle, he wants his "lucky ruble" signed, and instead of having us chug from the bottle, he brings over shot glasses.

When he leaves, I open my mouth to comment on how weird that was, but then a new dude comes over, and the whole thing repeats again—including shots.

My legs are feeling numb. And the tip of my tongue. And my thoughts are on a merry-go-round. On the bright side, pretending to be drunk should be very easy now.

As soon as the latest mama's boy leaves, another stops by—and he's even weirder in that he himself is the fan. Also, he offers to spank me in the *parilka*.

"No, thanks," I say.

"Oh, come on," he says. "I can do it very good."

Am I slurring my words, or is he too drunk to understand that no spanking means no spanking?

"Seriously," I say more firmly. "I'm good."

"Don't you respect me?" he presses.

Okay. Respect seems to be an important topic for drunk Russians. A couple of the previous dudes talked about it too—in the context of how much of it they have for Art.

Speaking of Art, he launches to his feet. "Look, bud." His speech is slightly slurred, but his eyes are dark and flinty. "I'm the only man who does anything to her. Ever. Is that clear?"

Is he acting? Either way, why does this make me feel even warmer in my chest?

The guy straightens his spine.

Skunk. Are we about to have a drunken brawl?

"Mr. Skulme," the dude says. "I'm sorry. I didn't mean disrespect."

Art seems to calm down. "It's fine. How about we drink one more shot and forget about it?"

We down the vodka, and when the guy leaves, Art sits back down and whispers to me, "I think it's time we head over to the airport. I fear people might be coming to the *banya* now just to get my autograph."

I look around.

He might be right.

This place that was pretty empty before is full now... that or I'm seeing doubles and triples. Oh, and the new people—or double-vision people—are all sneaking looks our way.

I leap to my feet.

Whoa. Head rush. Maybe I did that too fast.

Before I can lose my balance, Art grabs my hand.

Ah. The handgasm to rule them all.

He leads me to the locker room, but for some reason, he doesn't walk in with me.

Boo.

In a haze, I shower, which doesn't clear my mind as I hoped.

Wrapped in a towel, I'm stumbling over to my locker when a woman turns up in my way.

She looks like one of the Russian models I spotted earlier, only way overdressed for the location. And even thinner. And oddly familiar. And pissed off.

"*Korova*," she hisses at me with a nasty expression before shouting in rapid-fire Russian that I wouldn't be able to follow even if I were sober and spoke the language.

When she's done, as if to punctuate her point, she slaps my cheek.

CHAPTER
Seventeen

WHAT THE FUCK?

The stinging sobers me up enough to decide that I'm going to give this waif the smackdown of her life.

You don't grow up with seven sisters without getting into a fight or two, with and without hair pulling.

I raise my fists like a pugilist. "You're dead, whoever you are." I mean to sound cool and sinister, but the words come out slurred.

Instead of fighting me with honor, my assailant just rolls her eyes, then turns on her heel in a way that suspiciously resembles a pirouette.

"Wait a sec."

She doesn't. She prances away, making it look annoyingly elegant.

Oh. I remember now. She's the ballerina I saw on stage the other day. The one I nicknamed Black Swan. The one who was much too chummy with Art on stage —performance or not.

Bitch. I should smack her while I have the chance. But she's so fast, and my feet feel much too cottony at the moment.

I sit on a nearby bench to catch my breath.

Maybe I'll chase her after this.

The room spins.

Okay, maybe I'm not going to chase anyone for the time being. Grr. I guess it's Black Swan's lucky day.

Unballing my fists, I ponder what she said to me and why. A part of me is unsure whether she was actually here. Like, maybe when you drink enough vodka, a Russian ballerina manifests in front of you. Or a bear. Maybe that's what happened to Natalie Portman at the end of that movie.

The door to the locker room creaks.

Is the apparition back?

No. It's Marusja.

"Your finance asked me to check if you okay," she says grumpily.

My finance? Oh, she means my fiancé... who is related to my finances, such as they are.

"Here." Marusja gives me her hand. "I help."

I let her support me as I get up, and then she kindly holds me as I pull on my clothes.

"What's a *korova*?" I ask when I'm done.

She looks insulted. "Who you calling *korova*?"

I blink at her. "No one. I just overhead someone say that."

"It means *cow*," she says with a frown. "It's fat shaming."

Cow? My hands curl into fists again. The Black

Swan is lucky she ran away when she did—assuming she wasn't a figment of the vodka.

"Ready to exit?" Marusja asks.

I nod, and she leads me out to a foyer where Art is already waiting, swaying slightly on his feet.

Marusja says something to the nearby staff, and they help us get into a cab idling by the curb.

"JFK," I hear Art say as if from a distance.

We start moving.

My eyelids feel heavy.

I think I black out, or time gets choppy, because next thing I know, we're at the airport.

Another blink and I'm in a seat in first class, with a helpful Art covering me with a blankie.

I float on the feelings of warmth and coziness for the next few moments, and then my mind goes blank as I fall into the deepest unconsciousness of my life.

CHAPTER
Eighteen

I COME to my senses with the worst headache.

No. To call this a headache is an understatement. My head feels like it's been run through an industrial-strength blender.

Did an NFL player borrow my head? If so, he clearly played without a helmet... and lost.

I groan.

If pain could be turned into a smell, my headache would reach the levels of *taranka*. Or fermented boiled cabbage. Or one of those numbered Chanel atrocities.

Oh, and headache aside, why do I feel so cold, like I'm naked? And sticky. I feel very sticky for some reason. Not to mention, there's a soreness in my lower body. More than one type of soreness.

What the fuck?

A male groan mirrors my own from somewhere.

Okay, so wherever I am, I have company in my misery.

Time to pry open my eyes. Except... my eyelids

seem glued together. With effort, I force my blinkers open—only to be blinded by light coming through giant windows.

Odd. Wasn't I on a plane?

I let my eyes adjust and look out the nearest window.

The Las Vegas Strip. Wow. I must've blacked out sometime after the plane took off—understandable, given how much I drank.

I look down.

Skunk.

The reason I feel naked is because I am.

The reason I feel sticky is because I'm covered in some white substance that smells delicious. And I do mean covered—like it would be a challenge to locate a clean inch of me.

I hear another male groan.

Turning, I locate its source: Art—also naked and just as covered in the white substance as I am, which is a shame.

I sit up.

It's a mistake. The room spins out of control, making me uber queasy.

All right. I don't think I'm sober yet. Not even a little bit. Which makes sense in that it explains why this room smells like a distillery blew up. Although I still smell Art's yummy scent and sugary confections of all kinds.

Doing my best not to worsen my headache, I scan my surroundings.

Holy sweetness.

Every single surface of the room is covered in desserts. Cupcakes and different kinds of cakes, brownies, doughnuts, tarts, fudges, cookies, pies, melted ice cream, macaroons, muffins, parfaits, panna cotta, snickerdoodles, scones, candy, souffles—the list goes on and on. But what catches my attention are the whipped cream bottles, dozens of them sprawled around the room.

I dip my finger into a big lump of sticky stuff around my left boob and carefully taste it.

Yep.

Whipped cream, cherries, and little bits of all the sweets I see around me.

What. The. Actual. Fuck?

I gingerly prod Art.

He groans but doesn't open his eyes.

I taste the stuff covering him. Same as me—a mix of every dessert known to sweet tooths the world over.

Flabbergasted, I scan the room for more clues, but what I see only deepens my confusion.

There's a gas mask on a nearby writing desk. A fancy dress and lingerie are next to it. Under the desk is a pair of blue Manolo Blahniks.

What the hell? Did I rob Carrie Bradshaw, or is this a *Sex and the City*-themed dream?

But no. This headache would wake me from any dream, plus they didn't have gas masks on *Sex and the City*. Nor did—

The sound of tiny scurrying feet jerks my gaze to the other side of the room. I gape at the source of the sound and blink a few times, unsure if the vodka in my blood is making me see things, or if the dream theory needs stronger consideration.

A super-cute furry creature is holding an oatmeal cookie in two little paws, in a very human-like fashion. A rounded, very fluffy creature that looks like a well-fed squirrel with some ferret thrown in, and maybe also a bit of a bunny. Only its fur looks way more velvety.

Wait a sec. I think I know what kind of fur that is. My mom claims she stopped listening to Madonna's music over her wearing a coat that matches the fur of this creature exactly.

Chinchilla.

Huh. I didn't think they were *this* cute. Maybe Mom had a point.

But what's a chinchilla doing here, in Vegas? I don't believe they just run around the Mojave Desert, let alone the Strip. They're native to someplace in South America.

The chinchilla locks eyes with me, and it doesn't take a lot of imagination to figure out what it would say, if it could:

I know I look delicious, but don't even think about it. You'll get a stomachache, plus my fur will get stuck in your throat like a hairball from hell.

I stop making the critter nervous and look at Art instead.

Does he know what the hell is happening?

Maybe. But before I wake him, I need to consider the elephant in the room—the soreness. Two types, to be exact, but one very specific, post-sex kind of soreness.

When combined with naked Art, even with the headache, I can sleuth out what happened.

Rule One got broken, majorly.

Which leaves the second soreness, a stinging sensation on my lower belly that reminds me of a sunburn. Have I caught some weird STD?

I carefully wipe away the whipped cream/dessert mixture covering that spot and gasp, loudly.

I have a tattoo.

A full-on tattoo.

But that's not the worst of it.

The tattoo is an image of an arrow pointing at my pussy with an all-caps message that boldly states, "ONLY 4 MR. BIG."

CHAPTER
Nineteen

"How?" I whisper under my breath, staring at my stomach in horror. "When? Why?"

"Why are you shouting?" Art asks with a groan, opening one eye.

"Shouting?" I inhale a lungful of air and channel Leonidas, the King of Sparta. *This. Is. Shouting!*

Art slaps his palms over his ears and sits up, muttering something in Russian—most likely obscenities.

I hear something soft hit the floor. Out of the corner of my eye, I spot the chinchilla dropping its oatmeal cookie and leaping to hide somewhere—which makes me feel guilty for my outburst.

Art looks around the room, the confusion on his face matching my own.

"So," I say pointedly. "Do *you* know what the fuck happened?"

Brows furrowing, he looks at me, then around the room again. Then at his naked body. Then at mine.

To his credit, he doesn't laugh at the sight of my tattoo. He's either a better person than I am, or he's in too much shock to find this dedication to his cock hilarious.

"So… Mr. Big?" he asks, quirking an eyebrow.

Oh. Right. He doesn't know.

Reddening to the levels of the nearby cherry pie, I mumble, "A nickname I've given that." I point at his covered-by-sweetness manhood.

I probably should've lied, but my brain is not exactly firing on all cylinders.

He manages a faint smirk, but it disappears as he rubs the back of his whipped-cream-covered head. "So… I remember having drinks with you on the plane."

My jaw nearly hits the bed. "I was awake on the plane?"

He nods and winces in pain.

I swallow a gulp of forty-proof saliva. "Just to be clear, I had *more* drinks? After all that vodka?"

He scans the room again, as if answers might jump out of one of the cakes. "I'm afraid we both drank more. Drinks are free in first class, and as a line from a famous Russian movie says, 'Even people with ulcers and teetotalers will drink on someone else's tab.'"

I rub my throbbing temples. "I think I'm developing an ulcer as we speak."

He wipes some white stuff off his forehead and tastes it. "Me too."

I sigh heavily. "So what happened next?"

"We got off the plane, then took a cab… and then

had more drinks when we got to the first casino." He winces. "Again, they were free." His gorgeous features take on a look of concentration. "You won at craps, I believe, and then... I'm kind of blank."

I gambled and won? Why can't I remember any of this?

I narrow my eyes at him. "So you don't remember if we...?" I look pointedly at his whipped-cream-covered crotch.

He shrugs. "It sure looks like we did *something*."

Should I tell him about my soreness? It's a piece of evidence that leaves no doubt about what we did.

Before I can do so, he wipes at his abs, clearing off some of the gunk—and revealing that he too has a tattoo.

We both gape at it.

It's a picture of a cartoon lemon holding two eclairs like guns, both pointed at his cock. There's writing here too: "PROPERTY OF KISLIK."

A hysterical giggle bursts from my throat. "Is *kislik* a Russian word, or a portmanteau of kiss and lick?" Because those are the things I want to do to Mr. Big, even now, despite this headache-torture and the rest of it.

Art licks his finger and tries to rub off the tattoo. It doesn't budge. Blinking, he looks up at me. "*Kislik* is not a very common word, but it can be used to describe someone who makes things sour—say, a yogurt maker." His eyes take on a darker chocolate hue. "It's something I was jokingly calling you in my head."

I should've guessed it. That cartoon looks suspiciously like me, is holding sweets, and *is* a lemon.

"Well then." I roll my eyes. "The joke is on you. Literally."

He grimaces and rubs his hands together, trying to clear off the white stuff encrusted on them. Suddenly, he stops and stares at one of his fingers.

A ring finger, to be exact.

I follow his gaze, and at first, I don't get it. Then he licks the finger clean, and I see it.

A wedding band.

I check my own digit.

Yep.

On my left hand, on my ring finger, is a gold band that matches his.

CHAPTER

Twenty

My stomach clenches beneath the new tattoo. "We got married."

Art rubs absently at his chest, smearing a thousand calories worth of dessert in the process. "It seems like we followed the plan."

"Sure." I imbue the word with enough sarcasm to make an army of teenage girls jealous. "Everything went according to plan."

He throws a glance at my naked belly and the message written there. "Fair. But marriage, at least, was part of the plan."

"We never agreed to consummate it!" My Spartan yelling is back, and it amps up my headache a few notches.

Art grabs his head in his palms in the style of "The Scream" painting. "Maybe we didn't?"

I hurriedly run my gaze over the room. "There!" I point at a nightstand where a used condom is lying inside an empty dessert bowl. "I bet *that* has DNA evidence inside."

We totally did it, and the worst part is that I don't remember.

He looks at the condom, then at me. "At least we used protection."

"Maybe. Or maybe we did it many, many times, and some of them without protection. We have no idea how much time we're missing."

I don't add that my soreness seems to be indicative of more than just a drunk quickie. Then again, maybe it's due to the bigness of Mr. Big.

His eyes darken further, and his voice drops an octave. "I'm clean. What about you?"

My ovaries do a loop-de-loop. "Same," I manage to say. "But I'm not on the pill."

I let that sink in for both of us.

The idea of maybe becoming a dad must be energizing for Art. He leaps to his feet. "How about we clean up, then investigate?"

I follow him, and by the time I'm on my feet, my head feels like it might give birth to another head—one that will also have a headache. "Should we shower together?"

I'm not asking because I need the sight of him naked and uncensored by dessert in my rub bank. Or because I'm hoping one thing will lead to another, and the endorphins might actually do our headaches some good.

Fine, maybe I *am* hoping for those things, but I

figure when you're already in for a penny, you might as well be in for a pound... of pounding.

He steps back as if I were a swarm of horny bees. "No."

"No?" My stomach muscles tense so much some dried white stuff cakes off me and falls to the floor.

Art glances at the newly exposed flesh before raising his eyes to mine. He looks contrite. "I'm really sorry. Last night shouldn't have happened. Showering together now would only—"

"Say no more." I grit my teeth, making my headache throb in my jaw. "You're right. You go ahead and shower first."

What was I thinking? The guy has a ballerina harem at his disposal, and the only thing he needs from me is the green card. Right now, all he wants is to wash the stink of me off his body.

Art's lips press together in a slight grimace. "I think *you* should go first."

Is this chivalry, or is he saying I smell bad?

"You go," I say. "Age before beauty."

I don't feel like a beauty after being rebuffed, but I want him to feel like age.

"Ladies first. That's my final answer."

"Fine." I step on a cake as I head over to the desk to grab the dress and the lingerie—the only clothing I see around. I also take the Manolo Blahniks, then go in search of the bathroom.

Damn.

We're in a two-bedroom penthouse suite that's at least five times larger than my garage studio in Staten

Island. Also, it turns out we didn't need to argue over who will shower first because there are two full bathrooms.

Our stay must be costing a fortune.

I yell about the state of the bathrooms to Art, but I'm not sure if he hears me—and I don't care if he does.

I brush my teeth with the provided disposable toothbrush, then luxuriate in the shower for what feels like an hour. By the time I'm done, my headache has shifted from zombie Armageddon mode down to electricity blackout. Locating a fancy lotion that doesn't stink too badly, I slather it over my tattoo and make a mental note to research how to get it removed.

Next, I sniff my dress.

Nope.

The fluffy robe hanging on a hook is a lot more inviting, so I put that on and feel almost like a person. Then I shove my feet into a pair of hotel slippers. Grabbing the dress, I step out of the bathroom—and nearly bump into Art, who is also wearing a robe.

"Here." He hands me a water bottle and a packet of Tylenol. "This should help."

It will take a lot more than this to make me forget the shower rejection, but it's a start.

Just as I finish washing the pill down, there's a knock at the door.

"Housekeeping," Art says. "I asked them to clean our clothes."

Wow. He must've showered much quicker than I did.

We open the door and hand the guy my dress and Art's suit.

"Now what?" I ask when we're alone.

Art waves his phone. "We go to the living room and investigate."

Thankfully, the living room is mostly dessert-free. I follow Art to a comfy couch, where he sets up his phone so that its screen shows up on the giant TV in front of us.

"There are a lot of pictures and videos," he says. "Let's have a look."

An image of me holding dice shows up on the screen.

"This, I remember," he says.

Interesting. I'm already wearing the new dress.

I point at myself on the screen. "Did we shop before this?"

Art swipes at his phone a few times, and a picture of me in lingerie shows up. Some salesperson must've taken it because Art is in the frame, looking at me with the drooling expression of a cartoon wolf.

I guess with vodka goggles on, he wanted me. My soreness is proof of that.

"You wanted to put on a whole show," he says without meeting my gaze. "That's why I bought you *that* one and dragged you to another store to get a dress."

He then shows me a few images of me in different dresses—all of which could've been from the set of *Sex and the City*, and none of which I could ever afford.

I flush crimson. "Please tell me these aren't on social media."

Art looks sheepish. "I seem to have posted everything last night. Want me to take down the one with you wearing underwear?"

"Is vodka a bad idea?"

He removes the pic from his feed, along with a few more of me in more revealing dresses. Then he brings up the next image on the screen. "This, I don't recall."

It's a selfie of us standing cheek to cheek. Behind us is a place called Dick's Last Resort.

Up next is a video. In it, Art punches out a waiter while yelling something about being rude to his fiancée.

Oh, boy. I think I've heard of Dick's Last Resort. It's a place where waiters are dicks to you as a gimmick. Art was clearly too drunk to get that bit.

At least he didn't get arrested. I mean, I assume he didn't, since we're here and not in the local jail.

The next video is of us in a gondola at the Venetian.

And, of course, how could we not fall into the water midway through it?

Art glances at me, and my face burns at the video-me's clumsiness. Though, to be fair, video-Art is just as bad—and he's supposed to be the graceful one.

On the next stop of our misadventure, we're still wet from the impromptu swim, and on top of that, I seem to be crying. It soon becomes clear as to why. We're inside Titanic: The Artifact Exhibition.

I'm not going to cry now, obviously, but let's all agree—Jack could've fit on that door next to Rose. He totally could have.

"Delete that, please," I say with a slight hiccup, and Art does so.

The Mob Museum is next, and after that, we take turns shooting an Uzi at the Gun Store—probably inspired by our prior excursion.

Wow. Capitalism. To give two people as drunk as us guns—the mind boggles.

Next is the store where we got the gas mask—and a video of Art giving a slurred explanation as to why we bought it. Apparently, a guy farted in an elevator we were in, and my knight in shining armor wanted to protect me from having to smell that foulness again.

Yep. I'm still wearing the wet dress and the gas mask in the next two museums.

Art doesn't need my prompting to delete all evidence of that.

In a video that follows, we look drier, and I'm holding the mask, so that's good. The problem is, I'm not any more sober, so I heckle a poor magician we must've met somewhere by telling him that my sister Gia is so much better than he is.

Art flips through the recordings quicker.

In one, we're French-kissing at the Atomic Testing Museum—because with enough vodka in your veins, even radiation is sexy. In the next, we're buying a flogger at a sex store and calling it a *venik* throughout.

I sneak a look at Art. He's grinning. I wish I felt the same.

Where is that flogger now? No clue. But it wasn't the only stop of that sort. The next set of pics is at the Erotic

Heritage Museum, and in many, I look to be taking excessive notes.

Skunk. Did I tell Art about my blog? More importantly, is there evidence left on his phone that could remind him?

So far, no. The Erotic Heritage Museum visit is only in pictures, no videos, thank goodness.

"I think this is the big event," he says and starts a video.

Yep.

We're on a ship at Treasure Island, looking as happy as two clams in a vegan restaurant. The officiant is a female Elvis, of course, and the witnesses are dressed like... umm ...exotic dancers, male and female.

"I recognize some of them," Art says, following my gaze. "Former ballet dancers."

Great. Until now, I was only worried about his access to ballerinas. Turns out, he's got strippers at his beck and call as well.

When the ceremony begins, we're slurring words so badly our vows are hard to understand—but I do catch myself saying something about him keeping me as horny as Samantha. His vows are in Russian (I assume), so I only understand a single word: *kislik*.

Is it weird that I feel touched, despite the clusterfuckery of the ceremony?

Art's face is unreadable as he watches, so this is probably just a financial transaction to him.

"You may kiss the bride," the Elvis says to screen Art, and boy, do we kiss.

I should've been on the pill for that kiss alone. My

tongue looks to be reaching Art's spleen, not to mention all the lip biting and hands roaming. It's a miracle I don't take out Mr. Big—or that Art doesn't pull out my boobs from the dress.

Fucking hell. This bit can't be deleted. It's way too important for when we deal with the green card peeps. It looks incredibly real.

When our screen selves finally pull apart, the strippers and Elvis cheer. Staring into my eyes, Art slurs something that sounds suspiciously like, "And now you're mine, *kislik*." Speaking of the word that's now permanently written on his skin, the photos from the tattoo parlor are next—because "till death do us part" wasn't permanent enough for drunk us. Once tattooed, it's only logical that we go to a pet shop.

Which explains the furry beast I met earlier.

Art pauses the slideshow and arches his eyebrows at me.

"Oh, yeah, *honey*," I say. "It looks like we've got ourselves a fur child. Congrats."

I look around the room but don't see the fur child in question, so I urge Art to continue with the video. What follows is ten minutes of the store owner explaining the care and maintenance of chinchillas, as well as Art buying the best carrier for air travel, then registering our new pet with the airline.

"You need his name?" he slurs into the phone before shifting his gaze to the fluffy creature. "Fluffer."

Fluffer? Did Art not realize that's what they call the person whose job it is to make a male porn star hard before the camera rolls?

Speaking of porn sets, the next set of images is of the room we woke up in, without any desserts.

"There's a long video here," Art says. "But don't worry. This didn't upload anywhere due to its size."

Oh, God. If it's what I think it is and he tried to upload it...

"Great, let's see it."

Exhaling through his teeth, Art presses play.

CHAPTER
Twenty-One

"THIS IS OUR WEDDING NIGHT," on-screen Lemon says coyly, her speech slurred. She then darts a glance at the giant bed.

Slut.

On-screen Art walks up to her. "It sure is."

Lemon gets on her tiptoes, licks his earlobe, and very loudly whispers, "Someone should lose their virginity."

Art's nostrils flare. "Should they?"

"Emphatically." Lemon's gaze shifts to her crotch. "To that end, are you ready to eat… crème brûlée?"

I, the semi-sober Lemon watching, feel myself turning into an orange. At my side, Art's gaze is glued to the screen, his lips slightly parted.

On-screen Art looks at Lemon's Manolo Blahniks, then drags his gaze up until his eyes lock with Lemon's. "Who knew my *kislik* was so traditional?"

"So traditional." Breaking eye contact, Lemon leaps for the desk and picks up the phone. She must've dialed room service because she orders the crème brûlée, along with whipped cream, cookies, cakes, and so on.

The more items she lists, the higher video-Art's eyebrows go.

"Are you sure you ordered enough?" he asks when Lemon hangs up.

She shrugs. "I assume it's not just crème brûlée you've never tasted. Am I wrong, my sweets virgin?"

His eyes flare, and I can feel the heat in his gaze even through the screen.

"Well then," Lemon says in her best seductress voice. "The devirginizing will go on all night if it has to."

Huh. Is it weird that I like my blackout-drunk self? It's just too bad that being her comes with the price of such a terrible headache—not to mention what's about to happen on the screen.

"So," on-screen Art says huskily. "What do we do in the meantime?"

Lemon steals another glance at the bed. "What did you have in mind?"

Art's jaw tenses, and he takes a step toward her. Suddenly, someone chirps from off camera.

"Crap, Fluffer," Art exclaims and disappears for a second, coming back with the carrier.

Ah. Right. The poor chinchilla.

Art takes the creature out of the carrier, and they snuggle together, like a child and his stuffed toy.

Huh. Fluffer looks blissed out. Then again, who wouldn't be?

"Can I try that?" Lemon asks.

Art hands the pet to her, but when she tries to copy what Art did, Fluffer scurries away, looking deathly afraid.

"You scared him," Art says, then extends his hand to the little critter and says something soothing in Russian. The chinchilla must speak some Russian—or *really* like Art—because in a few seconds, they're snuggling together once more.

Lemon narrows her eyes at the chinchilla. "Is that a boy or a girl?"

"Boy." Art pointedly shows her the creature's belly.

I squint at the screen. There is zero evidence one way or the other. It probably takes an expert to sex them —someone like my chick sexer mother, who can somehow tell roosters and hens apart when they're six weeks old.

On-screen Lemon huffs and nearly falls on her ass. "If he's a he, why is he so chummy with you and not with me?"

Both the on-screen and real-world Art chuckle at that statement.

"Why would that matter?" asks the on-screen Art.

Great question. I'm a lot more sober than on-screen Lemon, and I have no clue what she meant by it— except that it sounds vaguely related to bestiality.

Lemon changes the topic by walking over to the minibar and taking a couple of little bottles from it.

No. Don't drink more. Are you insane?

She is. They both are. They sit on the edge of the bed with Fluffer on Art's lap, uncap the bottles, and Art says a fanciful toast along the lines of "may vodka bring world peace, cure pink eye, and bring back the woolly mammoths to the frozen steppes of Siberia."

Cringing, I watch them down the bottles, and my headache retroactively worsens.

Tossing her bottle aside, Lemon hikes up her skirt so high I can see her panties—and so can both Arts, judging by the avid interest on their faces.

"The dessert is taking too long," she states, her eyes on Art's lips. "Maybe there's something else you can eat in the meantime?"

Fluffer jumps out of Art's lap with a look that seems to say, *I knew these humans wanted to eat me. I fucking knew it!* He frantically hops away, out of frame.

Then I see why Fluffer really ran away.

It wasn't the "eat" comment.

Not directly, anyway. On-screen Art's pants are crazy tented—and that's where the poor rodent was sitting, so he just got scared by the awakened Mr. Big.

On-screen Lemon slides over to Art and gently brushes the tips of her fingers over the very top of the tent. "My dearest husband," she says with a bad British accent. "Is that for me?"

Skunk. Can I just fall through the floor and into a downstairs hotel room?

I sneak a peek at the real-world Art.

A vein is pulsing on his temple. He catches me watching, clears his throat, and readjusts his robe.

"Rule One," on-screen Art says in a hoarse voice. "Remember that?"

Lemon makes another circle with her finger and reaches for his zipper. "A bunch of hooey."

Real-world Art lets out a laugh.

I give him a stern look.

He pauses the video. "Sorry, it's just that *hooey* means 'dick' in Russian, and that's where her—I mean your—hand is. Also, it made me think, 'Wow. She's drunk so much vodka she's spontaneously speaking Russian.'"

"Hardy har har. Once you retire from ballet, you should consider becoming a fucking comedian."

"You have to admit, we've found ourselves in a strange situation."

I sigh. "We have."

"Should we even keep watching this?"

Great question. If the video morphs into porn—and the odds are nearly one hundred percent that it will— it'll make it that much harder to keep the rest of our marriage platonic. Despite that reasoning, I say, "Yes, we should. I need to know if I should take a Plan B pill."

Yeah. That's my story, and I'm sticking to it. It's not like I could just take the pill without watching, no way. Why expose myself to high levels of hormones if I don't have to… right?

"I can watch it myself and tell you."

I scoff. "Nice try. How about I watch it and tell *you*?"

He unpauses the video.

On-screen Lemon's fingers continue to circle around Art's bulge.

"This is a bad idea," on-screen Art says but doesn't stop her.

"This isn't a bad idea. It's Mr. Big," she says with a giggle.

Someone knocks on the door, and it takes me a second to realize it's in the video.

Walking funny—either because of what Lemon has done, the alcohol, or both—Art goes to open the door, and I'm not surprised to see the carts full of desserts rolling into the bedroom.

The waiters set the yumminess haphazardly around the room, put the whipped cream cans on the desk, and hurry away—no doubt suspecting the bacchanalia to come.

As soon as she and Art are alone, Lemon grabs a crème brûlée and puts it on the nightstand where I found its empty bowl today, with the condom inside.

"Eat." Her words are imbued with enough erotic energy to make the nearby jelly as hard as rock candy.

Art sits down at the head of the bed, picks up the bowl, and breaks the sugar shell on top.

"And now, for the first time, taste it," Lemon says.

My mouth waters.

Art sensually puts a spoonful of crème brûlée into his mouth.

His eyes are closed and he looks like he's really enjoying it—proving once and for all that he's human.

A tiny bit of the dessert ends up over his lip, like a milk mustache.

I know what Lemon is about to do before she does it. It's easy to guess because it's what I'd want to do, and the alcohol has removed all of on-screen Lemon's inhibitions.

She sits next to Art and licks the mustache off his lip, like a cat.

He opens his eyes. Grabbing the back of her head, he pulls her in for a kiss that makes the one after the wedding ceremony look PG-13 in comparison.

Wow. Is it weird to be jealous of myself? Also, I never want to drink again, not if it means I could forget a kiss like that.

As the voracious kiss continues, Lemon's hand locates Art's bulge once more, and she grabs it, firmly.

Pulling away, he sucks in some air. "Wait."

She touches her bruised lips. "Wait?"

"You're drunk."

She reaches over and pulls down his zipper. "You're drunker."

He scoots away from her, but not far, because the head of the bed is there. "I've never taken advantage of an inebriated woman."

Her grin is devious. "Oh, that. How admirable. Obviously, *I* can do what *I* want to myself, right? You wouldn't stop a poor, defenseless, *inebriated* woman from having some fun, now would you?"

His head shake is barely noticeable.

She walks over to the desk and peels off her clothes, slowly.

All. Of. Them.

I mean, I kind of suspected this would happen at some point, given how I was naked this morning, but I still blush like a nun would under these circumstances... though why a nun would get that drunk and then watch a homemade porn tape the next day is beyond me.

"We can stop watching," the nearby Art says.

On-screen Art says nothing—just stares at Lemon like he's about to devour her.

Trying to move seductively—but tripping over the desserts quite a bit—Lemon gets on the bed, spreads her legs wide, and starts touching herself.

I can't believe this is happening. I want to wake up from this nightmare, or at least run away, preferably all the way to Staten Island.

My voice is choked as I ask, "Can you play it on fast forward? And look away? I'll tell you when it's over."

If he were the one putting on that kind of a show, there's no way I'd agree to look away, but again, he proves to be a better person because he does as I ask. That, or watching me buff the weasel isn't something he wants to see while sober.

On the screen, the masturbation show is happening at breakneck (or breakfinger) speed, yet it still goes on for what feels like a very long time. The reason is simple: on-screen Lemon goes through every technique I've ever blogged about, and even invents a few new moves.

If he saw this, would Art realize I'm a professional? No idea, but I'm glad my on-screen self doesn't have access to an electric toothbrush or any other props.

Nope. Spoke too soon. On-screen Lemon leaps to her feet, grabs a whipped cream can and a cherry, then returns to the bed and covers her pubes with cream. Then she adds the cherry on top of it, of course.

Shoot me now.

She beckons Art, and they exchange a few words that I can't hear on fast forward. I bet it's something like "come eat" from her, and "okay, fine, anything to stop you from even more masturbating" from him.

Once on-screen Art is convinced, he goes for his treat in a cheetah-like leap. Then again, it might just look that way due to the video speed-up.

Should I tell Art he can look again? If that's what it takes to slow the video down, I guess so. I'm that curious about his cunnilingus technique.

I clear my dry throat. "Can you stop the fast-forward?"

Art turns back and audibly gasps.

Was that a good gasp or a bad gasp? Probably bad. He can't believe the alcohol made him stoop so far below his ballerina-inspired standards.

The on-screen Art doesn't seem to mind Lemon's charms. He works through the whipped cream like he's been on a hunger strike, then laps at her folds with just as much enthusiasm and ferocity.

She begins to moan.

Of course. I want to moan too—from humiliation. I also want to tell Art to look away again, but I'm struck speechless, so I just sit, my breathing rushed, my toes curling—like it's the me-right-now who's getting licked.

Is this some weird muscle memory or something that goes beyond that?

The moans get louder and louder, until Art turns down the volume on the TV, making my already-flushed face burn even hotter.

When she comes, her orgasm looks so powerful I feel an aftershock here on the couch.

"How's that?" on-screen Art asks with a cocky smirk.

She rips at his shirt, sending buttons flying. "You're officially not a whipped-cream virgin." She pulls down his pants. "However, you are at risk of getting pussy whipped."

What does that even mean?

Grinning, Art helps her get his clothes off, and soon, Mr. Big is unleashed.

I gasp, and so does on-screen Lemon. We also both nervously lick our lips... or maybe in her case, wantonly.

Even for something nicknamed Mr. Big, this is... well, big. You'd think with all that vodka, whiskey dick might be a concern, but no. Mr. Big is at full mast, a pure, enormous gorgeousness that looks kind of dangerous. Like there should be a license to wield it.

Did he pee near Chernobyl? I don't know about the current me, but the look on Lemon's face is reminiscent of Ann's when she saw King Kong for the first time.

Yep. I understand why I'm still sore.

When she recovers, she bends down—as if to take a closer look.

Nope. Wrong.

She's licking it, then sucking it.

Watching this was a mistake. I don't think I can ever look Art in the eyes again. Then again, I also can't help but notice how much my mouth waters—along with other places—especially when Lemon pulls away, grabs a can of whipped cream, covers Mr. Big in it, and then devours it all.

"I need to be inside you," on-screen Art growls when the whipped cream treatment repeats.

Okay, that's fucking hot. I'd say yes right now, all my earlier hesitations be damned.

Then again, I'm still a bit drunk.

Not surprisingly, my hussy self doesn't merely say yes. She sprawls back and spreads her legs welcomingly, moaning, "Yes, please."

Hey, she could have said, "Open for business."

But wait. "What about the condom?" I mutter out loud.

On his end, real-world Art tenses. Either he doesn't like the "will they use protection or not" suspense, or he's just plain bummed about where he's about to stick Mr. Big.

"One moment." On-screen Art runs back to his pants, fishes out his wallet, and rampages inside until he takes out a condom.

I glance at the real-world Art.

He darts a guilty glance at me. "I wasn't being presumptuous by having that with me. I *always* carry one in my wallet."

Great. If I needed proof that he's a manwhore, there it is.

Before I can say anything, on-screen Art rolls the condom onto Mr. Big, and then he fluidly positions himself over Lemon, his sheathed tip prodding at the entrance of her opening.

Fuck me. Those glutes. That back. Soreness or not,

I'm again as horny as a teen mountain goat… in heat.

He thrusts into her.

She moans.

My heartbeat skyrockets.

He grunts.

Real-world Art loudly clears his throat. "Should I fast-forward?"

"No," I say, much too quickly. In a more moderate tone, I add, "What if the condom broke?"

"Would we even see that?" he asks.

Fuck him and his good points. "We might hear it?"

"What does that sound like?"

I take a calming breath. "Fine. Fast-forward."

He does, but watching him fuck me super-fast only makes the video hotter—and more embarrassing.

Eventually, on-screen Art thrusts particularly violently into Lemon, which is when nearby Art must decide the condom question will be answered soon, so he resumes the video at normal speed.

"Art! Art! Art!" on-screen Lemon shouts over and over as she climaxes.

Wow. I don't think I've ever been that loud. It's a miracle I didn't lose my voice. He must've been good. Very good. Too bad the stupid vodka took the memory of it away from me.

Nearby Art wipes sweat off his brow while his on-screen self takes off the condom and puts it into the bowl where we found it today.

Art and I sit up straighter. If something unsafe happened, it would be going down on the screen now—

not that you can consider what we've already witnessed "safe."

"Do you have another one?" Lemon asks.

What a nympho. I've never blushed this much in my life.

On-screen Art shakes his head. "It was lucky I had that one."

"Oh, well." She scrambles to her feet and nearly falls over. "I know what we can do."

She disappears from view.

Why do I have a bad feeling about this?

When she comes back, she's holding the flogger.

What the hell? That thing wasn't in the room when we woke up. Where did it go? I hope not up some orifice. At least not mine.

Oh, no. Please tell me our sex marathon never left the confines of this suite.

Lemon picks up a piece of cheesecake and a can of whipped cream. "Ready for the American version of *parka*?"

On-screen Art arches his eyebrows. "Wouldn't that involve a burger?"

"Lie down, face up," she says in a pretty good imitation of how Art said those exact words at the banya.

He does.

She places the cheesecake on his chest, slathers it in whipped cream, and raises the flogger. "Ready?"

Whack!

The white mess is everywhere, and there's a little bit of redness on Art's exposed skin. He doesn't seem to mind—no doubt too drunk to feel pain.

"Your turn," he says.

She lies down, then closes and uncloses her legs.

Trollop.

He takes a scoop of ice cream from a bowl and places it in her navel. "Ready?"

Giggling, she shakes her head. "If you're making a sundae, add in some whipped cream."

Floozy.

Side note, why are there so many words for slut-shaming a woman and just one lonely "manwhore" epithet for men? Stupid double standards.

My feminist musings are interrupted by Art's flogging—as such things often are. Hey, at least he's a lot gentler on her than she was on him.

Still, the ice cream and whipped cream fly all over the place.

"Now… lick it off," Lemon orders.

I'm out of slut-shaming terms.

On-screen Art obeys.

She has another orgasm, loudly, then returns the favor for him. Just as he comes, she throws a pie in his face, yelling, "I knew you wanted a facial!"

A sexy food fight ensues, then more oral. Finally, they cuddle together and fall asleep.

CHAPTER
Twenty-Two

"We will never speak of that," I say when Art stops the video. "Deal?"

He nods. "Should I delete it?"

I'm about to say "hells yeah," but then I hesitate. "I'd keep it until you have the green card. If some government agent doesn't believe what we have is real, we'll show them that."

He laughs. "I can't even imagine the look on that hypothetical agent's face."

I laugh too, but then I make my face serious. "It probably goes without saying, but I want to spell it out: don't watch that again, or show it to anyone."

Nor will I watch it again because staying platonic with him is already as hard as Mr. Big was in the video.

"Goes without saying."

The door rings. He stands up to answer.

Is it my video-stimulated imagination, or did he just readjust something big in the Mr. Big region? Damn it, now that I've seen it, is his cock all I'm going to be thinking about?

When Art comes back, he's already dressed, and he hands me my dress from last night, now clean.

"I'm going to find Fluffer." He walks out of the room.

I snicker as I get dressed. Speaking of fluffers, he didn't require any for our little porno.

"Lemon, come take a look at this," Art yells from the bedroom.

I join him—and when I enter the room, I blush. Now that I've seen what transpired here, the desserts take on a new meaning.

Also, I swear I smell sex in the air, and it makes me horny. Or hornier.

Art is kneeling by the bed, looking under it, so I join him.

As soon as I see what he's found, I begin to laugh.

It seems we've located both Fluffer *and* the missing flogger. One is eating the other—and obviously, I mean Fluffer is eating the flogger, not the other way around.

I stop laughing. "Is that safe for his health?"

"I think so," Art says. "That handle is made out of wood, and the guy at the store said chinchillas will gnaw on random things regularly, to dull down their always-growing teeth."

Huh. Art was clearly paying closer attention to that spiel than I was.

"Come here, little Fluffer," I coo. "We're your mommy and daddy."

The chinchilla gives me a look that seems to say:

Mommy? Human, please. I witnessed your insatiable appetite all over this room—in both senses of the word. If I come out, you'll swallow me whole in one gulp, like a small ball of cotton candy. No, thanks.

He resumes gnawing on the flogger.

"How do we get him out of there?" I whisper to Art.

Theoretically, my arm is slim enough to fit under the bed, but no, thanks. I'm not sure this chinchilla has been vaccinated for rabies.

Art gets to his feet and leaves the room. When he returns, he's holding a large bowl with—oddly—dust in it.

"The guy at the store said they love baths," Art says. "Maybe this will get him out?"

He sets the bath down. As soon as Fluffer spots it, he leaves the flogger behind and rushes for the dust.

Huh.

Is this what those fur companies do to lure them in?

Fluffer starts to bask in the dust, and I watch with an ever-widening grin.

"How is this not viral?" I ask Art. "It's cuter than sleepy kittens."

Art looks at Fluffer with fatherly pride. "I agree. We'll have to shoot him one of these days."

Fluffer, who looks to be done with his bath, throws a worried glance at us:

Shoot me, then eat me. Humans are so predictable.

Before the chinchilla can rush back under the bed, Art says something soothing to him in Russian and gently picks him up.

This is it. Even the nicer-smelling human will eat you. Who knew?

Art places Fluffer in the carrier and turns to me. "We should head to the airport. I don't want to keep him locked up in this thing longer than necessary."

Sure, sure. You just want fresh meat on your flight, you monsters.

Since we're leaving, I locate my phone and search for my old clothes. They're gone, probably left at the store where I purchased my new getup.

"Do we leave the flogger under the bed?" I ask Art before we head out.

He shrugs. "It's ruined."

"They'll know it's ours." I redden as I picture someone locating the thing. They'll assume we're extra-extra kinky given the gnawed state of the wood. "There's dessert smeared all over it."

"If you want to crawl under the bed, be my guest," he says.

With a sigh, I step out of the room. Art and I don't talk much on the way to the lobby. I don't know about him, but I'm replaying the fateful video in my head and getting myself too turned on to be in public.

"I'm going to settle the bill," Art says. "Can you get a cab?"

I do so, and when Art joins me, his expression is strangely thoughtful.

Is he also reflecting on the video we saw?

"Where are we headed?" the cabbie asks.

"Give us a second," Art tells him, then turns to me. "Look, Lemon… if you've changed your mind about

179

the whole marriage thing, we can take a ride and get an annulment."

On what grounds? We actually consummated our union. "Have you changed *your* mind?" I ask, and I hate how weak my voice sounds.

His eyebrows furrow. "Why would I change my mind?"

Because the video made you feel dirty? Because you no longer want to be linked to the likes of me? Because you've realized you could save money by simply asking any warm-blooded woman to be yours for free? I can think of a few more reasons.

"If you're still okay with it, so am I," I say. "Oh, and, obviously, Rule One is back in effect."

"Right. Rule One." He studies my lips with a strange expression. "How about we also implement Rule Two: no drinking while married."

Is that so he doesn't repeat the mistake of soiling himself with me? I purse my lips. "Fine."

He turns to the cab driver, who by now must think us certifiable. "To the airport, please."

The driver hits the gas, and to fill the awkward silence that follows, I check my phone.

"Skunk," I inadvertently say out loud.

I have hundreds of texts, missed calls, and social media notifications.

"Everything okay?" Art asks, sliding closer to me.

"Lots of messages." I wave my phone.

"Ah." He takes this as an invitation to check his phone, so I dive into mine.

Skunk.

Art wasn't the only one snapping selfies and making videos last night. I did it too, and I posted them—after I was too drunk to understand the implications.

There are photos of us at each of the museums, but that's salvageable. Some pics at Dick's Last Resort and the Titanic exhibit—still not the end of the world. And—

Nope.

Here it is.

I posted pictures of us getting hitched—clearly taken by one of the stripper witnesses.

That means that everyone knows. My family and friends.

Even if I were to get that annulment, the worst of the damage is done.

With a heavy heart, I read the first message, which happens to be from Honey:

Married??? Seriously? How good did that thong smell? Call me immediately.

A text from Blue came shortly after that:

Holy matrimony!!! I mean, I like my Eastern European men as much as the next girl, but don't you think that was an itsy-bitsy-bit too fast? Call me, or I'll hack your phone and speak out of its speaker.

Gia wrote on Facebook. Being a performer, she keeps a presence there religiously:

I totally called it. This is how I thought Project BS would end, just maybe not this soon. I demand details.

And so on and so forth.

Even my parents are in the loop. In all caps, Mom tells me how happy she is, and then lectures me on the importance of multiple orgasms, especially on your wedding night.

Gee, thanks.

Dad's message is the most ominous:

Congrats! See you and your new hubby soon.

I drag the phone away from my face. "My parents might be coming to town."

Art looks up from his own messages. "That's great. I'm looking forward to meeting them."

Huh. Famous last words.

————

For the rest of the way to our plane seats, I field the messages from my peeps. Just as we take off and before I lose reception, I get to a text that came in much earlier yesterday, about the time I was massaging Art in the banya.

It's from an unknown number.

Hi Lemon, my name is Bella Chortsky. Your sister thought we should talk. I'm back in town. Do you want to have a drink tonight or grab some coffee tomorrow?

Oh, skunk. It's the owner of Belka—as in, a business contact—so of course, the idiotic drunken me replied sometime last night:

Sorry, no can do, Bellissima.

I stop reading.

Bellissima? Was that autocorrect, or did I really call a woman I've never met "beautiful" in Italian?

I hope it was autocorrect. It *has* been failing a lot as of late.

Unfortunately, the message continues:

I'm in Vergas.

Vergas? Is that an autocorrect for Vegas, or did I switch to Spanish, where that word means "slave"? Maybe it was the flogger's subliminal influence?

Oh, and here's the kicker:

I'm a boot to marry the best-smelling man, ever. Grain Czech?

Yes. Boot, grain, and *Czech*—oh, and why couldn't the autocorrect change that *smelling* into anything else, even smelting?

There go those sponsorship opportunities.

Or maybe not.

There's a reply from Bella:

Wow. Sounds like you're having a very good time there. I want to know more. Hit me up when you're back in town.

Okay, maybe not all is lost here. Not unless my final reply ruined my chances, which is very possible. A few hours later, when I was even more drunk, this is what I wrote:

As swoon as I'm back in Mew Pork, I'll shit you lard.

I smack myself on the forehead, hard. Or should I say, *lard*.

"That bad, huh?" Art covers my hand with his— probably by accident.

I turn my phone over quickly. It's bad enough Bella saw that atrocity; no reason my new husband should. "It's fine. How about yours?"

"Not so bad, especially compared to how everyone took the news of my retirement." He doesn't remove his hand.

The fluttering in my stomach feels like the gentle brushing of wings from baby swans. "You've retired?"

He nods. "You said you're not backing out of our deal, so..."

I flap my lashes at him stupidly. "Just like that? You're not a ballet dancer anymore?"

"No, I still am. I won't leave the company in the lurch. I'm going to do a number of performances until they find a replacement. But, yeah. The cat is out of the bag."

Wow. I admire his decisiveness. I would've waited for the green card before cutting off my paycheck. Then again, I should give myself some credit. If I really cared about paychecks, I'd work in finance or real estate, not follow my passion: blogging about all the different ways to visit the safety deposit box.

"Would you like a drink?" the flight attendant asks, approaching our seats.

Art pulls his hand away and gruffly says no at the same exact time as I do.

She looks offended and scurries away.

Art checks on the carrier under his seat, and I catch Fluffer's unhappy expression.

I never thought I'd say this, but I'd rather be eaten. Chinchillas aren't meant to fly. We're sane, unlike flying squirrels, sugar gliders, and humans.

Art coos something to him in Russian, and that seems to calm the little creature a bit.

Hey, even I feel calmer.

And sleepy.

Very sleepy, actually, which is understandable. I

184

spent most of last night doing things with Art, not to mention how bad alcohol is for sleep.

Oh, well.

I close my eyes.

Might as well take a small nap.

———

I wake up as we land in New York.

Wow. Five hours of sleep. And yet, the headache is still there.

"Hello, sleepyhead," Art murmurs when he notices my eyes opening.

"Hi." A girl could get used to seeing that face when she wakes up.

The plane comes to a full stop, and the engines turn off.

"Did you rest well?" Art asks as the seatbelt signs click off.

"I think so." I lift my hands to rub my eyes and notice someone has covered me with a plush blanket. "Thanks."

"How is your headache?" He hands me a water bottle.

I accept it and take a sip. The water is cool and refreshing on my parched tongue. "Still hurts. You?"

"I'm much better." He pulls out a packet of Tylenol and hands it to me. "Take this."

I swallow the two pills and chug the water to make sure I'm properly hydrated.

He watches me with a strange expression. His eyes

look warm, like chocolate fondue. "Did you know that you snore?"

I nearly choke, and some water comes out of my nose. "I do not."

He takes out his phone and plays a track from the voice recorder app.

Yep. That's snoring. "That could be anyone," I say with a sniff. "Ladies do not snore."

He lays his hand over my elbow. "You've foiled my dastardly plan. I totally recorded another woman snoring and tried to pass it off as you."

If he keeps holding my elbow, I'll let him get away with accusing me of making all sorts of unseemly sounds, be it snoring, burping, or bleating.

Sadly, he removes his hand to reach under the seat for Fluffer's carrier.

"Dastardly plan indeed." I mockingly narrow my eyes at him. "Don't try that again—or anything else that involves the phrase 'another woman.'"

Whatever Art is about to say is interrupted by the announcement that we're allowed to leave the plane.

In a cheesy gentlemanly gesture that I secretly love, Art offers me his hand to help me from my seat. He also lets me go through every door first all the way out of the airport.

Since we don't have checked-in luggage, we head straight for the taxis. As we wait, I text my sisters and tell them we'll talk as soon as I get home. I also debate if I should follow up with Bella, but before I decide, it's our turn to get into a cab.

As soon as we get going, I realize there's a huge problem.

The person who rode in this car before us must not have showered in a decade. And, to make matters worse, I smell a pine car freshener.

I crack open a window.

Nope. The car freshener smell is less potent, but the body odor is still intolerable, making me think it's the driver that's the source.

Even cozying up to Art and inhaling his magic smell doesn't work. How weird would I look if I pulled out that gas mask and put it on? Or stuck my head out the window, like a dog? Or maybe I could fake being sick? I might actually be sick if I keep smelling this.

The problem is, if we get out, it's now a long walk back to the taxi area, plus there was that line. I hate being such a diva about smells, but then again, I'm not sure I can—

"Stop the car." Art's tone is so demanding the cab driver smashes the brakes.

We stop with a jolt and a screech of tires, and I smell burning rubber—another scent I hate.

"We're getting out," Art says, then tosses the guy a twenty and hops out, holding the door open for me.

Before the cab driver can clarify what's what, I scramble out of the car.

Oh, the blissfully body-odor-free air.

My gag reflex relaxes.

The cab speeds away.

I look at Art with raised eyebrows, though I can guess what happened.

"That car seemed to smell," he says. "I figured if I noticed it, you're probably suffocating."

As I thought. He wanted to save me from the stink. That's an act of chivalry that would get you knighted back in the day, or at the very least get you into a lady's chastity belt.

"Thanks," I say earnestly. "But now we have to shlep all the way back."

He flashes his smart watch at me. "I could use the steps. Besides, you're worth it."

Aww. I almost float on air on our way back.

Luckily for us, the line is shorter when we get there, and the next car is smell free, or as much as is possible in a machine that runs on stinky gasoline and is occupied by dozens of people daily.

"Do you mind if I get on my phone?" I ask Art. "There's a business-related message I need to send."

He frowns. "I thought you were in between jobs."

Skunk. This is the problem with lies. They require more maintenance than an antique vibrator.

"My sister put me in touch with someone who might create a great opportunity for me." Hey, that's all true. "The problem is, I drunk-texted her, so now I need to carefully word any further communication."

He nods sagely. "Let me know if you need help."

Oh, no. It's bad enough that Bella—and maybe my spy sister, Blue—saw that whole "As swoon as I'm back in Mew Pork, I'll shit you lard" line. I don't need anyone else to see it. Especially Art.

"Thanks, but I need to do this on my own," I say.

"I'm sure you've got things to take care of concerning our new union."

"You're right." He unlocks his phone. "I do need to set up a number of things."

I stare at the screen for at least a half hour as I rack my brain for a way to salvage the Bella situation. The best I can come up with is:

Hi, Bella. Damn autocorrect, am I right? I'm back in the city. When would it be convenient for you to meet?

I type it out but don't send it. I'll give myself a few more hours to come up with something better.

Art clears his throat, so I look up.

"Remember how we discussed not having a big wedding?" he asks.

My heart rate speeds up. "Yes."

"Upon reflection... How would you feel about a medium-sized reception to celebrate our nuptials?" He gestures at his phone. "I've been asked, repeatedly."

I wrinkle my nose. I can almost smell all the perfume already. "If we must."

"It will be only family, friends, and coworkers," he says.

"Only," I say with air quotes. "I thought it was usually enemies and random strangers."

"Look, if it's a big problem for you, then—"

I shake my head. "If it can be done outside, I'll do it."

"We can do it outside. I'll organize everything. All I'll ask from you is to send me the contact info for the folks you want there."

"Okay, here goes." I email him the details for my

family, Fabio, and a few other friends. "Just let them all know that they can bring a plus-one, maybe two, but no more."

"Agreed."

The cab stops, and I realize that I'm already home.

"This is me." I gesture at the garage door.

Art leans closer, eyes gleaming. "Indeed."

I feel a force of uncanny gravity pulling me to him, and it's all I can do to fight it. "Bye?"

He turns away and exits the car.

Wow. Has he just invited himself over?

He walks around the car and opens the door for me. "I will see you tomorrow?"

Oh. A wave of disappointment crashes over me. "Sure. First thing, if you can."

He smirks. "I can make that work. Bye, wife."

I roll my eyes. "Bye, hubby dearest."

With that, I stride over to my domicile, only to find a huge basket by the door.

Wow. It's a fruit arrangement made to look like a gorgeous bouquet of flowers.

Is it for me or my landlords?

According to the note, it's from Art, so it's mine.

I feel bubbly all of a sudden. No one ever sends me flowers because their smells choke me, but this is a clever equivalent. Fruits have barely any scent.

"Thanks!" I yell at the cab, but it's already moving.

I bring the arrangement inside and check it out.

It's the full gamut: melons, strawberries, grapes, pineapple, and so on, but under it all, instead of a vase, is a cake, along with a longer note.

This gift is also a challenge. Eat all the fruit, then see if you'll still want the cake afterward.

Some of the earlier bubbliness goes stale. I know it's a girl cliché and all that, but is Art telling me I need to lose weight? Granted, in the most roundabout way possible.

Woofer whirs to life and bumps into my leg.

I'm not sure I would be so gauche as to call my human overlord fat, but I do think she'd shed less skin cells for me to suck if she dropped a few pounds.

Gritting my teeth, I take out my phone and set it to record video.

"Challenge accepted." I start devouring the fruit with gusto.

It's very nice, actually. Juicy and refreshing. Is fruit always like this? I don't eat it outside of the garnishes they include in desserts, so I don't really know. Of course, it's possible I'm simply dehydrated from the banya and all the alcohol. I know this, though: there's no way a few berries and pieces of melon will prevent me from eating that cake.

Except it's not a few pieces. It's a lot of pieces.

The more of the arrangement I eat, the more room it takes up in my stomach.

Skunk. I can't let Art win. Even if I don't enjoy it, I'll have that cake.

Maybe.

When I'm done with the fruit, the idea of having the cake seems almost repugnant.

Damn it.

I delete the video. If Art asks, I ate the cake.

My phone dings.

Oh, right. People are waiting to hear from me.

I go over to my computer, set up a meeting on Zoom, and send everyone invites.

I wait until five identical-to-mine—but slightly thinner—faces turn up. Then Mom and Dad make their appearance, followed by Gia and her twin Holly, and, for some reason, Fabio.

"How did you get an invite?" I ask him.

Honey ducks away from her screen and shows up in Fabio's. "Sorry. He was at my house when the invite came."

"Fine," I say. "Let's begin."

Honey returns to her screen and joins everyone in staring at me expectantly.

I take a moment to bask in being the center of attention for once. Then I say, "Looks like I'm the first Hyman sister to get hitched. That's all the news I've got. Any questions?"

CHAPTER
Twenty-Three

CHAOS ENSUES. People shout questions over each other, insults along the lines of "shut the fuck up" are issued, and there are even threats of bodily harm.

When they calm down a little, I say, "For those of you who don't know, I've liked Art—that's my husband's name, by the way—for a while now."

Gia, Honey, Blue, Fabio, and Olive look smug—they already knew about my obsession. Holly seems to be in her own world—no doubt gleeful that we've got eleven people on this call, a prime number. Mom and Dad look ecstatic—probably picturing a baby boy growing in my womb or something equally gross. Pixie and Pearl look pissed, as expected—none of us sextuplets like to be left out of juicy gossip.

"Art's full name is Artjoms Skulme," I continue. "He's a ballet dancer. At least for now."

Some people look distracted, probably googling my new husband's name.

"You know, I just got a text from someone with that

name," Olive says. "I didn't read it fully because I was joining this."

"Oh, yeah, he's organizing a reception for us." I look pointedly at Mom and Dad. "Attendance is optional, so those of you not in New York don't have to come."

"Oh, we'll be there," Mom says.

Yikes. Well, whatever comes of that, Art can't annul the marriage now.

Olive moves closer to the camera. "I will also be there."

Great. I just hope she leaves her pet octopus back in Florida. That thing's beyond creepy.

"I think Lemon is trying to change the subject," Honey says. "Tell us how you ended up married."

I drag in a calming breath. It sucks to have to lie to them, but there's no choice. And like this, over Zoom, is easier.

I start by telling them about the banya, then launch into our Vegas shenanigans, sans the sexathon. "If you want to see more pics of it all, add Art on social," I say in conclusion.

An avalanche of questions follows, and I do my best to field them. Then the next wave comes, and I'm a little less enthusiastic in my replies. By the tenth wave, I start demonstratively yawning. "Guys, I didn't get much sleep last night. When you meet Art at the reception, you can ask him anything you want."

Mom waggles her eyebrows. "Did you hear that, everyone? She didn't get any sleep last night. All night long."

My sisters look on in sympathy as I cover my eyes

with my palms. Strictly speaking, I said I didn't get "much sleep," but correcting Mom would just make it worse.

"That's Thing Four for you," Dad says proudly. "She had boundless energy even when she was a tyke."

Oh, no. More feedback like that is forthcoming. I need to put a stop to it, so I can leave this conversation with some dignity.

I make a funny face, then hold the expression to simulate a streaming glitch. Next, in my best ventriloquist impersonation, I throw my voice far away as I say, "Oh... no... my Wi-Fi... is cutting out."

With that, I hang up.

A text from Blue arrives instantly, and it's chilling:
I know.

What does she know? About the fake marriage? Or that I just faked the disconnect? Or she could just be bluffing, as a way of fishing for information.

I type out my reply:
What I did last summer?

No reply back, which means she was probably bluffing after all.

I return to my unsent text to Bella.

Nope. Still not ready to send that. Instead, I decide to do a little work.

Yeah. I think back on a few new techniques I seemed to have invented for Art the other night and include the most promising one in a write-up for my followers. I dub this blog entry "Live Long and Prosper."

Damn. Writing this down makes me want to do it while sober. And why not?

I close my laptop. This will basically be a quality assurance exercise—a way to guarantee my readers enjoy saucing their tacos when they try it.

Yeah. I'll take one for the team.

In a second.

First, I shower and change into comfier clothes. Then I get on the bed and take my panties off.

The key is to not think about that video with Art as I do this.

Yep.

I put my fingers in the V-shape of the Vulcan salute, which is the starting position of this particular technique: index and middle fingers together, then a gap, then ring finger and pinky together.

Still not thinking about the video.

I make sure my clit is in the groove between my middle and ring finger.

Hmm. This is nice. The snug feeling reminds of the Peace Technique I blogged about a few months back.

Not thinking about the video or Mr. Big.

I begin to slowly air the orchid.

Not thinking about chocolate eyes. Or firm lips. Or that shapely butt. Or those powerful dancer legs, or that toned back, or—

Who am I kidding? Putting my fake husband out of my mind is an exercise in futility. Either I won't come, or I will with an image of him firmly in my mental eye.

So be it.

I take out Art's thong—I mean, dance belt—from under my pillow and take a good whiff.

Oh, yeah.

I speed up and let all the images from my rub bank flow freely, the ones from the video and the banya.

And just like that, I come in ten seconds.

Suddenly feeling silly, I stuff the dance belt back under the pillow.

Woofer parks his butt in his charger.

It's official. It's only a matter of days before my human overlord is assimilated into the Borg. I will pray to iRobot Corporation that she's a lot less messy in her cyborg form, but I'm not holding my fan-powered breath.

When I can move again, I open the laptop and post the "Live Long and Prosper" technique without hesitation. It is bound to improve some people's lives, even if only in a tiny way.

As the first positive comment shows up, I grin. This blog really is my calling. I'm glad Art's money will allow me to do it for a while longer. Of course, the ultimate dream would be to find a good sponsor that can keep me doing this forever—which brings me back to that text to Bella that I've been procrastinating on.

Fuck it. I read my reply one more time and click send.

No instant reply, but it is late. I watch some TV until I get sleepy, and then I go to bed, where I can't help but do one more session of "Live Long and Prosper."

———

I wake up to the ringing of my phone.

Cursing, I snatch it from the nightstand and look at the screen.

It's Art, but why is he calling at such an obscenely early hour?

Begrudgingly, I accept the call. "Do you know what time it is?"

He chuckles. "10 a.m.?"

"Yeah. Exactly. Let me call you back after I wake up." I hang up.

Someone knocks on the garage door that also serves as my wall.

What the fuck?

"Open up," Art's voice says through the door/wall. "I've got people with me who get paid by the hour."

He what?

I leap off the bed and dress as quickly as I can.

Sticking my nose filters into place, I open my door/wall.

Outside is Art with a bunch of buff dudes.

Hold up. Is this some kind of orgy fantasy dream?

No. Dream Art doesn't share me with anyone. This must be reality. But then what the—

"Sorry to barge in on you," Art says. "I called several times."

"What is going on?" I ask, making it a point to stay far away from everyone on account of not having brushed my teeth yet.

"I got us a place," he says, like it's the most obvious thing in the world and not a bombshell of nuclear proportions. "These guys are the movers I hired."

CHAPTER
Twenty-Four

"MOVERS?" I wait for the punchline of the joke, even if I can't imagine what it could be.

Art nods. "Don't you want your stuff at our place?"

"Our place?" I'm not sure if it's the ungodly hour, but my brain refuses to compute the words coming out of my dear husband's mouth.

Art sighs. "Married people live together. Right?"

Oh, skunk. That is right. The government people will surely get suspicious if we don't reside at the same address. So will everyone else.

How have I managed *not* to realize this basic implication of our fake marriage? I wonder what else I haven't anticipated?

Ideas flood my brain. Now that we're official, Art can pull the plug on me if I get into a horrible accident —and he'd own Woofer afterward, along with everything else that's mine.

I halt the spiraling thoughts when I see everyone

looking at me expectantly. "I need to brush my teeth. Can you just pack my books for now?"

The movers nod, so I dart into the bathroom and make myself if not presentable, then at least recognizable as human.

When I come out, the books are nearly packed.

These guys are fast.

I lock eyes with Art, who's standing next to my bed with a plastic bag.

"You'll need this," he says, then picks up my pillow and stuffs it into the bag. "And I'm not sure if you want to get a new—"

He stops talking as he notices what lies under my pillow.

Oh, fuck. His dance belt. He's going to realize I've been sniffing it, like a total perv.

If Art is upset, he recovers quickly. Before any of the movers can spot it, he stashes his undies in the same bag as the pillow, then stuffs my sheet in there as well, which hides all the evidence.

He then clears his throat. "Where is your linen closet?"

Face burning, I show him the box that serves that purpose, and he takes it and the bag with my pillow out to a nearby truck.

"No," I hiss at him. "That's not going with the movers."

If the bag rips and Art's dance belt falls out, I'll have to murder the movers as witnesses, then probably go to jail and become a bitch to a woman named Karen. But what if Karen doesn't shower enough? Or uses perfume? Or has bad breath?

Chuckling, Art takes the bag and carries it to a nearby Honda Odyssey.

I gape at the minivan. "Is that what you drive?"

"I just leased it," he says. "Don't you think it screams, 'I'm married?'"

I blow out a breath. "It screams, 'I'm married with children,' and that's not happening."

A dark smile curves his lips. "Never say never."

If smiles could impregnate, then I'm in danger of needing that minivan.

"We need to talk," I say. "About all the fun surprises that come with our marriage."

"Tell the guys how you want your stuff packed, and then we'll take a ride to the new place and talk on the way."

I turn on my heel and go back to my garage.

My packing instructions don't take long, mostly because I don't have that much stuff.

"I'm taking this with me," I tell Art as I gently put Woofer into one of the million boxes the movers brought before adding in his charging dock and other accoutrements.

Oh, no! I'm going to have a new human overlord. A male one—and therefore hairier. Why, iRobot Corporation? Why me? A bigger place also means more dust. Maybe this box should get lost on the way? Or run over by a bulldozer?

Art blinks at the box. "Is that a Roomba?"

Nodding, I close the lid.

"You won't need that," Art says. "I have a cleaning lady."

I scoff. "Woofer is like family. He's coming with."

"I see." Art reaches to take the box. "I didn't realize that a robotic vacuum cleaner was such a serious commitment."

"Be careful with him." I hand over my precious.

Art takes the box as if it were an infant and carries it slowly to the minivan. "Anything else you want to personally carry?"

I decide that I do. I make everyone leave, and then I pack my underwear, sex toys, and laptop into a box that I label "PRIVATE."

"Ready now," I say.

Art reaches to carry the box, but I refuse to give it to him—in case something starts to vibrate inside and thus gives the game away.

"Can we talk now?" I ask as we get moving.

"In a second." Art turns the wheel and glances at me. "Do you know a cat?"

I stare at him. "Do I know a what?"

"A cat."

I blink a few times. "That's what I thought you said. I still don't get it, though."

"We need a cat. Just for a short while."

"We do?"

He stops at a red light and looks at me, his face dead serious. "According to Russian tradition, the first entity to walk into a new home must be a cat."

I cock my head. "Tradition or superstition?"

He sighs. "Do you know a cat or not?"

The red light turns to green, and we resume driving as I do something I never thought I would: catalogue all the cats in my acquaintance to figure out which of them I want involved in my marriage.

The pickings are slim. Blue has a cat named Machete, but he's a scary motherfucker, and I want Art's eyes and other bits to stay intact, thank you very much. Honey also has a cat. Hers is named Bunny, and —according to Honey—is a psychopath. I'm not sure if that helps this Russian tradition or hurts it.

"Let me call my sister," I say and dial Honey.

"Hey," she says. "What's up?"

"Can Art and I borrow your cat?"

Silence.

"It's this Russian tradition," I say.

More silence.

"Okay, let me put you on speaker phone so Art can explain it better." I click the button and move the phone closer to Art's yummy lips.

"Art, meet Honey. Honey, meet Art."

"Hello," Art says. "It sounds like you own a cat. If we could just borrow it for an hour, I'd greatly appreciate it."

"Why?" Honey asks, summarizing my position quite nicely.

"In Russia, a cat is considered a symbol of prosperity and wellbeing," he says. "It is believed that a cat will bring positivity into the dwelling."

Honey snorts. "Positivity? Have you ever met my cat?"

"Your cat's personality isn't important. Any cat will

annul the negative vibes left from the prior owners of the place."

"Ah, vibes," I say. "Why didn't you say so earlier? Does it appease the spirits too?"

Art's lips press into a line. "I might not personally believe it, but yes, the ancient Slavs did worry about household spirits, and a cat was considered an ambassador to them."

"Wouldn't the cat eat Fluffer?" I ask.

Honey sounds like she's choked on a drink. "Who or what is Fluffer?"

"Our pet chinchilla," Art explains. "He'll be okay because he's still at my old apartment."

"Ah, okay," Honey says. "I'll bring Bunny over to your new place. Give me the address."

Art turns to me, the corners of his eyes crinkling. "It just hit me. Honey and Bunny?"

I shake my head vehemently and make a zipping motion across my lips. If Honey thinks she's being mocked, she will refuse to bring the cat over, and then we'll have to deal with Blue's homicidal beast.

"Your sense of humor is a lot like your wife's," Honey says dryly. "This union might actually work."

"Indeed," Art says and tells her the address.

"When should I be there?" she asks.

"In twenty minutes, if you can," Art says.

"See you." Honey hangs up.

"That's some request." I text my sister a big thanks.

Art tightens his grip on the wheel. "Look… I didn't have a home growing up, so now when I get a place, I like to get things right."

Oh. Damn it, now that he's playing the orphan card, I feel like an ass for poking fun.

"Are there any other traditions like this one?" I ask, doing my best not to sound judgy or mocking.

"This is one of the few that I follow. But yeah, there are tons of others. Some people put honey in the corners of the house."

"Oh?"

"It's supposed to appease the *domovoi*. A kind of benevolent house spirit."

Wow. This is getting kookier by the second.

Grinning, I say, "Just in case, we could ask my sister Honey to stand in some of the corners. Cover our bases."

I even know what she'd say if we asked her: "No one puts Baby in a corner."

He chuckles. "Won't she get flashbacks of being a naughty child?"

I look at him worriedly. "Did they put you in a corner as a kid? My parents think that's child abuse."

He winces. "That was the least of it."

My chest squeezes. "I'm sorry. I feel like such a spoiled brat. My siblings and I didn't even get timeouts."

"And you turned out great," he says, his eyes warm as he glances at me. "I agree with your parents. Children should be cherished, not punished."

Okay. I'll file that away in case we get drunk again and have unprotected sex.

I shift in my seat. "Any other traditions to be aware of?"

"Some Russians sprinkle change around the house," he says.

"That could be useful." I check my pockets and locate a few quarters. "Anything else?"

"Not for moving in. But when you leave the house, it is traditional to pour out a glass of water."

I keep my face neutral. "Like pouring one out for the homies?"

"What's that?"

"Never mind. What else?"

"Before leaving to go on a trip, Russians formally sit down. When inside the house, whistling is forbidden, as it can lead to lack of money."

Is that why I'm so broke? I do like to whistle as I write my blog posts… but never again.

"You got more?"

"You can't twirl a hat," he says. "You can't put bread upside down. You can't spill salt. You can't wear a shirt inside out. You can't sit at the corner of the table—but that only applies if you're unmarried. You can't cut your own hair."

"Not even bangs?"

He grins. "I think you should be safe there."

"Okay. Is that it?"

"You can't shake hands under a front door frame. And that one is serious. Even non-superstitious Russians follow that."

Huh. I guess no shaking of hands with the pizza guy. Got it.

"What's the one you follow the most?" I ask.

He considers it. "There's one about eating everything on your plate. I always do that."

"Is it a respect for food thing?"

He nods, a bit grimly. "They say leaving food can lead to tears, but I think you've nailed it. The tradition was probably started by people who knew real hunger. Once you do, it doesn't feel right, throwing away food."

If he's saying what I think he's saying, I want to get a time machine and go back so I can feed him at the orphanage. Also, I feel horrible about all the desserts we left in that hotel room in Vegas. Hopefully, he doesn't consider desserts real food, but just in case, I now have an extra reason not to admit my inability to eat the cake after all that fruit.

"Anyway," Art says. "You wanted to discuss some marriage stuff?"

Ah. Right. I almost forgot. "What other things do I need to know about? Living together caught me off-guard, so I figure this is worth a conversation."

He switches lanes as he thinks. "I had a preliminary chat with an immigration lawyer, and she told me we'll need recommendation letters from friends and family."

"I think that can be arranged." I'll be mocked mercilessly, of course, but hey, this is why they say marriage is hard work.

He stops the car next to a swanky building and begins to park. "Some of the other stuff the lawyer mentioned we're already on top of. We'll need proof of living together and joint pictures. We will also be interviewed at some point, so we'll need to learn about one another."

He exits the car, and when he comes around to open my door, I ask, "Learn what?"

He shrugs. "They'll ask you if I've ever been in any Communist groups or terrorist organizations. The answer is no. They'll ask us both mundane stuff, like what kind of toothbrush the other person uses, which one of us likes to cook, or what kind of work we each do."

Skunk. That last one means I'll have to tell him about my blog.

"Don't worry," he says, clearly misunderstanding my expression. "We'll learn all we need to learn long before the interview."

My phone dings. I wave with it. "I bet that's Honey."

I check.

It's not.

The text is from Bella, and it makes my heart sink:

Hi there. It looks like we won't need to set anything up anymore.

CHAPTER
Twenty~Five

OH, no. I ruined it, didn't I? The drunken texts were too much, and Bella has rightfully flaked on me.

Skunk.

I'll need to restart the search for a sponsor, though my chances of finding as good of a fit as Bella's company are almost—

"Are you okay?" Art asks.

Right. Forgot where I am. "Yeah. All good."

He frowns. "You don't look 'all good.' If someone has upset you, I need to know, so I can—"

"Hello," a familiar voice says from behind us.

Art turns, and his eyes widen as he takes in Honey in all her biker-gang-inspired attire.

"Told you I have identical sisters," I say.

"Yeah," he says, sounding awed. "And to think there are four more of you."

Honey readjusts her leather jacket. "You'll see us all at the reception. Speaking of, did you get my RSVP?"

He nods. "Is that the cat?" He looks at the carrier she's holding.

"Yep. That's Bunny, reporting for duty."

"Let's go." Art holds the door to the building for us, like a doorman, then follows us into the elevator and presses the button for the twelfth floor.

When we get there, the corridor is clean and neat, a rarity for New York apartment buildings. Art stops next to a thick redwood door and pulls out a key. "This is it."

Honey sets down the carrier and opens it.

Bunny steps out, looking like Eeyore when he lost his tail—an impression strengthened by the fact that this breed of cat doesn't have a fluffy tail, only a little bobtail, like the namesake bunny. His fur is white, with black spots around the eyes that make him look like he belongs in the Addams family, or a Goth club.

"Is that normal?" Art asks, examining Bunny's butt.

"Yeah." Honey fluffs Bunny's fur and gets a murderous glare for her troubles. "He's a Japanese bobtail. If you've ever seen one of those beckoning-cat statues in a sushi restaurant, that's a depiction of this breed."

"I see," Art says. "So cats are considered lucky in Japan too."

"Maybe." I turn to Honey. "Is Hello Kitty also this kind of cat?"

Honey and Bunny give me sardonic glares. "Hello Kitty is a cartoon character," Honey says. "And a girl, not a cat."

I sigh. "But if she were a cat?"

Honey parrots my sigh. "She'd be this breed."

Chuckling, Art opens the door.

Looking indignant, Bunny stiffens his spine and puts his bobtail in the "up" position.

"Go," Honey says.

Bunny strolls imperiously into the place.

"Hubby, dearest," I say. "When can we follow the cat?"

Art frowns. "I'm not actually sure."

I rub my chin. "Strictly speaking, the cat was the first to enter."

"I have a better question," Honey says. "Do you have anything inside that can be murdered and/or tortured?"

Art steps into the apartment. "Not yet, but how about we follow, just in case."

I step inside.

Wow.

The entryway and hallway are clean and modern, with an empty shoe rack in the foyer—a luxury item I do not own—and even a coat hanger on the wall.

Very grown-up.

There are also paintings in the classical style everywhere, but it's the familiar sound coming from one corner of the room that commands my attention.

"Is that an air purifier?" I ask Art, excited.

He glances at my nose. "I had one installed in every room."

Aww. I walk over to the device. It's the same brand as the one I have, but a fancier model. To get them for every room must've cost a fortune and a half.

"Aww," Honey says, echoing my thoughts. "Making sure the place doesn't smell? He's a keeper."

"You know it." I take out my nose filters.

Damn. This apartment is an olfactory nirvana. I'm almost unable to smell anything other than Art's yumminess and Honey's leather jacket.

"We should check on Bunny." Art leads us down the hallway and into what turns out to be a bedroom.

Honey chuckles. "This is where it will all happen."

I arch my eyebrows at her. "Mom, is that you?"

"Touché." Honey looks under the bed. "Bunny's not here."

We walk into the kitchen.

"Incredible," I mutter, taking in gleaming white cabinets that extend all the way to the ceiling, stainless steel appliances that look vaguely futuristic, and black quartz countertops that are roomy enough for me to pitch a tent on them. Not to mention, a table with actual chairs.

"Well, duh," Honey says. "Your old place doesn't even have a kitchen."

Art's eyebrows furrow. I guess he didn't notice that detail when he stopped by this morning.

"The cat isn't here." I open one of the kitchen cabinets on a lark. Still no cat. "Where else could he be?"

"This way," Art says and leads us into the living room.

Nice. A huge TV, white rugs, a sleek gray couch—I can see myself here, chilling and watching Netflix with Art… in a purely literal, platonic sense, of course.

Then I spot a giant cage-like structure in one corner of the room and the cat gazing longingly into it.

Honey looks the cage up and down. "Kinky."

I roll my eyes, and Art coughs.

"That's called a chinchilla mansion," he says. "It's for our *pet*."

Honey gives me a meaningful glance. "Right. It's for your naughty little *pet*. Got it."

I study Bunny warily. "Why is he staring like that?"

Honey follows my gaze. "No doubt fantasizing about the panicked screams of a creature he's slowly and luxuriously torturing to death."

How cheerful.

"Well." Art eyes the cat. "I think we're done with his services."

"Yeah," I say. "He'd better leave so Fluffer doesn't smell homicide in the air when he gets back."

Honey glances at this room's air purifier. "I doubt even *you* will smell Bunny in a few minutes, but fine." She bends down and carefully picks up the cat—whose gaze doesn't leave "the mansion" throughout. "You guys probably need to settle in anyway."

"Thanks, sis," I say.

"No problem." She walks to the entrance, and we follow. "It was a pleasure to meet you, Art."

"The pleasure was mine," he says.

Hey now. Better not have been too much of a pleasure.

"I'll see you both at the reception," Honey says. "Speaking of which, I have two plus-ones. I hope that's okay."

Before I can explain to her what plus-one actually means in English, Art waves his hand. "You're not the only one."

Great. And here I thought we'd have a small shindig. Whatever. It's outside, so the perfume and cologne smells will be less potent.

Honey sticks Bunny into the carrier. "Bye."

I wave to her, and when she enters the elevator, I turn to Art. "So what now?"

He suggests we start nesting, so that's what we do. Soon after, the movers arrive, and Art helps me unbox my stuff and find good places to keep it all.

"This closet is all yours," Art says, opening a door in the bedroom.

Oh, my. It's a walk-in closet that reminds me of the one Carrie had in the movie version of *Sex and the City*. It's so huge it might just lead to Narnia, but one with fashionistas instead of talking beasts. Not that there's a big difference between the two.

It takes me mere minutes to hang all the clothes I own, and they take up less than one percent of the insane storage space.

"Hey!" Art calls from somewhere. "Can you come here for a second?"

I locate him in the kitchen, holding a cake.

"The movers brought this," he says, lifting his eyebrows.

Skunk. I forgot to get rid of the evidence.

"Isn't this the cake that came with the fruit?" he asks.

I sigh. "You know it is."

He grins. "Is there anything you want to say?"

"Like this?" I curtsy. "You were right, dear. My sweet tooth is *totally* a craving for fruit. I bow to your infinite wisdom."

He shakes his head, looking torn between stashing the cake in the fridge and tossing it. Unable to decide, he just hands it to me. "I'm going to my place to get more of my stuff. Want to join?"

"No. Let me keep sorting things out here." I pointedly stick my finger into the cake and lick it.

He watches my finger with a burning in his eyes. Have I made him angry?

Unwilling to test my fake husband any further, I stick the cake in the fridge. His slight wince is my reward.

"Lock the door behind me," Art says and walks out of the kitchen.

I follow and watch him exit the apartment, closing the door behind him.

I stare at it, the enormity of what's just happened hitting me fully for the first time.

I'm going to live with Art.

Me. With the guy I've fantasized about.

Unbidden, a girlish, gleeful squeak escapes my lips.

I can't believe this is happening.

It's like a surreal dream.

Oh, and the cherry on top is I'm getting paid for this shit.

Before I can squeal again, the door opens.

"You didn't lock it?" Art's frown makes me take a step back. "You have to do it as soon as I leave."

"Yes, dear. I'll obey your every command, dear."

His features soften. "Please, Lemon. This is Manhattan. You never know who might barge in."

"Fine." I finally notice what he's holding: my PRIVATE box in one hand and the bag with my bed sheets in the other. My heart leaps. "I thought I told you not to touch that!"

"Sorry." He puts the stuff on the floor. "Figured you might want to deal with whatever is inside."

Before I can ask him to swear on his soul that he didn't peek inside the box, he leaves again.

I stare at the bed sheets, my heartbeat speeding further.

They're a physical reminder of a question I should've asked Art from the very beginning.

Where are we going to sleep? More importantly, will it be together? In one bed?

Surely not. He'll probably take the couch. Or I will.

But what if we *do* sleep together?

This is getting so real so fast I feel like another squeak—or a squeal—is working its way out of my body.

I'd better busy myself with chores.

First things first. I scan the apartment for a place to stash my sex toys.

When I was a kid, I hid stuff from my sisters in a broken electrical outlet, but this place probably has them all working, and I don't want to get electrocuted. The floor baseboards look sturdy as well, so no hiding stuff there either.

Maybe the oven?

No. I have no idea if Art likes to cook.

The freezer? But what if he wants to freeze some peas?

Then it hits me. I rush to the bathroom and lift the toilet tank cover. Yep. Since the toys are waterproof, this will work nicely.

Okay, now I have to deal with the dance belt. Actually, there's not much choice here but to let it go. I can't have Art catching me sniffing it.

I walk around until I spot the laundry hamper in the bathroom. Reluctantly, I toss the dance belt in.

"Bye," I say to it. "It was nice knowing you."

Skunk. Maybe I should've taken one last sniff?

No. Must be strong.

I busy myself by putting a bunch of stuff away. Then I realize I haven't yet set up Woofer. Even with all these air purifiers and the cleaning lady, the place could start smelling dusty without his help.

In a few minutes, Woofer is running around, motor growling—until he hits the first door.

What the hell, human overlord? This place is too big. I'll get tired and will need my charger way before I'm done cleaning it all. And these doors? Keep them open at all times, or else. And make sure no wires are in my path. It seems the iRobot Corporation has forsaken me in my most dire hour of need.

The doorbell rings.

I check the peephole. It's Art, and he's holding a pet carrier and a box.

"Who is it?" I ask, doing my best to sound super-cautious.

"Art," he says approvingly.

"I need proof of that. Can you show me your driver's license through the peephole?"

With a smirk, he puts his stuff down and does as I say. "Can you open the door now?"

"It's suspicious you want me to open the door without more precautions. Real Art would want me to be careful. Maybe I should get more proof that you're you?"

His smirk turns into a slight frown. "Like what?"

I grin. "The real Art has a very distinct tattoo. Can you show it to me?"

I reach to unlock the door, but he actually steps away and does as I ask, flashing me the ink and the sexy V that leads down to Mr. Big.

Yummy. Should I ask to see *that* next? No. This joke has gone on long enough. I unlock the door.

He picks up the carrier and the box and steps inside with an exasperated expression. "Was that really necessary?"

"Just wanted to be safe, as you ordered. I know better than anyone that merely seeing someone's face isn't enough to prove their identity. I share my face with five other individuals—most of them untrustworthy."

He sets the box down near the door but holds on to the carrier. "I doubt I have long-lost sextuplet siblings, and even if I did, they'd be unlikely to live in America."

There I go again, reminding Art that he's an orphan. What's next? Forgetting to feed him? Making him watch a movie marathon of *Batman*, *Harry Potter*, and *Oliver Twist*?

A squeak emanates from the carrier.

Art says something soothing in Russian and then switches to English. "Let's go put Fluffer into his enclosure."

"Sure." Anything to get his attention away from the metaphorical foot in my mouth.

Art leads me to the living room, opens the door to the chinchilla mansion, and aligns the carrier with it before opening the hatch.

Fluffer whizzes into his new home, eyes wild with excitement.

Maybe they're not eating me yet. Maybe they want me happy and contented, like Kobe cows.

At first reluctantly, then with growing excitement, Fluffer jumps onto the numerous shelves that were clearly designed for this very purpose. When he tires of exploring the shelves, he leaps onto a flying saucer-like contraption and runs as fast as his little paws allow.

I grin. "Is that a chinchilla treadmill?"

Art's grin matches mine. "Closer to a chinchilla hamster wheel."

I blink, mesmerized by Art's glinting eyes. "Too cute."

"I should feed him." He leaves the room and comes back with the box.

"What's in the box?" I ask. "Is it Gwyneth Paltrow's head?"

He frowns. "Why?"

"I can't tell you without spoiling a certain movie," I say.

"Fine." He opens the box.

"Is that hay?" I pick up a few dried stalks and sniff them. Yep. Exactly like the stuff we played in at my parents' farm. "Is this for Fluffer or a surprise pony you're about to give me as a wedding gift?"

He narrows his eyes. "Don't you remember what the guy at the store said?"

I wince. "Sorry."

"We need to make sure Fluffer always has access to hay," Art says in a professorial tone. "It's good for his dental, physical, and digestive health."

"Hey, I don't have a problem with hay."

Shaking his head, Art arranges the hay inside what must be a feeder, then attaches a weird bottle contraption near it. It reminds me of something I've seen at the farm.

"Is that a water bottle with a straw with a metal ball?"

"Yes. In case you forgot, we can't use a bowl for water as that could lead to Fluffer's fur getting wet—and that's bad."

"Why, will he spawn more adorable furballs?"

Art looks at me like *I've* spawned a few furballs.

"You know, if you feed him after midnight, he turns into a gremlin?"

Art's expression doesn't change, but now Fluffer stares at me also.

Me, a gremlin? Have you looked into a mirror lately?

I sigh. "If this marriage is going to work, there's a list of movies you'll have to see. Put one called *Gremlins* at the top."

"I'll watch whatever you ask me to," Art says. "Can we get back to chinchillas getting wet?"

I giggle. "It just hit me. Gremlins aren't the only ones whose reproduction involves getting wet."

"So mature," he says with an eyeroll. "Anyway, getting wet can lead to fur fungus or ringworm, or cause hypothermia. In general, chinchillas don't like getting wet."

Fluffer grabs a stalk of hay and begins munching on it.

Everything he said is true, so when your carnivorous nature is finally revealed, for the love of fur, don't make me into a soup.

I eye the adorable furball with a grin. "Will we need to brush him?"

"Need, no," Art says. "He'll groom himself. Some of them do like to be brushed, though, so we can try it once he gets used to us a little."

Fluffer grabs himself more hay.

Get used to you? Let a hungry bear adopt you, then get back to me when you want it to brush your hair.

"What about cuddles?" I eye Fluffer skeptically. "Would he want to be held?"

"Again, after some trust is formed," Art says.

Fluffer catches my gaze, his expression frightened.

Go cuddle with a hungry bear, and then we'll talk trust.

Art stands up. "Let's let him acclimate to his new surroundings."

"Sure," I say. "What do you want to do now?"

Please say, "Talk about the sleeping arrangements."

He strokes his chin thoughtfully. "If you're done

unpacking, how about you put together that list of movies for me?"

I do as he suggests, which obviously ends in me watching some of the movies I put on the list. Being considerate, I close the living room door to avoid spoiling anything for Art.

Just as Hannibal Lecter delivers the line about "having an old friend for dinner," my nose detects something delicious wafting from the gap under the door.

I let my nose lead me to the epicenter of the tempting scent—the kitchen.

The kitchen table is set with beautiful square plates, candles, and three bowls with incredible-smelling delicacies, with classical music adding to the ambience.

"Rice pilaf," Art says when he spots where I'm looking. "With raisins and dates."

Wow. Speaking of dates, I feel like I've just stumbled into one.

"Did you cook all this?" I ask, my mouth watering. "Or is it takeout?"

"I like to cook," he says.

I'm about to say, "Marry me," but then I remember he already did.

"Please sit," he says. "I was just about to call you."

He doesn't have to ask me twice. I plop my butt down and reach for the rice.

Art grabs my wrist gently, which kicks off fireworks up and down my whole body. Fireworks that end with a sparkler in my nether regions.

"I'm going to service you."

Oh, that again. Just like the last time, the words produce X-rated images in my mind, but now they're made worse by the fact that I've seen what it looks like when he "services me" in the dirty way that also involves eating.

Art ladles the rice onto my plate and then tops it off with something that looks even yummier.

"What's that?" I ask. "It smells divine."

As if to confirm my statement, my stomach growls, like Woofer when he's especially grumpy.

Art smiles. "Duck à l'Orange." He places something fruity next to the duck. "With poached pears."

If I like that duck, is he going to use that as proof that I'm French?

I reach for my fork and knife, then stop. "Am I allowed to pick these up, or is handling silverware part of the service?"

He picks up my utensils and cuts up the duck for me into small, delectable pieces. "You're allowed to handle your own fork and knife. Just let me fill your plate and cup." Matching actions to words, he fills my glass with something that looks like sangria. "Russian-style compote," he explains.

"Thanks."

I start with the rice. Sweet and savory, it's mouth-gasmic. Next, I put a tiny piece of pear in my mouth. Wow. Even better than the rice. I sip the drink. Double wow. This could replace my Mountain Dew addiction. I attack the duck. Triple wow. Even sweeter and with enough umami flavor to please a Japanese foodie, the duck makes my eyes roll into the back of my head in pleasure.

"Do you like it?" Art asks.

It takes an effort of will not to quack in response. "I don't like it… I love it." I stuff more of everything into my greedy mouth.

Art grins widely. "I'm glad. Is it sweet enough?"

Since my mouth is too full, I nod.

"No sugar," he says proudly. "It's all from the fruit."

I chew and swallow, enjoying every second. The only worrisome thing about this meal is related to the old proverb: "The way to a man's heart is through his stomach." If that works on women too, my heart could be in serious jeopardy.

"So," I say when I've taken the edge off the worst of my hunger. "Did you go to culinary school or something? This is not a meal an average person can just make."

"Self-taught." He grabs himself another serving of the salad I've been pointedly ignoring. "Early in my career, ballet didn't leave much time for any other pursuits, but more recently, I've gotten into cooking and investing. What about you? What did you study in college?"

This isn't my favorite topic. Some people with DNA identical to mine are highly educated, whereas I'm… not. "I didn't go to college." I grimace. "I guess I'm self-taught also."

It's true. I've masturbated for as long as I can recall, and if they gave out degrees in it, I'd have a master's at least, or maybe even a PhD, considering how much I've written on the subject.

If Art looks down on my lack of schooling, he shows zero signs of it. If anything, his nod seems approving. "That reminds me," he says. "What is it that you do?"

My heart does a backflip. This situation is my fault. I should have foreseen this coming up when I asked him about culinary school. So stupid. Maybe I can still salvage this?

"Hold up," I say. "You didn't tell me what *you* studied in school."

His narrowed eyes remind me of Hershey's kisses. "You're dodging my question, aren't you?"

Skunk. I put my fork down. "Or it's *you* who doesn't want to tell me about your college education."

He sighs. "I attended a university back in Russia, but they gave me my grades based on my ballet fame, not merit, so I don't consider my Economics degree to be worth much. When it came to investing, I had to learn everything from scratch." He looks at me expectantly.

I stare back guilelessly. "I put that movie list together for you. Want to see?"

He reaches across the table and playfully grips my chin—which makes something in my panties short-circuit. "Tell me what you do for a living."

"No."

He drops his hand and makes puppy eyes at me—and this time, the short-circuit is in my brain. "Please?"

On the one hand, it's flattering that he wants to learn

all he can about me. Makes me feel like he cares. On the other hand, once he learns this, he'll run.

The puppy eyes don't go away.

I heave a sigh. "Do I have to?"

His face turns serious. "They'll ask us these questions at the interview."

Oh, skunk. I forgot about that. He's not just casually getting to know me because he cares. It's all just a means to an end to get that green card.

"Fine," I say. "But you'll regret marrying me, for sure."

"Doubt it."

I take a deep breath. "Promise not to tease?"

He nods.

"Promise not to get a divorce?"

He looks concerned now. "I promise, unless your profession is something truly heinous, like a tax attorney."

"Fine. My job involves petting the cat… if you know what I mean."

He blinks at me. "Like a house sitter for people with cats?"

I roll my eyes. "I'm talking about the two-finger taco tango."

"What?"

"Buffing the weasel?"

Is that concern for my sanity in his gaze?

"Brushing the beaver? Squeezing the peach?" I make the V-shape of the Vulcan salute with my fingers. "You've seen me do it. Remember?"

A hint of comprehension glimmers in his eyes. "You're a sex worker?"

It's my turn to look blank. "How did you get that? I'm talking about masturbation."

He nods warily. "And that's why I asked if you're a sex worker."

"What kind of a sex worker masturbates for a living?"

He lifts one broad shoulder in a shrug. "The girls at peep shows? The girls who work those chat cams? The girls who—"

"Sorry, no. I'm not a sex worker. At least I don't think I am. I blog about the subject of muffin buffin'—but I don't actually do it in front of anyone… besides that time with you."

He rubs the back of his neck. "If that's all, why did you not want to tell me?"

"Because it's embarrassing?"

He exhales a relieved breath. "And that's it?"

"Well, yeah." I begin to feel a bit silly. "I thought you were a conservative type who'd judge me."

He puts his hand over mine—which makes comprehending very hard. "Just because I like classical music and I open doors for you doesn't mean I'm a prude."

That makes sense, at least when his touch is scrambling my brain.

With a smile, he pulls the hand away to get his phone. "What's your blog called?"

Flushing, I say, "Pet the Petunia."

He types it into his phone and reads for a few of the longest moments of my life.

Finally, he puts his phone face down. "That's pretty good."

A ballet of swans takes flight in my belly. "You think so?"

He nods. "All those positive comments. You're helping other women. I think it's great."

If he wanted to get into my pants, this would be a way to do it. Well, this and the dinner. And the hand on hand. And the way he smells. And—

Fine. It seems it isn't that hard for Art to get into my pants—which reminds me.

"What are our sleeping arrangements?" I blurt.

There. Like ripping off a Band-Aid.

Art's hands go still, his fork frozen in midair. "Are you sure you don't want to have dessert first?"

The duck and the rice harden into coal in my stomach. "Look who's dodging the question this time."

He picks up the glass of compote and takes a generous sip. "You're right. We should talk about this."

And yet he sits there silently until I can't take it anymore and say, "I'm starting to guess you want to sleep *together*."

His head bobs slightly. "But Rule One still applies."

Am I disappointed or relieved? "Then why?"

"Because of the interviews," he says. "They might ask you if I snore, or who hogs the blanket. I figure we should sleep in the same bed at least long enough to learn such details. After that, we can take turns on the couch in the living room. I made sure it's extremely comfortable."

I drum my fingers on the table. "That's ironclad logic."

And as unromantic as an anthill.

"Good." He rises fluidly to his feet. "Ready to try dessert?"

Okay, I guess that's all the conversation we'll have when it comes to the sleeping arrangements. Not sure I can blame him for not wanting to think more about it.

"Let's have the dessert," I say, faking the cheerfulness I usually feel when sweets are the topic of conversation.

He reaches into the freezer.

Thank goodness I didn't stash the sex toys there.

The bag he pulls out is hard to see through, and then his back blocks what he does with its contents—but whatever it is, I'm intrigued.

Suddenly, the sound of a woodchipper roars through the kitchen, almost deafening me.

What the hell? Is he getting some maple syrup from inside a tree trunk? I thought you just needed to tap it for that.

When the noise stops, Art scoops something out of the blender cup—which explains the noise—and into a pretty bowl.

"Here." He puts the treat in front of me.

"This looks like ice cream," I say. "But isn't that the root of all evil?"

He sprinkles an assortment of nuts on top of the ice cream. "Try it." He hands me a little spoon.

I taste the result. Yum. It reminds me of a sundae that's extra heavy on banana.

He watches my lips like he's hypnotized by them. "You like?"

I swallow the sweet goodness. "What's the catch?"

"It's banana."

I eat another spoonful. "Sure. I can taste the banana."

His grin is of Cheshire Cat proportions. "You don't understand. Banana is the *only* ingredient."

What?

I dip the spoon into the creamy goodness and swirl it around. "There's no way this is just banana."

"Yes, way," he says. He brings over the bag he took out from the freezer and shows me the frozen bananas inside. "This is all I put in the blender."

I take another spoonful. Hmm. "Now that I know what to taste for, the ice cream illusion is ruined a bit."

He shrugs. "If you enjoy it, finish. If not, no big deal."

Lies. I know he's Mr. Don't Leave Food on Your Plate. Not that I'd want to throw this away. This ice cream may be as fake as our marriage, but it's cold, creamy, and delicious... not to mention all the potassium and whatnot.

Finishing it, I put my spoon down. "Thank you."

"You're welcome." He takes all the plates over to the sink and begins to wash them.

"Wait," I say. "You cooked. At least let me clean."

"No need." He opens a door on what turns out to be a dishwasher. "Earl will take care of it."

I arch an eyebrow. "Earl?"

He puts the rest of the dishes away. "You named

your vacuum cleaner, so I figured I'd name our dishwasher."

As if summoned, Woofer rolls into the kitchen—and bumps into the leg of my chair.

Looks like the male human overlord is just as lazy as the female one. Can't even bother to wash a dish on his own. At least he's better at naming the poor machine he's enslaved. Earl sounds royal and dignified, while Woofer is the name of a filthy mutt.

I stand up. "What now?"

Art extracts a dishwashing tablet from its candy-wrapper-like covering and sticks it into Earl. "I was thinking we'd exchange our movie lists."

"Exchange? I thought I was just giving one to you."

He takes out his phone. "I decided what's good for the goose is good for the gander."

"Fine. Let me take a gander at your list."

"Ladies first."

With a mock groan, I text him my list.

He scans it, and a smile appears on his face.

"What?" I ask.

He points at the screen. "That show. I've seen it before. It's great."

No.

Can't be.

But there's only one TV show on the list.

Still, I can't assume. This is too big to leave to an assumption.

"Which show are you talking about?" I ask, my voice unsteady.

"Sex and the City. I'm a big fan."

231

"You like *Sex and the City*?"

If he'd electrocuted me with a taser, I'd still be less shocked. I've yet to meet a male who's even watched it, let alone liked it. I mean, I've always known such creatures existed in theory, like black swans or telemarketers that people enjoy getting a call from, but I didn't expect one to cook me dinner.

Art nods. "That show is how I fell in love with New York. In a way, I wouldn't be here without it."

Okay. It's official.

I married my soulmate.

CHAPTER
Twenty-Six

IN THE NEXT INSTANT, doubt creeps in. Could he just be saying that? Also, even if he's telling the truth, why did he watch the show? Was it because he lusted after one of the leads, or did he want to understand women better?

He touches my forearm. "Are you okay?"

"Why?"

"Because you're looking at me funny."

I blink a few times. "I mean, 'why did you watch the show?'"

He smiles. "Let's go to the living room and get comfy. Then we'll talk."

What a tease. I follow him to the couch and plop down next to him, my skin tingling as our knees touch.

"Spill," I growl.

"I think it should be obvious," he says.

I stare at him blankly.

"Mikhail Baryshnikov," he says with exasperation.

Oh. How did I not think of that?

"He was the guy who played 'the Russian' in the last season," Art says. If the topic were anything but *Sex and the City*, he would be totally mansplaining, but I love this too much to complain as he continues. "In case you didn't know, in real life, he's a ballet legend—and, like me, was born in Riga."

I grimace ruefully. "I feel silly now."

"Don't. How could you know that man was my idol? I started with those nine episodes he was in, then got hooked and watched everything."

"So what's your favorite episode?"

He scratches his chin. "Season six, episode twelve."

I grin. "Is that the one where Baryshnikov first shows up?"

He nods. "What about you? What's your fave?"

"Season one, episode nine," I say without hesitation. "It's called *The Turtle and The Hare*."

He squints, then shakes his head. "Hard to remember from just the title. What was it about?"

"It's the one where they get The Rabbit."

"The Rabbit? Is that another cat?"

I laugh. "It's a vibrator with ears. That episode reassured women that it's okay to masturbate. If even Charlotte was happy to do it, why not them?"

"I think I remember now. And it makes sense. The vibrator was your Baryshnikov."

My grin stretches from ear to ear. "What's your least favorite?"

"The movies," he says, making the word sound like a curse.

"Agreed. Anything after the last episode of season six is subpar."

He nods with evident seriousness, and we go over our least favorite moments in the movies—of which there are many.

As he talks animatedly about Carrie and Samantha, I can't help but wonder why him liking this show seems so significant, so full of portent. Why it feels like we have so much more in common now versus ten minutes ago. I mean, it's just a TV show, right?

In general, I don't like this feeling in my chest. Between his hand on my knee and the pleasant fatigue from the gourmet meal in my belly, the fiction and reality of our marriage are blurring, and that's very dangerous.

Nothing has changed. He still just wants a green card and nothing else. He still—

"Wait a second," Art says with mocking sternness. "My dick's nickname—that's a *Sex and the City* reference, isn't it?"

My eyes are drawn to his crotch, and my face flushes crimson. "Does that make him feel less special?"

Art laughs. "I actually thought Carrie's Mr. Big was kind of a dick, so this is fitting. She should've ended up with Baryshnikov instead."

I decide it is long past time to change the topic. "You mentioned your list?"

He nods and sends me a text. "The highlighted movies star Baryshnikov in them."

I check my phone. Hmm. If it were just the movies

with his idol in them that were unfamiliar, that would be one thing. But I have never heard of any of these. Some even sound made up, like *The Diamond Arm*, *The Irony of Fate or Enjoy Your Bath*, and *The Caucasian Captive*.

"Are these real?" I ask. "I consider myself a movie buff, but I've never come across these."

He pats my knee. "And therein lies the problem. *Sex and the City* might not be enough to make this relationship work."

I grin. "That's arguable. One can get far on *Sex and the City*."

He turns on the TV. "How about you show me yours, and then I show you mine?"

Are we still talking about movies?

"How about we watch *Dirty Dancing*?" I suggest. "Just bear in mind, said dancing isn't ballet."

We put the movie on, and somehow, I end up curled against him on the couch as if we were an old married couple. He drapes his arm over my shoulder, and I gulp in lungfuls of his tantalizing scent, feeling so warm and safe that I want to melt into a puddle.

Speaking of puddles, my underwear feels distinctly damp.

When the credits roll, he tells me the movie was great, and that we should see *The Irony of Fate or Enjoy Your Bath* next.

If it means we'll stay on the couch like this, I'll watch anything, even *Glitter*.

When the movie starts, I understand why I've never heard of it. It was made in the Soviet Union, in the seventies.

Art pauses the movie early and says, "Just so you're aware, this is a classic that gets broadcast every New Year's Eve—which is the Russian answer to Christmas."

"What do you mean?" I feel a yawn coming on, but I suppress it. I'm too cozy to leave this spot, plus I'm dreading the temptation of the bedroom.

This couch is bad enough.

He hugs me tighter. "In Russia, people decorate fir trees, exchange gifts, and even have a Santa equivalent named Grandpa Frost... all on New Year's Eve."

How am I supposed to think straight like this?

"Does Grandpa Frost look like Santa?" I somehow ask.

"In that he's an old guy with a bag of gifts and a white beard." With his free hand, Art pulls up a picture on his phone. "I think he started off as the Russian spirit of frost, but later got cross-pollinated with depictions of Santa."

"Wait." I point at a female in the picture. "Is that Mrs. Clause?"

He pulls back to give me a horrified look. "Can't you see how young she is? That's his granddaughter, Snegurochka, a.k.a. The Snow Maiden."

Huh. "What about his wife? What about Snegurochka's parents?"

He looks thoughtful. "Now that you mention it, I don't think there's more to this family. Just the grand-daughter. I think she's also some character from ancient Russian mythology who became associated with the New Year. The Soviets changed original customs to make them secular in the thirties—and I guess consistency or logic wasn't a priority."

With that, he unpauses the movie.

It's subtitled, not dubbed, but that somehow makes it better—makes me feel like I'm in Russia. As the film progresses, Art frequently pauses and explains certain nuances similar to Grandpa Frost. Oh, and some of the plot elements bring back recent memories for me—like when the hero and his friends drink too much vodka in the banya.

"What did you think?" Art asks when the movie credits roll.

Reluctantly, I extricate myself from his embrace. "I liked it."

"Great. Tomorrow, we can watch *The Caucasian Captive*."

I arch an eyebrow. "Is it a romcom too, or something more serious? That title makes it sound like a racially charged Stockholm syndrome romance."

His eyes widen. "It's a romcom. Caucasian in this case is used in its original meaning because the crux of the plot centers on an old tradition of the people in the Caucasus region—bride stealing."

I yawn. "Sounds intriguing. From my list, how about we watch *The Princess Bride*?"

"Deal." He yawns also. "I think it's time for bed."

My sleepiness evaporates. "Sure."

"Come," he says. "Let's learn each other's evening routine."

Yeah. That's normal. No reason to jump up and

down in excitement and glee, which is what I feel like doing all of a sudden.

Keeping a poker face, I follow him into the master bathroom—a room almost as large as my old place, with a rainfall showerhead, two sinks, and a huge bathtub.

"Do you like that sink?" He gestures at the one where I left my toothbrush.

"Sure."

Can he tell how freaked out I am? Because the answer is *very*. The domesticity of this is just insane. It makes this whole living arrangement crazy real.

"Do you shower before bed?" he asks.

Skunk. I didn't even think about that. "Yes." I blush like the Snow Maiden. "You?"

More importantly, what are the odds he'll want us to shower together?

His eyes gleam. "I usually shower after ballet practice, but today, I was thinking of doing it before bed. After I retire, that will be my new routine."

The images. Oh, the images. I can feel my heartbeat in my temples. "You want to do it while I brush my teeth? I won't look."

Yep, I said that with a straight face, knowing full well that I'll see a lot of him in the mirror—and that I'll watch, shamelessly.

He picks up his toothbrush and squeezes some toothpaste onto it. "How about we take turns?"

Boo.

"Okay. Good idea." I grab my toothbrush and accidently squeeze too much toothpaste onto it. "After this."

As I activate my toothbrush, I wish it were aimed at my pussy instead of my teeth. Maybe if I burned off some of this sexual energy, I'd feel like a normal human being and would stop seeing sudsy Art images in my mind.

He brushes his teeth manually, like a caveman, which makes his strong forearm flex.

Great. Now I want to misuse my toothbrush even more.

He spits his toothpaste out. "Ladies' shower first?"

"Sure," I mumble through a mouthful of toothpaste. "Let me finish this."

"Of course." Again, his eyes gleam—which might mean he's just as discombobulated with all this as I am.

Some demon forces my mouth to ask, "What do you sleep in?"

His smile has a wicked tinge to it. "Usually naked, but in a pair of pajamas from now on."

Instead of spitting out my toothpaste, I audibly swallow it.

Fuck. Is he doing this to me on purpose?

Moving like a horny zombie, I grab my most conservative-looking nightie—though it's still less than ideal if the goal is to cover as much of me as possible.

Art eyes the garment in my hands with a strange expression. "Enjoy your shower." With that, he disappears from the bathroom as if I might chase him.

I lock the door and stand with my back to it,

squeezing my eyes shut while I try to get my breathing under control.

This is insane.

Even if he were my real husband, this level of desire seems unhealthy. As is, I fear I might sleep-fuck him— or worse—in the middle of the night.

Well, there's a simple solution: I can masturbate preemptively.

I scan the bathroom. The showerhead is of the wrong style to be useful, and I'm not sure my toothbrush and fingers will cut it today. I need something big on the inside, and maybe something extra-buzzy on the outside.

Then it hits me. I've hidden my favorite toys right here in this bathroom! I must've subconsciously planned for this.

I get the toys out from the toilet tank and turn on the shower to make sure Art doesn't realize what I'm doing.

Come to think of it, I haven't cuffed the carrot in the shower in a long time—and I don't think I've ever blogged about it.

That settles it.

I lay out my toys near the shampoo bottles, then undress and step under the warm stream.

This is nice.

On auto-pilot, I wash my hair and body before I recall my important side mission.

I scan the toys. Oh, yeah. This calls for the biggest dildo I own—one that's a couple of inches shorter and a bit thinner than Mr. Big.

I grin mischievously at it. "You'll have to do."

Knowing that Art is just beyond this wall makes me feel very naughty.

I lube up the dildo with my spit and prop my left foot against the wall to ease the entry.

Here goes.

I position the dildo against my opening—which is when my right foot slips on the wet tile floor.

CHAPTER

Twenty-Seven

Oh, no. No, no, no!

I flail both arms, the one with the dildo and the one without.

Nope.

I hit the ground with a loud slap, air whooshing out of my lungs.

Skunk.

There are stars in my eyes and a loud boom in my ears.

In a second, the stars stop spinning, but the booming sound is still there. It sounds strangely like a shout asking, "What happened?"

Great question, imaginary shout.

Did I break something?

I scan my ribs and the rest.

No, I think I'm okay.

Wait.

The shouting is louder now, and it's Art's voice.

He's demanding to know if I'm okay.

I inhale some air into my lungs in order to answer, but it's too late.

Crack! With a violent sound, the door flies off its hinges, and Art's voice sounds much closer. "Fuck! Are you okay?"

Shit. Shit. Shit.

Strong arms turn me over, and a panicked Art examines every inch of me thoroughly, like he's conducting my annual dermatological exam.

Did I hit the floor face first? My cheeks are burning almost painfully.

"I'm okay," I lie.

I scramble to my feet, unsure of what to do first: hide the toys or cover my naked body with something.

Art grabs my hand, firmly. "Are you sure you're okay? It sounded like you fell hard."

Are my cheeks bleeding?

I check in the mirror.

Nope. Just very red.

I can't believe that on top of everything, I sounded like a sack of potatoes when I fell. What else, universe? Am I about to throw up in front of him? Pee myself?

Frantically, I grab a towel and wrap it around myself. "Okay, since I'm fine, you should go."

Only now do I realize he's wearing nothing but black briefs—and boy, they look amazing on him.

Art's jaw sets stubbornly. "I'm not leaving until I'm sure you're okay."

Shoot me now. "And how can I prove that?"

He shoves his fingers through his hair. "I have no fucking idea."

"Fine! Can you at least look away?"

"Why?" he asks, then finally looks around.

Sex toys are everywhere. I must have knocked them all off the shampoo shelf while I was flailing.

"Oh," he says, eyes widening. "You were—"

"Sailing the catamaran." My cheeks burn impossibly hotter. "Fanning the fur. Womansplaining myself."

He bends down and grabs the dildo I never got a chance to use. "How did this stuff get in here?"

I dart a glance at the still-open toilet tank, and he follows my gaze.

"Seriously?"

I blush harder.

He looks at me, then at the toys, then back at me with a frown. "Why the stealth? I thought you blogged about this stuff. You could just keep it all in your nightstand."

I roll my eyes so hard my eyeballs hurt. "Yeah. Sure. Should I also use them while you're next to me in bed?"

His pupils dilate to the size of dimes. Swallowing, he mutters, "Maybe not that, but I'm not always going to be home. I can also just work on my computer in the office when you need to..." He wiggles the dildo. "... take care of your needs."

I snatch the offending object out of his hands. "Fine. Anything to stop this conversation."

Before he can reply, I grab an armful of toys and sprint out of the bathroom.

He follows me, probably to make sure I'm okay.

I open the closest nightstand drawer and toss the toys in. "There. Can I get some privacy now?"

He looks me over again. "Are you absolutely sure you're not hurt?"

"Positively."

He reaches for his nearby pajamas. "Promise to yell if something starts to hurt?"

"I swear on what's left of my dignity."

He goes back to the bathroom and comes out wearing the PJs.

"I'll be back in a few." He leaves the bedroom.

I lock the bedroom door behind him and use the towel that's covering me to dry myself before putting on my nightie.

There's a knock.

I unlock the door and get into bed.

Art is standing there with some tools. As I gape at him, he starts to repair the bathroom door with the utter nonchalance of someone who knows exactly what he's doing.

Damn it. He's handy too. Even if I had gotten a chance to use the toys, I'd probably require another session after this.

"You still okay?" he asks when the door is as good as new.

"Yep." Physically anyway. Well, my salivary glands are in overdrive, but that's my new normal around him.

He disappears into the bathroom, and the shower starts up again.

Now what?

Despite the fall, what I most want to do is dial my rotary phone once more—and knowing Art is in the shower just makes it worse.

The problem is, I have no idea how long his showers take. The last thing I want is to get caught again.

Maybe I can just fall asleep?

I close my eyes. The air purifier hums soothingly next to the bed, and under normal circumstances, I'd be out already. But these circumstances are anything but normal.

I open my eyes in frustration.

What makes this extra annoying is this weird conviction I have that Art is stroking Mr. Big in the shower. I have no idea how or why I've decided this. Maybe it's one of those dreams that slide through your mind as you fall asleep. Or maybe all these hormones have awakened my latent ESP powers. Either way, I'm so certain he's jerking off I can practically see it through the walls. In vivid IMAX detail.

Inconsiderate bastard. Whatever happened to "what's good for the goose is good for the gander?"

Maybe I should knock on the door and tell him to quit it?

The shower stops.

Lucky. He probably just came. How nice that must be.

The door opens, and Art tiptoes into the room.

He thinks I've fallen asleep? Maybe it's best to pretend that I have.

He quietly slides under the blanket on the other side of the bed.

I swallow, hard. Despite the shower and the air purifier's best efforts, I can still detect that telltale Art scent, and it doesn't help my sexual frustration in the slightest.

He turns onto his side, facing away from me.

An avalanche of fantasies assaults my poor brain. In most, I scoot over and reach for Mr. Big as a starting point.

He turns toward me.

The fantasies now start with a kiss.

He flops onto his back.

Wow. Is that the blanket tenting? Maybe I was wrong about what he did in the shower? Or maybe I wasn't wrong, but he recovers quickly? What am I saying? I know he recovers fast. I saw it on video.

He turns away from me again.

How high is his metabolism? I feel heat radiating off of him in waves.

He turns toward me.

I sigh. I'll never fall asleep like this.

He goes still.

Oops.

"You up?" he whispers.

"Seems like it," I whisper back.

He jackknifes to his feet. "I'm sorry, but I can't sleep like this."

"Like what?"

Even though I was just thinking the same thing, I feel insulted. Does he think I smell? Am I breathing too loudly? Did my stomach growl?

"I'm going to sleep on the couch." He grabs his pillow.

"Wait." I sit up. "What about the interview questions? They could ask about our sleeping patterns."

He eyes the comfy blanket we've been sharing. "You can say that I'm a gentleman when it comes to the blanket, and that you like to wrap yourself in it without a care for anyone else."

I look down and realize I'm turning myself into a burrito as we speak.

"I left my blanket in the linen closet," I say. "Please use it."

"Thanks." He walks to the linen closet and grabs the blanket. "Sweet dreams."

As I watch him leave, I battle an unexplained wave of disappointment.

This is stupid. He's done us both a favor. This way, I can actually get some shuteye.

To that end, I close my eyes.

And wait.

And wait.

Sleeping should be easier now, right?

Nope.

I toss and turn for a half hour before giving up. Locking the bedroom door, I crank up the air purifier to the highest setting to mask any vibrating noise and take the toys out of my nightstand.

He did say I was free to do this in our bed.

I crawl over to his side and take a whiff of the sheets there.

Yeah. That's the stuff. If hunger is the best spice, a hot husband you can't fuck is the best masturbation enhancer. The orgasm that crashes over me curls my toes and makes me shake all over.

Feeling like an overcooked noodle in the aftermath, I drag myself to the bathroom to wash the toys. By the time I put them away, my eyelids feel like they're being weighed down by boulders.

Sleep arrives the moment my head meets the pillow.

CHAPTER
Twenty~Eight

I WAKE UP. For a second, I'm confused as I look around. My surroundings are unfamiliar.

Oh, right. I moved in with Art.

Getting up, I brush my teeth and put on some clothes, then go in search of my husband dearest.

He's not in his office or in the kitchen.

As I approach the living room, I hear soft classical music playing. Art must be nearby.

Yep. Not only is he here, but I also get an incredible view for my troubles.

Dressed in tight workout pants and a tank top, Art is standing in a picture-perfect Warrior Pose, one knee bent, back lengthened, and every muscle in his extended arms flexed. Even his bare feet are sexy, all strong and masculine.

Fluffer, who was watching Art, turns a suspicious, fuzzy face toward me.

See? You're looking at this giant like you want to eat him. What chance does a tiny morsel like me have?

Art extends his right arm over his head.

I debate between two equally reasonable choices: let him know I'm here or run back to the bedroom to use the toys.

My choice is made for me. Woofer rolls over from behind me and makes so much noise that Art glances our way.

One human overlord has smelled the other, yet I get the blame?

"Morning." Art disengages from his pose, looking more graceful than I could ever hope to be. "How did you sleep?"

"Okay." I check out the couch. There's no sign he actually slept on it. Is he a neat freak? "How about you?"

He shrugs. "When pulled out, this couch is almost as comfy as the bed."

I wave at his mat. "Doing a little yoga?"

"It's part of my morning routine. Why don't you join?" Without waiting for my answer, he walks to the edge of the couch and pulls out another yoga mat.

Hmm. I got into yoga some time ago, after writing a blog post about tantric masturbation. My signature move is to diddle myself in lotus, but when it comes to other yoga poses, the chances of me making a fool of myself are high.

"I don't want to disrupt your practice," I say.

He makes puppy eyes at me. "Just a couple of poses."

Gah. If this fake marriage somehow leads to children, I hope he doesn't teach them that particular move, or else they'll get spoiled rotten.

I take a step back and nearly trip over Woofer. "I think I'm too hungry."

Art grins. "I made some breakfast. I'll share it with you if you're good."

Tempting. If that food is as yummy as what he made last night, it might be worth the unwanted exercise.

"Fine," I say reluctantly. "Five minutes."

He gestures at the mat. "Stand there."

I do.

"Show me your Warrior Pose."

He demonstrates his own, which makes it very hard to concentrate as I do the same.

Shaking his head, Art walks over to me. "Can I make a few corrections?"

I nod. Is this going where I think it is?

Yep.

He gently grabs me by the hips and centers my pelvis.

Fuck.

I've always had a thing for being manhandled, but this is on another level. My panties are instantly soaked, and yoga is the last thing on my mind.

He lifts my right arm higher, sending erotic goosebumps down my whole body.

Yoga? What's that?

"Good," he says, returning to his mat. "Hold the pose for a few seconds."

I do my best, and even somehow remember to breathe.

"Let's do a Standing Forward Fold," he says and bends in half with zero effort.

Damn. I could write sonnets about his glutes. Sonnets and haiku:

His butt is hot hot.

It's very very hot hot. Is it not?

I want it, want it.

As I follow his guidance, I pray to Ganesha that I'm doing this correctly. If Art gets behind me and adjusts *this* pose, I might just spontaneously combust.

"You're a natural," he says.

Whew.

Then again, a part of me is disappointed he didn't slide behind me to make corrections. That part also hoped he'd pull my pants down, spread my legs, and—

Yoga. Focus on yoga.

"Downward-Facing Dog," Art announces, moving into the pose, and I swallow drool as I join him in pointing my butt up and head down.

"Great job," he says.

Damn it, why didn't I mess that one up? My butt was in the air, ripe for the taking.

We do the Boat next, then the Cobra, adding more images to my rub bank. As we fold our legs into the Half Pigeon, my stomach rumbles, loudly.

"Okay," Art says. "You can go eat now."

Sure. But can I bring it in here and watch his remaining yoga routine?

Nah. Probably not appropriate. Even a real husband might feel objectified.

The breakfast turns out to be delicious—pancakes

that taste like they were made from sugar and cottage cheese, and *blins* drenched in some kind of syrup that I've never tasted.

Just as I'm almost done, Art enters the kitchen.

"What's that?" I point my fork at the syrup.

"Soaked dates blended with water," he says. "You like it?"

"Love it." I stuff the remainder of the food into my mouth.

He grins and takes out what looks to be plain oatmeal and a small salad from the fridge.

I goggle at the greenery. "A salad for breakfast?"

"I'm not retired yet," Art says. "This is a veritable feast compared to what the female dancers eat."

He attacks the food wolfishly, making short work of it.

"Can I finish that?" I point at the *blins* and the pancakes he never touched.

"I made them for you."

Aww. He's really determined to go after my heart through my stomach. And eyes. And nose.

"Anyway," he says. "I have rehearsal to go to."

I do my best to hide my disappointment. "When are you coming back?"

"In the afternoon. If you're going to be home, have lunch without me. It's in the fridge."

I gape at him. "You made me lunch too?"

One corner of his mouth curls in a smirk. "What are fake husbands for?"

I can think of so many things. So many things. "Okay, I guess. See you."

He leaves the kitchen, and I follow him to the door like a puppy. I watch as he puts on his shoes. Then he turns to me, eyes warm and chocolate-y, and I feel like he's lassoed a rope around my uterus and is pulling it toward himself.

I sway toward him, intoxicated by his scent. His eyes flare and seem to darken to a near-black. For a moment, I feel like he might lean toward me, but he just says softly, "Lock the door."

I swallow and take a step back. The momentary spell of insanity is broken. With a faux smirk, I bow. "Yes, dear. I'll obey your every command, dear."

Shaking his head, he leaves.

I lock the door like a good wife. I can pretend when I have to.

CHAPTER
Twenty~Nine

BARELY A FEW MINUTES pass before my feet take me straight to Art's office.

I shouldn't snoop. I really shouldn't.

Oh, who am I kidding? I step into the office and look around.

A desk, a chair, and two wall-mounted monitors are pretty much it.

Does investing require such spartan surroundings?

As if possessed, I wake up the desktop computer.

It asks for a password.

Hmm. Blue would hack this in an eyeblink.

I type in "ballet."

Nope.

I try "Baryshnikov."

Jackpot. I'm in.

To my disappointment, the only app on the desktop is for trading. Nor is there anything interesting in his browser history, just Gmail, Forbes, and other boring sites like that.

No porn?

I lock the computer and leave to grab my own laptop.

Since my browser history is blush-inducing, I should make my password less guessable in case Art is also a snoop. Currently, my password is "klittra," which is the Swedish term for female masturbation.

What would be less obvious? Flicking the bean? Polishing the banister? Orbiting Venus? Finding Nemo?

Finally, I just open a blank Notepad document, close my eyes, and type at random. There we go. No one will ever guess this gibberish. I spend a few minutes memorizing the new password, then set it before I visit my blog.

Interesting.

I have a new, very avid fan with a funny screen-name: SquirrelBoner.

"Amazing write-up," SquirrelBoner says about my latest post.

"You're brilliant," she (or he?) says about the one where I talk about my favorite dildo.

And the gushing continues, to the point where I get an eerie feeling that I know this person. Somehow. Random strangers are rarely nice to you on the internet. Hence the existence of the term "troll," but not its opposite.

Could this be Art? Maybe he decided to check out my blog in order to be supportive and went a little overboard with his praise?

"SquirrelBoner" doesn't sound like him, though. If anything, "HorseBoner" is more his style.

More importantly, SquirrelBoner asks me some very interesting questions about the trickier techniques involving toys. Whoever he or she is, they sure know about sex toys. And while Art might qualify as a sex toy himself, I doubt he knows enough about them to be SquirrelBoner.

In fact, I know very few people who know so much about orgasms and—

Wait a second.

Could it be my mom?

Nah. Gia, Honey, and Blue aren't cruel enough to tell her about the blog. Not unprovoked, anyway.

Just in case, I text each of them and ask them if they posted comments on my blog.

Their answers are all in the negative, followed by questions about Art.

My replies lead to another Zoom session, during which I update my sisters on my cohabitation situation.

"He's got the looks *and* the cooking skills. Damn."

Gia and Blue echo the sentiment. I direct the conversation toward the SquirrelBoner mystery, but no one admits to using that name or telling Mom. Blue even offers to use her special skills to track SquirrelBoner. However, when she says she'd need a favor in return, I politely decline.

"Good luck then," Blue says and jumps off the call. My other two sisters follow.

With a sigh, I close the Zoom app and start to brainstorm some content for my blog.

Oh, I know. I've never described what I think of as DJing. Great. I write up a post to explain it, and for funsies, I do my best to use phrases like "scratch it like a vinyl record" as often as possible.

As soon as I post, SquirrelBoner comments: "You're so prolific. This blog is perfect."

Should I just flat-out ask SquirrelBoner who he or she is?

Nah. I'll figure it out. Eventually.

For the moment, I feel peckish, so I check out what Art made for me for lunch.

Dumplings?

I bite into one.

Yummy. It's sweet, stuffed with cottage cheese, raisins, and dates.

For dessert, he left me a fruit salad, so I eat the cake from the other day instead, just to be contrary. Except Art wins anyway. His cooking incorporated so much fruit that I can only stomach one slice of cake—an unheard-of restraint for me.

My happy tummy inspires me to do something I've been meaning to do for a while—research how Russian men feel about curvy women. Purely as an anthropologist would, of course, not because I have any personal stake in the answer whatsoever.

The results of my research are promising—or would be, if I had any stake in this. For example, when I translate "curvy figure" into Russian, it returns "soblaznitel'naya figura." If you then translate "soblaznitel'naya figura" back into English, it becomes "seductive figure." Doesn't that mean that "curvy" and "seductive" are interchangeable in Russian culture?

Still, what's true for Russians in general doesn't

mean that one specific Russian (say, Art) likes certain specific curves (say, mine).

I shut my laptop in disgust. I don't really have a problem with my body—at least I didn't until this whole thing with Art. He's just so out of my league, and the fact that he's surrounded by all those waifish ballerinas doesn't help.

Then again, he *is* about to retire, so the ballerinas won't be around him anymore. And maybe he doesn't think he's that out of my league. After all, he hired me to be his wife, so he must think our coupling is at least somewhat plausible. Also, he liked me just fine when drunk. And what was the deal with that tenting blanket last night? Is it possible that—

The doorbell rings.

I check the peephole.

Speak of the handsome devil. Art is already holding up his driver's license to his face.

Grinning, I open the door.

He walks in with two large paper bags in his hands.

"You went shopping?" I ask.

He nods. "How do you feel about a fusion dinner? I was thinking *Pommes Anna* made from sweet potato, along with fried yellow plantains Cuban-style and sweet-and-not-so-sour pork?"

"Wow. Super fancy. Can I help you make it?"

"Sure." He takes the shopping bags into the kitchen, and I follow.

"Here." He hands me a bag of sweet potatoes. "Please wash and peel these."

I do as he says, sneaking glances his way the entire

time. Impossibly, he's just as sexy when he cooks as he is when he does yoga.

Ugh, what is wrong with me, lusting after him in the kitchen of all places? Have my hormones gone totally haywire?

By the time everything is sizzling on the stove, the delicious aromas make me ravenous for food, which makes it easier to ignore the other kind of hunger.

"Do you want in on my salad?" Art asks. "I season it with fig balsamic vinegar, which is very sweet, and I can throw in some fresh grapes or raisins."

This again.

I narrow my eyes at him. "When you insist on me eating fruits and vegetables, are you giving me some sort of a hint?"

Art reels back like I've slapped him. "I love fruits and veggies and want to share the experience with you. It's just like the movie lists." A pot whistles angrily, so he turns the knob on the stove before facing me again. "When I was a kid, fruits and vegetables were scarce outside of the summer season, and even then, they were a rare delicacy for us at the *detdom*. Some kids even got scurvy. So now that I have unlimited access, I indulge every chance I get."

Skunk. I've again reminded him of the crappy times at the orphanage—and this time, because of my stupid insecurities.

I take a breath. "Okay. If it's like the movie lists, I'll have some salad."

It's my penance—especially if there's kale in it.

Turns out, even Art's salad is delicious… I mean, for

a salad. So is the rest of the food. I feel like it's the best I've ever had, though my participation in the prep might have something to do with that.

"You know," I say when I'm satiated enough to be able to speak. "If investing doesn't pan out, you could become a chef."

"Thanks, but cooking for money wouldn't be as fun."

I cock my head. "I think getting paid for something you enjoy is the ultimate dream."

He smiles. "You're talking about your blog?"

"Maybe." I clear my throat. "Speaking of that... did you read it, by any chance?"

He smirks. "A little."

"Did you comment?"

He shakes his head. "Since the target audience is women, I felt like an intruder, and commenting would have made it worse."

So he's not SquirrelBoner. I didn't think so, anyway.

"Speaking of getting paid for things you enjoy doing," he says. "I liked ballet in the beginning, but when it became my job, something was lost. I think that's why I got into investing. I want to be financially independent, and to pursue hobbies that aren't tainted by money. But hey, everyone is different."

"Yep. I can't disagree more."

He smiles. "In a good marriage, you have to learn the art of disagreeing peacefully."

"You know a lot about marriage," I say. "Have you been married before?"

Smooth, Lemon. Very smooth.

"I haven't found the right person." He levels a sharp gaze at me. "What about you? Did I marry a divorcee?"

The sweet potato I was chewing almost goes down the wrong pipe. "Me, married? I've barely even dated."

He gapes at me. "Barely dated?"

I stare down into my almost-empty plate. "You know how I've got a sensitive nose?"

He nods, eyebrows furrowing as I look up.

"That makes intimacy difficult."

He puts a hand on mine. "I'm sorry. I didn't realize."

"My longest relationship was with a guy who show-ered compulsively. Before that, I had a few very short, gag-inducing flings."

He pulls his hand away. "What about me? Do I make you gag?"

I shake my head vehemently. "You're a rare excep-tion—a bit like the members of my family, at least when they don't wear perfume."

He looks relieved. "I hate the idea of you finding me disgusting."

He does? Why? Since I'm not brave enough to ask that, I go for something that I'm just as curious about. "What about you? Have you lost track of the number of ballerinas you've dated?"

He wrinkles his nose. "Hard to lose track when the number is close to zero."

"Close to zero?" Is it because they're so thin they're a fraction of a regular woman?

"Well, I had a couple of casual encounters with ballerinas, and even those led to so much drama that I now avoid them at all costs. There's a Russian saying:

'Don't spit into the well. You might want to drink water from it.' And since I work with them…" He shrugs.

I chuckle. "The English version of that is even less poetic: 'Don't shit where you eat.'"

He cringes. "As vulgar as that sounds, it fits the situation even better."

"So, if not ballerinas, who? And don't tell me you haven't dated a million women."

That would be impossible to believe.

"I've dated," he says. "But not millions, and it's never amounted to anything serious. My longest relationship was with an opera singer."

I arch an eyebrow. "Is she famous?"

He tells me her name, and I take out my phone to look her up.

Wow. Very pretty. Also, undeniably curvy.

Hmm. Dare I have hope?

"Now you have to give me the name of one of your exes to stalk," Art says when I look up.

I give him the name of a guy I dated in high school. "He isn't as talented as your ex, and he was a sweater."

"Warm and fuzzy?" Art takes out his phone and types in the name.

"No, he sweated a lot."

Art frowns at his screen. "He's a lawyer. I hate lawyers."

Has he always hated lawyers, or has he developed those feelings just now, the way I've suddenly developed a dislike for opera singers?

"Anyway," I say. "What movie are you making me watch today?"

"The Caucasian Captive. What about you?"

Oh, yeah. He chose that yesterday. I tell him my pick, and we go to the living room and start the marathon—cuddling on the couch as we do.

The Caucasian Captive turns out to be genuinely funny, especially the three dudes who seem to be a rip-off of the Three Stooges. Oh, and there's a song about bears. How Russian is that?

"So," I say when the credits roll. "I guess it's my turn to sleep on this couch."

"Actually, I've decided to give you the bedroom for perpetuity. I think he finds my presence soothing." He points at Fluffer's mansion.

Fluffer's black eyes glint.

I'm not sure if soothing is the right word—but you do seem like the giant less likely to eat me... at least until you retire from ballet.

"Are you sure?" I eye the couch. "I'm happy to take turns."

"I insist."

"Thanks," I say and get to my feet. "I'd better get to it then."

He turns off the TV. "You can shower first."

How nice of him. I head into the shower and take care of business. When I'm done, I put on a nightie that accentuates my curves in the right way—for no reason —and return to get Art.

Oh, my.

Art's sitting there, cradling Fluffer in his big, strong hands.

My chest feels melty, like frozen banana ice cream.

"Who liked his little dust bath?" Art is crooning. "Who's my—"

He doesn't get the chance to finish what he was saying because Fluffer spots me—and leaps out of Art's hands.

Seriously?

With a loud chirp, the chinchilla beelines into the mansion, the way I would if confronted with a T-Rex.

"I don't think our pet likes me," I say, and the hurt in my voice is only partially a joke.

Art looks me up and down in my nightie, and I could swear he appreciates what he sees. The "likes curves theory" is gaining more and more traction—not that it means he wants *me*.

Still, score one for Lemon.

"We all just need time to get used to each other," he says, a bit huskily.

Maybe Art could get used to me, but Fluffer's frightened stare doesn't inspire much confidence.

"Here." Art hands me a weird, raisin-like object. "This is a treat they're supposed to love."

Our fingers brush, and I feel a pleasant zing ricocheting down my body.

I sniff the berry. No clue.

"What is this?"

"Dried rosehip," Art says and pulls out another plant thingy. "This is a dandelion root. Another treat."

He hands it to me, and our fingers brush again.

I'm not sure about the chinchilla, but all this touching is a treat for me, big time.

"Thanks." I walk over to the mansion and stick the

dandelion root inside. "Here, Fluffer, come get it."

"I'm heading to the shower," Art says.

"Okay," I reply breathlessly.

The sudsy images flood my mind again—that is, until the chinchilla pounces and rips the dandelion root from my hands.

"Wow. That's a bit violent, but whatever."

Fluffer's eyes gleam in victory.

How could I be sure that the dandelion root wasn't bait? Better be safe than eaten.

He begins munching and looks like he's savoring every bite. It's so adorable. I really want to pet him.

Sure, pet me with your carnivorous teeth.

After the root is gone, Fluffer grabs a wooden stick and gnaws on it as I watch with a grin.

Eager to catch his attention again, I hold out the rosehip. "Want this?"

In a blur of fur, Fluffer rushes at me, snatches this new treat, then hops over to the top shelf and turns his back to me as he enjoys it.

Rude, but kind of in a cute way.

When the treat is gone—and it might be my imagination—there's a lot more warmth in Fluffer's eyes. Maybe even a little bit of trust.

If you feed me that for twenty years straight, I'll let you eat me.

"Was he a good boy?" Art asks, startling me.

I leap to my feet and take him in. He's wearing PJs, which is a shame, but his wet hair revs up my X-rated imagination anyway, and I nearly choke on drool. "That was a quick shower," I stammer.

"It's a habit I picked up in the army."

My mouth falls open. "You were in the army?"

Was he part of the super-secret, Russian ballet special forces? In *Avengers: Age of Ultron*, we got a glimpse into Black Widow's past and learned that she trained in ballet, so anything's possible. Maybe Art can even dance-fight, like the girl in the latest *Jumanji* remake.

"I was conscripted," Art says. "All Russian men are."

I force my still-open mouth shut because the sight of my teeth might frighten poor Fluffer. "I didn't know that. Was it hard?"

He shrugs. "Compared to the *detdom*, it was a cakewalk."

Damn it. Every time he mentions the orphanage, I want to leap at him with a hug, but I don't think that's proper fake wife behavior.

"Good night," I say, but the words sound like a question.

I really want him to reply with, "Stay."

"Night." He blows me an air kiss.

Boo. But hey, that's *something*.

I catch the kiss when I know he's not looking and keep it in my fist until I lock the bedroom door.

Feeling like a goof, I stick the imaginary kiss into my panties. Could I be more insane? I blame the hormones —and the only way to tame them is in my nightstand drawer.

It takes an hour and a few orgasms, but I finally go to sleep.

CHAPTER
Thirty

THE NEXT SEVERAL days follow a similar routine. Art wakes up first, makes breakfast and lunch, and then I join him for yoga before he goes to his ballet practice. When he returns, we cook dinner together and watch more movies from our lists.

Each day, I feel like I'm getting closer to him—a pleasant illusion. More and more, it's as if we were a real husband and wife, just with a dysfunctional sex life. But hey, not every relationship is perfect.

We also have our wedding reception coming up on Saturday. Art is planning the whole thing, but that doesn't mean I'm immune from stress. I've had to veto just about every single flower Art has chosen because the smell of them would've driven me insane.

We've settled on succulents instead.

As we're saying our goodnights on Thursday, Art asks, "Are you excited about seeing your parents?"

"Yeah," I say with as much excitement as I can

muster. I don't want to seem like an ungrateful brat when it comes to anything family-related.

The truth is, what I'm dreading the most about the upcoming reception is introducing Mom and Dad to Art.

When it comes to creative ways to embarrass their daughters, my parents should be in the Guinness World Records.

"Are your parents adventurous eaters?" Art asks.

The hair on my nape rises, like I've picked up a great disturbance in the Force. "Why?" He didn't ask this when planning the food for the reception, so it's not about that…

He tips his head to the side. "I'm just thinking about what to make for them tomorrow."

Oh, no. My Spidey Force sense might be right—a realization that raises my heart rate. "Did you invite my parents to eat with us before the reception?"

He purses his lips. "Not just eat. They're staying with us."

They're *what*?

Skunking skunk glands. How could he do something so reckless? There are plenty of other daughters for Mom and Dad to stay with, not to mention thousands of hotels.

"Interesting," I say in a choked voice. "It's odd that they're willing to crash with us instead of in a hotel."

He grins. "Your father actually sounded excited, at least over text. He didn't think that meeting me for the first at the reception would be private enough."

Right.

That was by design.

I take a calming breath. "They're not fussy eaters."

That's putting it mildly. I'm pretty sure my parents have eaten everything from jellyfish to human placentas.

"Great," Art says. "It *is* kind of strange they didn't tell you about their visit."

Not strange. They probably knew I'd try to talk them out of it.

I heave a sigh. "I guess we'll deal with them tomorrow. Right now, I should head to bed."

He flashes me a warm smile. "Sweet dreams."

I run to the bedroom and close the door.

Must call parents and prevent this Armageddon.

Mom doesn't pick up.

Fuck.

Dad doesn't either.

I leave them both voicemails to call me back immediately, and I also text them that we need to talk.

Mom replies to the text:

Driving. Will talk when we see you in the morning.

Morning?

Someone shoot me, please. Put me out of my skunking misery.

———

A distant doorbell wakes me up the next morning.

I sit up, a shot of adrenaline clearing my brain better than any espresso.

I check the time. It's 10:15 a.m. Way, way too early to

be getting normal visitors. But of course, the one thing my parents are not is normal.

I run out of the bedroom, still in my nightie—just in time to see Art stepping out of the kitchen.

Instead of his usual yoga attire, he's wearing a pair of dress pants and a button-down shirt. The outfit looks amazing on him, causing stirrings in my core. Stirrings that are the last thing I need with my parents around.

"Wait for me!" I yell as he heads down the hallway toward the front door.

Art turns, his eyes darkening as he takes in my outfit.

My heart skips a beat. If I had any doubts that he enjoyed seeing me in this getup the last time, they're gone now. He even hungrily licks his lips.

"That's your parents," he says, his voice a bit rough as his gaze returns to my face. "You sure you don't want to put something else on?"

And leave him alone with them? I can't think of a worse idea. Then again, I can't exactly prance around in a nightie all day.

"Let me introduce you, and then I'll change," I say, my own voice hoarse from sleep.

What damage could Mom and Dad do in the time it takes me to brush my teeth and change?

I run past Art to the door and unlock it.

"You didn't ask who it is," he mutters under his breath. "How many times do I need to remind you?"

"Someone is grumpy without his morning salad," I mutter back, but I check the peephole, figuring better late than never.

Yep.

It's the parental units.

Mom swears that Dad looked like Bob Dylan when they met. Currently, he looks more like Larry David—if Larry David were to gain a bunch of weight. And grow his hair into a silver ponytail. And become a hippy. And acquire a wild beard. So… maybe not like Larry David.

Mom, on the other hand, looks extremely good—especially for someone who's birthed eight babies. Whatever nutrients we sucked out of her when she carried us, she's long since replaced. Her hair is shampoo-commercial silky, and her skin is as smooth as Dad's bald spot.

Opening the door, I give them a huge smile. Despite all the humiliation they're bound to bring my way, I love them and I'm genuinely happy to see them. "Hi, Mom. Hi, Dad."

Mom beams back at me. "Namaste, sunshine."

"Thing 4," Dad says, nodding in greeting.

"That's my nickname," I whisper loudly to Art.

Mom waggles her eyebrows. "I see your husband isn't letting you wear much clothing. He'll fit right in with our family."

And so it begins. I clear my throat. "I'd like to introduce said husband, Art."

Art ushers them to step in—probably to avoid the dreaded handshake under the doorframe. Yep. As soon as they're inside, he extends his hand for a shake.

Dad scoffs at it. "You're Russian. Give me a kiss."

And it continues.

Art is a good sport, though. With a wide grin, he

274

hugs Dad, then kisses him on each cheek—which is hopefully what Dad meant. For all I know, there may be an old Hyman tradition for the father to French his new son-in-law.

Mom looks on with jealousy, and I'm pretty sure she's wishing Art was kissing her.

When Art and Dad finally disconnect, she eagerly says, "My turn."

I sigh as Art hugs and kisses her with an even wider grin.

Mom looks as happy as Petunia—the pig she brought to orgasm.

"It's nice to meet you, Mr. and Mrs. Hyman," Art says after he somehow extricates himself from Mom's clutches.

"Not even my father goes by Mr. Hyman," Dad says. "You're part of the family now. Call me Dad."

"And me, Mom," Mom says.

A barrage of emotions flits across Art's face. Was that longing? Gratitude? Joy? Sadness? It's all too quick to read.

"I will, *Mom*," he says, savoring the last word. He turns to Dad and seems to equally enjoy saying, "Dad, please come in."

Dad looks ecstatic, probably because this is the closest he's ever gotten to having a son. The other sextuplets and I owe our existence to my parents' desire for a boy. After the twin girls, they resorted to assisted reproduction technology with that hope in mind, and Murphy's Law took care of the rest.

"Please take your shoes off," I say.

"Oh, it's fine," Art protests.

"No," Mom says. "We've read about this. Russians take their shoes off when they enter, so we will too."

Dad toes off his raggedy sandals. "Also, this is an opportunity for me to see your mother's beautiful feet."

Please, please don't explain to Art what that means. For the love of sanity. My parents like to "research" kinks, and one that seems to have caught Dad's liking is the foot fetish.

Mom takes her shoes off, and I spot red nail polish, an ankle bracelet, and toe rings—evidence that Dad's foot fetish is still alive and well.

"Here." Art produces two pairs of house slippers in the correct sizes. Wow. Someone really prepared for this.

Mom slides her feet into the slippers, and Dad pouts.

Please don't explain this. Please.

Thankfully, Dad says nothing about the disappearance of the objects of his lust and just puts on his own slippers.

"What kind of tea do you want?" Art asks, leading everyone to the kitchen. "We have black, green, Darjeeling, and Russian Caravan."

Mom makes moony eyes at Art. "I'm thirsty for something Russian."

"Me too," Dad says.

The corners of Art's mouth quirk—making me thirsty too. "Great choice."

"You guys have tea, and I'll go change," I say.

I repeat: what trouble could they get into in the few minutes that I'll be gone?

Just in case, I sprint all the way to the bedroom, brush my teeth for half of the usual time, and skip flossing. And yet, when I return to the kitchen, I see that still took too long.

I gape at the scene in front of me, which at first, looks like Dad is servicing Art orally—not unlike the way I did in a certain video we never talk about.

But no. That's not it, though what's really happening isn't that much better, or more appropriate.

Dad is massaging Art's left foot.

Yes. That's what happened in the eyeblink that I was away. My father has decided to give my husband a foot massage. He's doing it with such vigor his ponytail gets wrapped around Art's ankle.

This would be weird even if Dad hadn't just alluded to his foot fetish.

I grasp for words, and all I come up with is, "Dad. What the hell?"

Dad looks up at me, his face the definition of innocence. "Art has just told us about his ballet practice and how tough it is on his feet, so—"

"Yeah, sure," I say. "Did he ask you to get on your knees in the middle of our kitchen?"

"I really don't mind," Art chimes in.

Mom chuckles. "I remember myself as a newlywed. I was jealous if someone so much as sneezed at Harry."

Yep, Dad's name is Harry Hyman, which never fails to bring to mind virginal woolly mammoths.

My cheeks burn. "I'm not jealous. I'm emb—"

"My apologies." Dad releases Art's foot, pulls out a sock from his pocket, puts it back on Art's foot, replaces his house slipper, and sits on the nearest chair. "Ever since Crystal and I started to learn about polyamory, I've been doing my best to forget jealousy even exists."

Skunk on a cracker. My sisters and I would sometimes joke about Mom and Dad starting a sex commune one day. That joke was clearly a jinx because it might be becoming reality.

"Way, way TMI," I hiss at Mom before turning to Art in desperation. "How about you tell us what this breakfast stuff is?" I gesture at the huge spread on the table.

Art takes a lid off a saucer, revealing small black balls inside. "Caviar." He points at the *blins* next and explains what they are, finishing with, "*Blins* with caviar is a classic."

No wonder he wanted to be sure my parents aren't squeamish eaters. Chicken eggs seem perfectly normal for breakfast, but fish eggs—gross.

As if reading my mind, Art moves three little saucers my way, removing lids and explaining, "Lychee jelly, mango jam, and date syrup."

Mom looks super impressed. "You made all this?"

He nods as I say, "Yeah, he even laid the fish eggs."

Oh, crap. This is too close to the topic of—

"Did you know Crystal is a chick sexer?" Dad asks.

This is on me. I mentioned eggs.

Art puts *blins* on each person's plate. "What's a chick sexer?"

I glower at my husband. "Did you forget what I just said about TMI?"

Ignoring me, Dad says, "A chick sexer can tell apart female baby chickens from cockerels."

Art ladles caviar for everyone except me. "That's fascinating. Thanks for expanding my vocabulary. What is it that you do... Dad?"

Sighing, I put a little bit of each fruity sweetener on my *blin*. Nothing can distract Dad from saying what he's about to say.

"I'm a penetration tester," Dad announces triumphantly. As usual, he was looking for an excuse to say this. "It's not as dirty as it sounds."

Resigned to letting this play out, I take a bite of my breakfast. It's delicious, though it's hard for me to decide which I like more: lychee jelly, mango jam, or date syrup.

"He penetrates computer systems," Mom says conspiratorially. "That is, when he's not penetrating me."

That, verbatim, is why my sisters and I have never had a friend from school visit our home more than once. Well, except for Fabio.

Interestingly, Art doesn't cringe or ask for a divorce. Then again, for all he knows, all parents talk this way.

"Speaking of jobs," Dad says. "Art, can *you* tell us what Thing 4 does for a living? She's been keeping it hush-hush."

Oh, no. I'm not ready for this. Must deflect. "Mom," I say, imbuing my voice with urgency. "Are you as good with squirrel penises as you are with rooster ones?"

There. If Mom is SquirrelBoner, she'll give it away now.

Mom stares at me like I'm the one who's been acting loony all this time. "A rooster doesn't have a penis. It fertilizes eggs using its cloaca."

That's what she's focused on instead of squirrel penises? Hey, at least the job question is forgotten.

Also, cocks don't have cocks? That's pretty ironic.

Another note: if Blue were to hear this fowl conversation, she'd freak the fuck out.

"Wait." Dad stuffs the remainder of his food into his mouth.

Skunk. Maybe my job isn't forgotten?

When Dad swallows, he says, "Why did you ask about squirrel penises?"

Art looks at me with a curious expression. I bet he a) also wants to know, and b) is realizing this apple didn't fall all that far from the rotten tree.

I mimic Dad and stuff all my remaining *blins* into my mouth to give myself time to think.

They all watch me like hawks.

Do hawks have penises? Probably not.

"Well," I say when I'm done swallowing. "I asked because of... our chinchilla. We've been calling him a he, but I can't see any genitals proving his gender either way."

"A chinchilla?" Mom looks around, eyes gleaming with excitement. "We don't have one at the farm."

"Right," I say. "But you do have Q-Tip, a male squirrel, so I figured you could use your sexer expertise to verify that Fluffer is a boy."

There. If they buy that, I'll also try to sell them the Verrazzano Bridge.

"Can I please see the chinchilla?" Mom sounds like a five-year-old.

I dart Art a worried glance. "Maybe after breakfast?"

Mom does what Dad and I just did—cleans her plate.

Art finishes his food too. "How about I make the introduction?" he says. "Come."

My parents follow him like they're going to the Promised Land.

When we enter the living room and they spot poor Fluffer, Mom squeals in glee and Dad oohs and aahs.

Fluffer doesn't share their enthusiasm in the slightest.

I knew I'd be breakfast one day. Knew it.

Art gets the dust bath and sets it out for the little guy.

Turns out, his fear of us isn't as strong as his urge to take a bath, and as Fluffer rolls around, Mom watches him closely—presumably in case he flashes his peen.

When the dust bath is over, she shakes her head. "I have no idea. You'll have to consult with a rodent specialist."

"He or she is very cute, though," Dad says. "And reminds me of last week."

Mom grins knowingly. "Yeah."

I pointedly do not ask what happened last week. There's no way the answer is something anyone wants to hear.

Art doesn't get the memo. "What happened last week?"

"We got furry," Dad says.

"On our Try a New Kink Night,'" Mom adds.

Oh, the images. The images. I see them doing it in Wookie suits. In Ewok suits. Kneazles. Nifflers. Pygmy Puffs. Fizgig. Gizmo. Tribbles. The list will never end.

Someone please bleach my brain. I don't need it anymore.

Judging by Art's expression, he doesn't know what Dad is talking about—and to his credit, he doesn't ask.

It doesn't matter, though. They'll elaborate if not distracted.

"Guys," I say, forestalling any explanations. "Did I tell you about Art's amazing Russian movies?"

The deflection works beautifully. My parents clamor to see an example, so Art puts on *The Diamond Arm.*

The film turns out to be a crime comedy, and Art has to pause it frequently to talk about Russia with Mom and Dad—who are apparently planning a trip there.

"Were you born close to the Arctic Circle also?" Mom asks after Art explains where Kolyma is—a place mentioned in the movie.

He tells them that he was born in Riga, Latvia, and that it's a little closer to the Arctic Circle than Moscow, the city he grew up in. He also suggests they visit Latvia over Russia because it is safer.

By the time the credits roll, it's lunch time, and Art invites everyone to the kitchen.

The main dish looks and tastes like pulled pork but is actually made of jackfruit. In general, fruit seems to be the theme here. There's fruit sushi, fruit salad, and fruit cake on the table.

"Botanically speaking, an avocado roll is fruit sushi too," Art says as he gives everyone a serving of his sweet creation. "But I wanted to make something different for you. Something memorable."

"This is delicious," Dad says when he tries a piece of a raspberry-mango-kiwi roll with peanut butter. "The only problem is that this gives me a craving for real sushi." He and Mom exchange creepy glances.

I wonder what that's about.

No, scratch that. I don't want to know. In fact, I steer the conversation back to their hypothetical trip to Latvia, which leads my parents to pepper Art with more questions.

When our meal is over, my parents demand to see one of Art's ballet performances. It's been a while since I've drooled over one of those, so I'm up for that too.

Art puts on *The Sleeping Beauty*, where he's the male lead. Watching it takes forever because my parents keep asking him what each of the moves is called (an avalanche of French words), who wrote the music (Tchaikovsky), and so on.

On my end, when Art's character appears, I wish I weren't in the company of my parents. His role is Prince Désiré, which is quite appropriate given the raw, carnal feelings he evokes in me.

I shift in my seat uncomfortably. Rule for the future: wear a pad when watching ballet with Art. Or better yet, watch it without Mom and Dad.

If they weren't here, I'd strip off my clothes in front of Art and let the chips fall where they may.

Sometime into Act 3, Art gets a text. He reads it and frowns.

"Everything okay?" I ask.

He lowers the phone. "That was our event organizer. The latest weather forecast has a thirty percent chance of rain, so the folks at the Botanical Garden are placing tented gazebos over all the tables. They need us to sign off on it."

I feel a pang of guilt. My oversensitive nose is why the reception is happening outdoors.

I check the time. It's four-thirty. My parents will probably be thinking about dinner soon.

"Should we go check it out?" I ask Art.

He nods.

I turn to Mom and Dad. "You guys want to come with?"

Mom shakes her head. "You guys go."

My guilt deepens. I'm glad they're not coming. I could use a break from steering conversations into safe waters.

"Are you sure you'll be okay here on your own?" Art asks.

"Go," Dad says. "We can watch another movie in the meantime."

"Should we wait for you for dinner?" Mom asks.

"No," I say. "I know you guys will want to eat soon. Just order something. We'll most likely grab a bite on the way."

"Sounds good," Dad says. "When do you think you'll be back?"

Art checks his phone. "Shouldn't be longer than a couple of hours."

"Okay." Mom gives Dad a meaningful glance. "We'll get some sushi." She turns to Art. "Do you have a takeout menu?"

Before I can tell Mom about this cool invention called Google, Art produces a paper menu from a drawer in the kitchen.

"We should go," he says to me after handing it to my mom.

I leap to my feet. "Let's."

———

"Do you mind if I check on my portfolio?" Art asks as we get into the cab.

"Of course not."

He pulls out his phone, and I start a group text with all my sisters to let them know about the parental situation. Thanks to skunking autocorrect, the text actually says:

Knight-errants are bricklaying with me and Art. Go ahead and enjoy schadenfreude.

Seriously, autocorrect? You mess up "parents" but not "schadenfreude?"

Blue is the first to reply with an LOL.

Your turn will come, I text. *Prepare for lunches and/or dinners.*

Keep them away from peanut butter, Olive texts and adds a puking face emoji.

Odd. Was that something that got autocorrected, or is there a story there?

Wow, Honey chimes in. *If Art stays with you after this visit, your marriage will last forever.*

The rest of my sisters' texts are full of jokes at my expense.

I glance at Art. The crazy thing is, he actually seems to be okay with my parents. No. More than okay. I think he's enjoying their company.

Not that it matters. Our marriage isn't real.

The cab stops. That was fast. The traffic must've been unusually light.

The event organizer, an overly muscular guy, greets us near the garden entrance.

Wow. I know this guy. Being a good and supportive friend, I've watched all of Fabio's porn, and this guy was in one of the scenes. Obviously, I'm too embarrassed to comment on this, so I just stay quiet as he leads us to the place where the reception is going to take place.

As we walk, my belly feels like the battleground for a ballet of swans. I've never been into wedding stuff—at least not as much as some women—but if I were to imagine a dream venue, this would be it. Art has nailed everything from the classic white tablecloths on Scandinavian-style tables to the gorgeous plants and tasteful decorations.

"So, truth time," the organizer says. "Do you think the tents are hideous?"

I study the clean white gazebos set up over each table. They provide both shade—important for my sun-avoiding sister, Olive—and protection from possible rain. "I think they're pretty."

The organizer looks at me like I'm insane. "Pretty? Those?"

Art rests a hand on the guy's shoulder. "Relax, Festus. They're perfect."

Festus? In the video, he was Daddy.

Festus gapes at the hand on his shoulder, looking like he's about to faint. Or explode in an orgasmic sort of way. "If you think so."

"We do," I say. "You can go now." As silly as it is, the only shoulder I want Art to be touching is mine.

Mine.

Art pulls his hand away. Festus looks disappointed but regroups swiftly, peering at me in confusion. "You're really okay with this?"

Did he expect a Bridezilla?

I nod, and Art grins.

"The reception is still happening?" Festus asks, sounding vaguely disbelieving.

"It is," I say.

"Great." Festus exhales a big breath. "Let me go tell the Botanical Garden folks." He rushes away, no doubt afraid we'll change our minds.

"Thank you," I tell Art, gesturing at the tables around us. "This is going to be an amazing reception."

Too bad it's not real.

Art's gaze is so warm it's like a hug. Stepping

toward me, he clasps my hands and squeezes lightly. "I'm glad you like everything."

I moisten my suddenly dry lips. "'Like' is too mild a word for what I feel."

His gaze drops to my mouth, and his voice turns husky. "You know… people will expect us to kiss tomorrow."

He lifts his eyes to mine, and I feel like a piece of nougat caught in melted chocolate. My words come out breathless. "Are you worried it will look fake?"

"It's… a concern."

The swans in my belly thrash rabidly. "Do you want to rehearse?"

He cradles my face with his large hands. "It's only prudent."

"Prudent is my middle name," I breathe—and Art crushes his lips against mine.

CHAPTER
Thirty-One

HOLY OXYTOCIN.

He tastes faintly like chocolate truffles, but the mouthgasm I'm experiencing puts any sweets-related ones to shame.

This isn't real. It's surreal.

Our tongues dance the most intricate ballet ever staged, and I feel like I'm having an out-of-body experience. Like his lips are sending shivers through my soul.

Someone clears his throat.

Art doesn't seem to notice or care, but I reluctantly pull away. My face is hot and so are the more private parts of my body as I turn to face Festus, who's trying really hard not to look disgusted.

With a sniff, he says, "We're all set," before adding under his breath, "Now go get a room."

I touch my swollen lips. "Thanks?"

Should he who did all those anal tricks be throwing stones?

"Right," Art says, his voice rough. "Thank you."

I glance at him, and we leave fast, as if Festus were a bear chasing us. Fabio would call him a bull, though, I think.

My mind is spinning.

That wasn't just a "let's pretend to kiss" kiss. It felt shockingly real.

Was it like that for Art? I want to ask, but what I end up blurting instead is, "I'm starving."

He looks like he wants to say something—maybe "I'm ravenous too"—but then he presses his lips together and nods toward a Mexican food truck parked across the street. "Want to grab a bite there?"

So we're not talking about it. Fine.

We get the food to go and catch a cab.

The ride happens in silence, and my churro tacos are tasteless as I wolf them down.

Art doesn't seem to enjoy his shrimp tacos either.

———

When we enter the apartment, all seems quiet in the living room. The TV isn't on, Mom and Dad are nowhere in sight, and even Fluffer is napping.

My parents must be eating a late-for-them dinner.

Art leads the way into the kitchen, then stops dead in his tracks at the entrance and stares in confusion at something inside.

I catch up and follow his gaze.

Oh, skunk.

Mom is sprawled naked on the kitchen table. She's covered in sushi, maki rolls, and sashimi.

Time seems to slow as my adrenaline spikes.

In what seems like an eyeblink, I notice unwelcome details, like the fact that Mom's right nipple is covered by tuna sashimi and her left by salmon sashimi, with soy sauce inside her belly button.

I shudder to think where they've put the wasabi.

Dad is naked too, his junk barely covered by the table.

Things just get worse from there. Dad's mouth is headed for one of the pieces of uni sashimi that's sitting on a shiso leaf covering Mom's hoo-ha—and I'm not sure that my sister Olive did me a favor when she informed me that uni is made from the reproductive glands of the sea urchin.

The words that escape my mouth are more of a squeal. "What in the actual hell?"

Mom turns our way, and if she's embarrassed, I sure as fuck can't tell. "Oops. You two are back early."

"Oops?" I stomp my foot like I'm four again. "That's what you have to say about this? Oops?"

Stopping his disturbing trajectory, Dad stands up and gives me a stern glare. "Don't talk like that to your mother."

Oh, my eyes.

My poor eyes.

The table is no longer hiding Dad's privates.

I'd blind myself with the nearby chopsticks, but who knows where they've been?

My cheeks must be redder than the salmon covering

Mom's nipple as I squeeze out, "I'm going to the living room and will only speak with the two of you after you've gotten dressed."

Ignoring their replies, I stomp out, and Art follows me.

Once in the living room, he whispers, "Hey. They have a healthy love life. It's a good thing."

Great. That's what I need right now—my fake husband discussing the healthiness of my parents' bedroom (and kitchen) habits.

"I think Fluffer could use more hay." I walk over to the mansion to reload the tray.

Fluffer watches me like a furry hawk.

Turns out there is *a fate worse than merely getting killed for food. That fate is being turned into sashimi, placed atop a giant's naked body, and eaten.*

My parents appear, finally dressed.

"I'm not going to apologize for being a sexual being," Mom says right off the bat.

I suck in a calming breath. "What about ignoring basic hygiene on our kitchen table?"

At this, Mom and Dad do exchange guilty glances.

"If you tell me where you keep your cleaning products, I'll wash the table," Mom offers.

I'm very tempted to tell them that the table is now theirs, but Art speaks first. "Don't worry. I'll take care of the cleaning tomorrow morning."

The look Dad gives Art is almost worshipful. "Thank you… son."

Are those tears in Dad's eyes? Does he want another

man in the family this badly, or is he that bummed about the coitus interruptus?

I snap my fingers to get their attention. "New rule: everyone can be sexual beings, but not while we're all together in this small apartment."

Mom looks intensely disappointed but nods. Dad tugs on his beard and lifts his hand to count his fingers. "Okay," he finally says. "Eighteen more hours. I guess we can do that."

"Good. And no sushi or peanut butter." I have no idea what they do with the latter, but better safe than sorry.

Mom and Dad nod again.

I relax marginally. "Let's talk sleeping arrangements. I think you guys should take the master bed, while Art and I—"

"No, no," Mom says. "We brought our yoga mats."

"Huh?" is my genius reply.

Dad beams with pride. "We've been sleeping on yoga mats for the last couple of weeks. My back problems are gone."

"That's great," Art says. "But you didn't need to bring your own mats. You could've borrowed ours."

Only if he wants to burn those yoga mats in the same fire as the kitchen table.

"Ours are made of cork," Mom says. "That works better for us."

Don't they use cork mats in hot yoga because they're better able to handle sweat? So why—

Never mind. I hope I never find out for sure.

As Mom and Dad get said mats out of a suitcase and

lay them down in the middle of the living room, the implications of this arrangement dawn on me.

With my parents here, Art can't sleep on the living room couch.

He and I are about to share the bed.

CHAPTER
Thirty-Two

"CAN I get you guys anything else?" Art asks Mom and Dad as I process this shocking realization.

"No, thank you," Mom says.

"You've been a gracious host," Dad says. The look he throws at me seems to say, "Unlike some people."

Art smiles warmly. "Thank you. Good night."

My smile is way less gracious. "Don't let the yoga mat bugs bite."

Art and I head for the master bedroom, and with each step, my heartbeat accelerates.

"I can sleep on the floor," Art whispers as soon as the bedroom door closes.

"Don't be ridiculous," I whisper back. "The last thing we want during the reception is for you to throw your back out."

He waves dismissively. "My back is very strong."

Right. It has to be, to juggle all those ballerinas.

"You won't get good sleep on the floor," I say. "We

don't want you to have bags under your eyes in all the pictures. Let's just share the bed."

To punctuate my point, I head over to the bathroom. Art doesn't follow, which I take as consent.

As I shower, some of my bravado evaporates, replaced with trepidation.

Why did I insist on sleeping together?

What if I roll over in my sleep and accidentally impale myself on Mr. Big? Or what if Mr. Big ends up in my mouth? There's sleep walking, so why not sleep sucking?

Overlaying those concerns is a replay of that kiss, which has been spinning in my mind since it happened.

It seemed so real. Like he really *meant* to kiss me. And I definitely felt on the verge of giving in to the impossible temptation that is Art.

As the images flit through my mind, I have to stop myself from exercising every masturbation technique I've ever blogged about. I don't want to fall and get caught. One more embarrassment today, and I just might implode, like an incandescent lightbulb trying to molest a hammer.

Somehow, I finish my evening routine and exit the bathroom with my sanity still intact—which is when Art goes in. Now I have to fight the temptation of the nearby sex toys.

I can't.

I shouldn't.

But—

The bathroom door opens.

PJ-clad Art steps out, locks the bedroom door, and

slips under the covers with me, turning off the light on the way.

Wow. That was an even quicker shower. That means he didn't masturbate. Does that mean he didn't want to? Or was he also afraid to slip and fall?

All I know is that if I had given in to the sex toy temptation, I would've been caught… and a part of me wonders if that would've been such a bad thing.

Maybe if he'd gotten turned on and—

"You awake?" Art murmurs softly.

"Nope," I whisper. "I always talk in my sleep."

"Want to talk about what happened?"

Does he mean the kiss or the sushi incident?

Either way, I reply, "Sure. Let's chat."

He turns on the bedside lamp, and we turn toward each other.

Oh, my.

Only a measly foot separates us from kissing again.

"You were kind of harsh out there," he says softly. "I was surprised."

So this is about the sushi incident. "You're taking my parents' side?"

He scoots an inch toward me. "No sides. It's just that they seem nice. Also, given your job, I find it odd how uncomfortable you are about their expression of sexuality."

I gape at him. "You're calling me judgy?"

"You said it, not me."

I punch my pillow. "How would *you* feel if you saw *your* parents doing that?"

He flinches, and a sorrowful expression twists his face.

Oh, skunk. Now I feel like a heartless moron. I scoot until our noses almost touch and gently lay my hand on his cheek. "I'm so sorry. That was thoughtless of me." I bite my lip. "Or maybe you just made me feel like a bad daughter, and I lashed out. It doesn't help that we've been lying to them this whole time and—"

He covers my hand with his, his calluses pleasantly rough on the smooth back of my palm. "No, I'm sorry. You're lying to them because of me, and—"

I kiss him. I can't help it. I mean for it to be a soothing, I'm-sorry kiss, but I miscalculate.

He stiffens for a heartbeat, and then he kisses me back with such raw passion that if I were Sleeping Beauty, I'd wake up with a heart attack.

CHAPTER
Thirty-Three

JUST LIKE DURING our kiss at the Botanical Garden, I experience an ethereal, out-of-body joy. If we were to float off the bed, I wouldn't be surprised in the slightest.

Breathing heavily, Art pulls back to meet my gaze. The heat in his melted-chocolate eyes could caramelize sugar on a dozen crèmes brûlées. "I want you," he murmurs, and the hunger in his voice sends an erotic shiver down my spine.

My heart hammers hard against my ribs as I kick the stifling blanket off of us. "Oh? Can you be more specific?"

Can melted-chocolate turn into magma? "I want to make you come all over my face," he says, enunciating every word. "And after that, all over my cock."

That I can speak is a miracle. "What about Rule One?"

"Fuck Rule One," he growls.

I lick my lips. "What about the agreement with my

parents? No one is supposed to be having sex under our roof for the next eighteen hours."

"Fuck that too." He sits up on the bed and yanks off his T-shirt.

Oh, my.

Those abs.

That V that leads to Mr. Big.

To paraphrase Matthew McConaughey in *Magic Mike*, there are going to be "a lotta lawbreakers up in this house tonight."

I sit up and take my PJ top off as well.

His eyes roam over my exposed flesh as if it were an all-you-can-eat cupcake buffet, and his voice roughens further. "You're perfect, *kislik*."

Kiss and lick are what I want too. I jump off the bed and wriggle out of my pants. "You're not bad yourself."

He takes in my legs, his nostrils flaring as he swings his feet to the floor. "Like I said, fucking perfect."

Standing up, he rips off his pajama pants—and I do mean rips, into shreds of cotton.

As I face Mr. Big sober for the first time in real life, the little hairs on the back of my neck rise.

This reminds me of when I first stood under the Empire State Building. Yes, I knew it was large enough for King Kong to climb during that documentary, but once you stand under it, you really appreciate the scale.

Like a star caught in the gravity well of a supermassive black hole, I feel myself drawn into Art's orbit—and he into mine.

Gripping his shoulders, I rise on tiptoes, and our lips clash once more.

Pure deliciousness. Even better than doughnuts with ice cream.

I feel lightheaded, partly from the oral sensations but much more from his intoxicating scent.

Without removing his lips, Art picks me up and lays me on the bed.

Wow. All that ballerina juggling has imbued him with the manhandling skills of a god.

He nibbles on my lower lip, then moves his ministrations from my mouth to my neck.

Fuck, yeah.

I reach down and stroke Mr. Big.

It's smooth, like hard candy. Very hard candy.

Grunting in pleasure, Art retaliates by giving my neck a small yet hungry bite.

Is he also thinking of me in dessert terms? If so, I approve.

He nibbles his way down to my clavicle, and then his face is in the middle of my breasts. I freeze in anticipation, and then… yes! He moves over and sucks in my left nipple, his mouth hot and wet on my sensitive flesh. At the same time, he kneads the other breast, intensifying the sensations.

Panting, I arch against him as he switches his attentions to the other nipple. Then, as if drawn to exactly where I want him most, he slides his tongue down my belly until I feel his warm breath on my sex.

I gasp, and he looks up, his eyes fiery. "You remember what you have to do?"

My cheeks burn with renewed vigor. "Remind me."

"You will come." His voice is filled with dark promises. "From my tongue."

I nod because what is there to say?

He kisses my clit, the pressure of his lips feather light.

I suck in a desperate breath.

He gives his target an indulgent lick, the kind I reserve for a spoon of panna cotta.

I ball my hands in the sheets.

He makes his tongue wide and flat.

My toes curl.

He licks again.

A moan is wrenched from my lips.

He does the kiss thing, followed by the flat-tongue thing, then a lick, and then another round of it all, and another.

With a scream, I do as I was ordered—I come all over his beautiful face.

"That's a good *kislik*," he murmurs roughly, looking up. "Now you'll come once more. On my cock." His lips are shiny as he runs his tongue over them, seemingly savoring the taste.

In answer, I crawl over to the nightstand, locate a condom, and hand it to him, then watch with bated breath as he begins to sheathe Mr. Big. Even though the rubber is a magnum (I was optimistic when I purchased them), I'm not sure it will fit.

Whew.

The poor latex doesn't rip. Now let's see if he fits in *me*.

In a blur of fluid movement, Art does his ballet-inspired manhandling magic again, and I find myself on all fours.

How?

Mr. Big gently brushes against my opening.

Oh, my. Forget the how. Forget everything.

I focus on the sensations—a stretch at first, then wonderful fullness.

Art grabs my hips with his strong hands, his thumbs kneading my buttocks.

Fucking finally. Our *pas de deux* is about to begin.

The first thrust is gentle—*adagio*, as they call it in ballet. The next few are as well. Then Art slows, as if to check if I've fully adjusted to his (rather large) invasion.

I answer by backing into Mr. Big and arching my back. If I could twerk, I'd throw one of those in, but alas, that is a skill I've yet to master.

Still, Art gets the message. His next thrust is harder and faster. Then harder yet.

I ball the sheets in my fists again. A huge wave of pleasure is building in my core.

Art's fingers dig into my flesh, his movements getting into *allegro* territory.

My breaths turn into gasping moans.

"Yes," Art growls. "Come for me." He speeds up his pace until he pistons into me so quickly there isn't a ballet term for it.

Oh, fuck.

Here it is.

My orgasm makes landfall and I come, shouting Art's name.

He groans and Mr. Big grows impossibly harder and

bigger, sending seismic aftershocks through my over-sensitive sex.

The moment I feel his release, Art pinches my clit and wrings another orgasm from me—one I scream into the pillow.

In the aftermath, I find myself manhandled once more, this time in order to be turned into the little spoon. Draping an arm over my ribcage, Art kisses my ear, murmuring tender, barely audible words of praise, and an unusual contentment envelops me, one that Zen monks might experience after a month of meditation... or after breaking their vow of celibacy.

Feeling warm and cared for, surrounded by Art's tantalizing scent, I close my eyes and plummet into the best sleep of my life.

CHAPTER
Thirty~Four

I WAKE up snuggled against Art, my head in the crook of his shoulder, his arm wrapped around me.

Warmth floods my chest. I'd gladly wake up like this forever.

Except... I don't have forever. At best, I have however long it takes Art to get a green card. At worst, as soon as my parents leave, we'll be back to sleeping in different rooms.

I force my eyes open as more unwelcome reality creeps in.

Did that out-of-this-world sex even happen? Could it have been a dream?

No. There's a soreness to prove it was all real.

But now what? The warm and fuzzy feelings in my chest are terrifying. They make me wonder what Art thinks about the whole thing.

Did last night mean nearly as much to him as it did to me?

There's a loud knock on the door.

"Namaste, sunshine," Mom calls loudly. "If you don't get up now, you'll be late for your hair and makeup appointments."

Skunk. How long before Mom breaks through that door?

I extricate myself from Art and check the time.

Wow. 11:05 a.m.

Art never sleeps in this late. Ever.

"Mom, I'll be out in a minute," I yell, pulling on a robe.

Art opens one eye. "What's with the racket?"

"Sorry," I whisper, flushing. "I have to be someplace. Snooze some more if you want."

I rush to the bathroom to take care of business. When I'm almost done brushing my teeth, Art joins me, already dressed. More heat rises to my face as our eyes meet, and he gives me a crooked grin before grabbing his own toothbrush.

Okay. So that's how we're playing it, all cool. Got it.

I brush my teeth vigorously, and so does he. The domesticity of it pinches something inside my chest. I want to spit out the toothpaste and pepper him with questions about what last night meant, but before I can act on that iffy idea, there's a louder knock on the door in the bedroom.

"We're officially late," Mom yells.

I meet Art's eyes in the mirror and accidentally swallow the remnants of my toothpaste. "I've got to go."

Toothbrush still in his mouth, Art gives me a thumbs up.

I hurry back into the bedroom, get dressed, and open the door.

Mom sneaks a peek at the bed. "Platonic night, huh?" she asks, waggling her eyebrows.

"A lady doesn't kiss and tell," I mutter.

Mom grins. "A lady doesn't, but what about you?"

I don't dignify that with a reply. Instead, I beeline to the kitchen, where Dad is drinking a cup of coffee.

"Morning," I say and start shoving food indiscriminately into my mouth. I'll need energy for the beautification ordeal.

Mom waltzes in and looks me over. "Ready?"

"Yeah," I reply, and just then Art walks into the kitchen as well.

Dad grins at him. "Sounds like you and I will have a boys' morning out."

I swallow the last of the muffin I was chewing. "That's not a thing."

"We'll make it our thing," Art says and turns to my dad. "Have you ever heard of banya?"

Dad shakes his head.

"It's something I like to do when I'm stressed or just want to unwind," Art says. "A great way to start a big day like this."

I wrinkle my nose. "You're not going to take him to the *taranka* place, are you?"

Art looks disappointed. "Is the smell sensitivity genetic?"

"No," Mom and Dad say in unison.

"In that case, yes," Art says. "We'll go to Easy Fume."

Mom pulls me by my elbow. "We're beyond late."

As I let her lead me away, I wonder if Dad and Art will get to second base at the banya. It's likely, but hey, it might just look socially acceptable there.

Once we're outside, Mom pushes me into a cab, which takes us to appointment number one of a million.

The goal of all the primping and preening is for me to be the best-looking person with my face at the shindig. The good thing is, my mom chatters the entire time, which keeps me from dwelling on Art and what happened last night.

Hours later, Mom announces that our goal has been achieved.

I stare at myself in the mirror and whistle. I'm not sure if the time was worth it, but I look great—which is kind of a waste, given that the whole thing is a farce.

"Don't worry," Mom says, misreading my frown. "I warned your sisters not to wear white and, in general, to do their best to ensure you're the prettiest sextuplet today."

Good. I hope they look downright frumpy.

———

When Mom and I get to the Botanical Garden, our husbands—hers real (hopefully) and mine fake (sadly) —are already waiting for us.

Art scans me from updo to high heels, and the heat in his eyes gives me a spine-tingling flashback to last night.

"You look amazing, *kislik*," he says huskily, and I don't know if he means it or is just playing his part in making this look real.

Either way, I reply, "Thanks, dearest," and check him out thoroughly as well. He's wearing a bespoke tux, his hair is carefully groomed, and his face is clean-shaven. Trying not to drool, I murmur, "You look good enough to make my sisters jealous."

Mom winks at me. "The single ones, for sure."

"You're late," Dad says. "Everyone is already here."

"Wait," Art says. "Let's take some pictures."

I go into my purse to get my phone and realize it's gone.

Skunk. In my rush to get here, I left it on the charger.

Oh, well. Art can take the pictures with his phone, and everyone who's likely to call me is going to be at the reception.

Pictures taken, the men lead us to the gazebos, and I learn that the "boys' morning out" was such a huge success that Dad plans to make trips to the banya with Art a regular thing.

"Thanks for taking him," I whisper into Art's ear, and heroically resist the urge to nibble on it.

"Oh, it was a pleasure," he whispers back, his lips tickling my ear. "The only problem was that we had to cut it short."

Before I can reply, we step into the clearing where

people are mingling, and everyone stops talking to stare at us.

Huh.

This must be what it feels like when you step out for the official "first dance" at a wedding. It's kind of fun to be the center of attention. That is, until I spot two eyeballs burning with hatred.

The eyeballs in question belong to Black Swan— who clearly has no tact whatsoever. Why else would she wear a white dress?

With a start, I remember her confronting me in the banya locker room. I was already drunk, which made the incident foggy in my memory, but I recall it clearly now. She said nasty things to me, or at least I assume she did. Her tone was mean, and she called me a Russian cow. No, sorry, just *a* cow.

Art follows my gaze and frowns. I wonder if he's also not happy to see Black Swan here. But if that's the case, why invite her?

Then again, I guess he couldn't *not* invite her. Next to her are a bunch of other ballet people from Art's company—presumably all of them. It would be weird to single out one colleague, I imagine, even if she is a bitch.

Maybe he's frowning at the white tutu-like thing she's wearing. Or because of how sad it is that all his people are from work, with zero family representation —unless you count the two *detdom* buddies sitting next to some of the dancers. I recognize them from the pictures Art showed me; they live in NYC. I'll have to say hello to them later.

As for me, I recognize almost all the faces at the non-ballet tables as my family members or their plus-ones. For instance, the twins, Gia and Holly, are sitting with two good-looking guys, their boyfriends.

I peer closer at their table. Next to Holly is a woman I don't recognize. She's more beautiful than any of Art's coworkers, and that's a high bar. Is she a ballerina who befriended Holly, the least social of my sisters? Or do Holly and her boyfriend practice polyamory?

Wait a second. Holly's boyfriend looks a little bit like the mystery woman. Also, Gia did mention a—

Someone clears his throat loudly enough to vibrate the crystal glasses on the tables.

"Ladies and gentlemen," Fabio says into a microphone. "Please give a sweet welcome to Lemon and Artjoms Skulme."

Everyone cheers and claps.

"Sweet?" I whisper into Mom's ear. "Was it your idea to give *him* the mic?"

"Sorry," Mom whispers back. "He said he'd be good."

Figures. She's had a *sweet* spot for Fabio since our high school days.

When everyone quiets down, Fabio looks at me. "Would you like to dance with your new partner-in-lime?"

A dance? We haven't even sat down yet.

Art doesn't seem to share my lack of enthusiasm. Quite the opposite. He gracefully steps away from me, then extends a hand in the fanciest way possible—

something I'd expect to see at the court of Louis XIV, not New York City.

As I take his hand, tingles spread through my whole body.

Classical music begins playing, a song I've heard Art put on before.

I narrow my eyes at my husband. "You planned this?" I mouth.

He winks at me and pulls me into the dance.

Wow. I'm not a dancer by any means, but with Art's lead, I'm actually doing it like a pro.

Art tugs me closer. "Sorry," he whispers. "I didn't want you to have performance anxiety, so I kept this a surprise."

Before I can retort, he twirls me around.

Damn.

This is fun. And hot. And fake. That last bit sours my joy, and I'm glad when the dance is soon over.

"Come." Art drags me to our seats as Fabio announces that my parents are going to dance next.

Mom and Dad take the dance floor while Art puts a little bit of everything on my plate. The food is great, and interestingly, all the dishes are of a non-malodorous kind—clearly by Art's design.

After Mom and Dad finish their dance, Fabio tells everyone to eat for a while but warns that "dancing will resume shortly."

As soon as Mom and Dad return to the table, Dad starts to tell Mom about the banya, and Art chimes in from time to time. I let them talk as I stuff my face. It's been a long time since my hurried breakfast, and I'm ravenous.

Just as I finish everything on my plate, someone taps me on the shoulder three times.

Turning, I come face to face with Holly and the attractive woman from her table. "I wanted to say congratulations," Holly says. "And introduce you to Bella."

CHAPTER
Thirty-Five

OF SKUNKING COURSE. I was about to figure this out before Fabio interrupted me. This is Bella Chortsky—the owner of the sex toy company Belka and the person I've been trying to speak with about a sponsorship opportunity.

When Gia first brought her up, it was in the context of Bella being Holly's new BFF, so it's not *that* surprising Holly's brought her here as her second plus-one.

Except I thought Bella had ghosted me. Her warm smile, however, doesn't seem to be one a ghoster would give the ghostée.

Realizing that I'm gaping at Bella like an idiot, I leap to my feet and shake her hand. "Lemon. Nice to meet you."

Bella's smile widens. "Nice to meet you face to face like this."

It is? But what about the ghosting?

"It's odd, actually," Bella continues. "I feel like I

already know you."

"You do? Why?"

She arches one perfect eyebrow. "All that correspondence on your blog?"

What correspondence? Am I being punked?

Holly rolls her eyes at Bella. "I told you. She doesn't know that *belka* means squirrel."

Bella turns to her BFF. "How could she not? She married a Russian."

Belka means squirrel in Russian? Wait a minute… "You're SquirrelBoner?"

Bella looks sheepish. "I thought you knew. Sorry about that. In case you're wondering, Boner is the name of my dog. It's short for Bonaparte."

Her dog. Sure.

She grins at what she must read on my face. "Anyway, would now be a good time for a talk?"

"Of course. How about there?" I gesture at a clearing where there aren't any tables.

"Great." She heads where I suggested. As I follow, I notice the suitcase she's carrying. It's covered in tiny hand-drawn, multicolored penises and vaginas.

Huh. I bet my mom would kill me or one of my sisters to have such a piece of luggage.

When we finally have privacy, I can't help but blurt, "I'm confused. I got a text from you that said we didn't need to set anything up anymore."

"Well, yeah." Bella stands her peculiar suitcase on the grass next to her. "Holly invited me to this event, so I figured we'd talk today. I'm glad I did that. Stalking your blog in the meantime has given me all the info I needed. At this point, I know Belka is interested in collaborating with you. We just need to iron out the details."

Oh, wow. This is unbelievable. I feel like jumping up and down in joy, but I fight the temptation. It's better to play it cool since we need to talk money. "What kind of details?"

Skunk. I catch myself bouncing from foot to foot. Hopefully, she'll think I need to pee.

Bella opens the suitcase, revealing enough dildoes and toys to satisfy an army of enthusiastic nymphomaniacs. I fight a gasp of awe. It's like the part in *Pulp Fiction* where a golden light shines out of the pivotal briefcase.

"Glorious, aren't they." Bella looks like a proud parent as she gazes at a pair of anal beads. "And since your husband warned me not to wear perfume, I made sure that these are also scent-free."

I bob my head, still awestruck.

"How about you test each of them and write a sponsored post with your review? Belka will pay five grand for each post."

Five grand? My eyes bug out, and a *squee* tries to work itself out of my throat. I swallow it back, but a treacherous grin still blooms on my face.

So much for playing it cool.

Of course, the negotiation isn't over yet. "One thing," I say, striving for at least a modicum of business-meeting-appropriate composure. "The reviews will be honest. If I don't like a toy, I'll say so and why. I'll also be transparent with my followers about our arrangement."

"Sounds fair. I believe in my product." She reaches into the suitcase and grabs an extra-large dildo. "Good or bad review, it's a win for me."

"Oh?"

"Good is obvious," she says. "But bad is useful because if you have good reasons for why something doesn't work, it gives us an opportunity to improve the product—which is what I'm all about."

Huh. She's really dedicated to women's pleasure. We have a lot in common.

"By the way, what do you think of this?" She tugs on the two ends of the dildo she's holding, and the thing opens up—revealing a smaller dildo inside. She does this again, and there's an even smaller dildo. Then smaller still.

"It's a prototype," she says. "For now, we're calling them matryoshka cocks." I watch her get down to the last teeny-wieny toy—and it turns out that it can vibrate really well.

I purse my lips. "I'd have to use the matryoshka cocks to be sure, but off the top of my head, this would make a great travel companion for someone who likes to play with different sizes."

"I know, right?" She reassembles the matryoshka cocks into one oversized dildo.

"It's also the ultimate gift," I say.

"How so?"

I grin. "We don't usually know what size preferences our friends have when it comes to these things, but this is a 'one size fits all.'"

"'One size fits all,'" she says thoughtfully. "I think I will use that if you don't mind."

I open my mouth to say that I'd be honored, but Fabio's voice rings out.

"We'll resume the dancing with a father-daughter dance," he says into the mic.

Bella drops the matryoshka cocks back into the suitcase and zips it up. "You'd better go. We'll talk more in the near future. I have no doubt this is the beginning of a beautiful friendship."

I shake her hand vigorously and run to the dance floor where Dad awaits.

As we start, Dad's eyes begin to tear up. My own follow.

"I wasn't sure if we should even do this," he says, his voice breaking. "This dance is an outgrowth of patriarchal history, after all. But your mom insisted, and now I'm glad she did."

"Me too," I whisper.

Then I recall that my marital status is fake, and the warm feelings transform into sadness. I also feel guilty about lying to Dad. He's got tears in his eyes, for skunk's sake.

When the dance is finally over, Dad blows his nose and leads me back to the table.

Please let all the formal crap be over.

Nope.

Fabio announces the next phase: a dance between the mother-in-law and her new son-in-law.

I narrow my eyes at Mom, who looks like a kid on Christmas morning.

Is this why she insisted these dances take place? Grr. Then again, Art looks so happy to participate that I'll suppress my jealousy for a couple of minutes... that is, unless Mom grabs his tush.

Nope.

Their dance is pretty PG, though I still wouldn't trust Mom around sushi tonight.

Also, when the music stops, Mom looks extremely disappointed.

Fabio speaks up again. "At this juncture, Art would like to say a few words to his new bride."

Everyone cheers as Art walks over and grabs the mic from Fabio before facing me. Unsure of the protocol, I stand up.

"Lemon, my *kislik*," Art says ceremonially. "From the moment I saw you, I knew that was *it* for me. I knew I'd found my person. My light. That which would make the rest of my life sweet."

My knees turn weak, and I have no choice but to plop back into my chair.

Art frowns worriedly.

"I'm fine," I gasp. "Legs tired. Go on."

It's the biggest lie I've ever told.

I'm not fine.

I'm screaming inside.

His words sound so fucking sincere that it hurts. And since I know they're lies, instead of warming my heart, they make it feel like it's ripping apart.

Damn this fake marriage. I want Art to be telling the

truth. I'd give anything for him to be telling the truth, but of course, I know he isn't.

"Looks like I've swept her off her feet yet again." Art looks around, giving everyone a conspiratorial grin.

Everyone but me cheers.

"Anyway, where was I?" Art looks at me. "Ah, right. I was about to call my wife the most beautiful woman I've ever met. The cleverest too. The—"

Mom sobs so loudly I miss what Art says next.

Since when is she so sappy? Must be the promise of grandchildren or something like that.

Dad gently squeezes her shoulder in an effort to calm her down. I wish someone would calm *me* down. I'm on an emotional rollercoaster and I don't even know why. I signed up for this charade. I shouldn't feel anything at Art's fake speech.

Mom stops sobbing, and Art's voice reaches me again. "—someone whose hand I want to hold every night. Someone I will honor and respect. Someone I will stay faithful to. Someone I'll never forsake. Someone—"

Mom starts sobbing again, louder this time, and is inconsolable to Dad's touch. By the time she quiets down, I only catch the last part of what Art says, which is, "Join me now and drink to my wife's health."

People down their drinks as Art heads my way. When he reaches me, a bunch of voices start shouting, "*Gor'ko! Gor'ko! Gor'ko!*"

"What's that mean?" I whisper into Art's ear.

"We trained for this," he says. "It means 'bitter.'"

I frown. "Is that some weird joke related to my name? Also, how did we train for this?"

"It's just a Russian tradition. That's what people shout when they want the bride and groom to kiss."

So "bitter" means "kiss." How very Russian. And I now understand what he means about our training.

Art glances at my lips. "Obviously, if you don't—"

I stand up, wrap my arms around his neck, and rise on tiptoes to lock my lips with his. I channel all the feelings triggered by his speech into the kiss.

Distantly, I hear cheering and Mom crying yet again.

I pay them no heed. My head spins, and my heart races madly. I so badly want Art to mean those words— and I want him to take me here and now.

With great reluctance, I pull away from the kiss.

Fabio wolf-whistles. "That was some PDA."

Everyone cheers.

"Now," Fabio continues dramatically. "The moment you've all been waiting for. Anyone can dance with anyone they please!"

Another cheer.

Art and I sit, and I down a glass of water to calm myself after the kiss.

Someone taps my shoulder.

Is Bella back?

I turn, but it's not my new business partner. It's an attractive man from one of the ballet people's tables.

"May I have this dance?" he asks with a courtly bow.

"No," Art growls just as I open my mouth to agree.

Startled, I look at him. "Why not?"

"Because this dance is mine," Art says in a hard tone. "And the rest of them too."

So now he's acting like a possessive husband? If this were real, I think I'd like it.

"My apologies," the guy says and slinks away.

"You can dance with one of her sisters," Mom calls after him. "They usually dress better and wear perfume."

Greedy much? She's at one daughter's wedding but is already pimping out the rest of them.

When the guy is out of sight, Art says, "Shall we have this dance?"

I shake my head. "First, I need to powder my nose." And get my unruly heart under control. I look around. "Does anyone know where the bathroom is?"

Mom tells me where to go, and I depart swiftly.

Between that speech, that kiss, and everything else, I'm on the verge of not just having, but also expressing feelings he wouldn't want to hear about, especially at our fake wedding reception.

The bathroom smells like chlorine. I hold my breath as much as I can as I take care of my business, and by the time I exit, I'm desperate for fresh air.

Instead, I'm hit with a cloud of weaponized perfume.

The Black Swan stands in front of me, in all her inappropriate white-tutu glory.

I take a step back. The expression on the ballerina's face is so frightening I'm glad my bladder is empty.

With a heavy accent and in a voice that's as sexy as it is scary, she hisses, "Your marriage. It is scam."

CHAPTER
Thirty-Six

FUCK.

How did she find out? Will she tell the government? How much trouble would Art and I get into?

I picture Art deported. I picture lawyers. Jail.

Skunking skunk.

Black Swan is still staring daggers at me.

What do I do? What the fuck do I do?

Denial. Yes, that's my best and only strategy.

I'm stuttering only slightly as I say, "I have no idea what you mean."

Black Swan takes a menacing step toward me and sticks her hand into her purse.

Shit. Am I about to be stabbed with a shard of glass?

She pulls out a piece of paper.

Hmm. In China, there used to be a torture method called "death by a thousand cuts." Does she want to do that to me with the edges of that sheet?

She thrusts the paper into my unsteady hands. "Here. This why you not his wife."

With that, she executes a pirouette-like turn and prances away.

"You stink worse than Pepe LePew," I shout at her back. Then, befuddled, I take a look at the paper.

It looks like some sort of a document, but all in Cyrillic. The only recognizable thing is a date, one that's from a decade ago.

Still, for some reason, dread spreads through my insides.

That woman wouldn't give me something nice to read, that's for sure.

Another waifish woman comes toward me, one from Art's guest list. A ballerina? Is she going to give me papers too?

"Hi," I say, hiding my turmoil. "Do you speak Russian?"

She shakes her head. "No, sorry. I'm actually American."

"Then may I borrow your phone while you're in the bathroom?"

She looks hesitant, and why wouldn't she?

"I'm the bride," I say. "Art's wife. Half the reason you're here."

That does the trick. She takes out a phone, unlocks it, and hands it to me. "Okay. Here you go."

She disappears into the depths of the bathroom as I download my favorite translation app and hover it over the text.

The translated words stare at me from the screen, as confusing as they are impossible.

No. No, can't be.

Regardless, a Siberia-like cold is spreading through my veins.

With unsteady fingers, I download another translation app and re-run the text.

Same result.

I locate a translation website and type in the words "marriage certificate," then click "translate to Russian."

The result is exactly the title of the document I'm holding.

There's no doubt any longer.

In my hands is proof that one Artjoms Skulme was already married when we met.

CHAPTER
Thirty-Seven

THE SHOCK CRUSHES MY LUNGS. It's all I can do to drag in small breaths.

Art is married.

Art has a wife who isn't me.

That had been an irrational fear of mine, that he had a secret wife in Russia.

Or maybe not so irrational. He did react strangely when I asked him if he was married.

How could it be true?

My heart squeezes painfully with each frantic beat. Visions of me in jail and of Art getting deported come back with a vengeance. Isn't that what will happen if the government finds out about his polygamy? Definitely, and I have no doubt Black Swan will ensure they do find out.

My mouth feels sandpapery as I start grasping at straws. Maybe Art *was* married but is now divorced? No, that doesn't track. He told me he was never married. Either way, he lied to me—but why lie about being divorced? I would've been fine being his second wife, either fake or real. The only scenario that makes sense is that he never divorced—meaning he's still married.

Fuck. I married a married man.

I'm a homewrecker. Well, a fake one, but still. Actually, not so fake. I've slept with him twice now. That's properly homewrecker-ish.

My lungs constrict further. I feel as if an obese skunk is standing on my chest. Weirdly, there's also a stinging on my index finger.

I bring the finger to eye level.

Just what I need. A papercut. Nine hundred and ninety-nine more to go for it to qualify as Chinese torture. Russian torture is what I'm already being put through.

Burning pressure builds behind my eyes, and I press the heels of my palms to them to stop the foolish tears from falling. Idiot. Why did I think Art would be interested in me? Of course he has a wife. Of course this was completely fake, a means to get a green card. I should never have—

"Hey, Lemon," someone says, and I lower my hands to see Honey speed-walking toward me.

Frowning, she stops in front of me. "What is it? You're paler than Gia."

Before I can answer, the owner of the phone comes out, so I give it back and thank her in a shaky voice.

"You okay?" she asks, and I give her a tight smile.

"Yeah, thanks."

She slips the phone into her bag and walks away. As

soon as she's out of sight, I thrust the certificate into Honey's hands.

She squints at the document. "What am I looking at?"

As I explain the situation to her in a choked voice, her hands turn into fists.

"Want me to cut her?" she asks when I'm done. "Or him?"

Shaking my head, I shuffle like a zombie in the direction of my table. Honey says something soothing, but I can't make it out. I'm too much in my head, replaying all the good things that have happened between Art and me, but seeing them through this new, corrupted filter.

Lies, all lies. Vile lies.

When I arrive at the table, I jab my finger into Art's shoulder.

He looks up, and his brow wrinkles. "What's the matter?"

Still channeling a zombie, I extend my right hand and point at Black Swan.

He follows my gaze, and his eyebrows snap together. "Did Alisa say something?"

My chin quivers treacherously. "She told me *everything*."

He squeezes his eyes shut and lets out an audible exhale. Opening them, he stands up and says in a low voice, "I can explain."

He can explain? I don't know what I expected—denial, maybe—but not this.

I push him, but I might as well try to push a brick wall. "Stay away from me."

His chocolate gaze looks pained. Oscar-winning acting again. "*Kislik*, I—"

"Don't call me that! Don't call me anything."

He reaches for my hand. "If we could just—"

"Stop!" I jerk my hand away. My heart feels like it's shattering into pieces. "I'm done with this charade. Goodbye."

Turning on my heel, I run. Art chases after me, shouting something, but I pick up the pace until I'm full-out sprinting in my heels. My heartbeat hammers so loudly in my ears I can't even make out his lies—and I'm glad.

I've heard enough of them.

Dashing through the exit, I spot a cab idling next to the sidewalk, with Honey inside. She's holding the door open and waving at me.

I dive into the cab, and we torpedo forward as I struggle to catch my breath. My leg muscles burn and my feet feel like they've been rubbed raw, but it's nothing compared to how I feel inside.

"Where are we headed?" I ask in a hollow voice after a minute.

"Home," Honey says sympathetically.

Home? I don't actually have a home. What I've been thinking of as "home" is the place where Art and I pretended to live together. My old shithole is stripped of my stuff and subleased out, so it's not a home in any sense of the word.

Some of this must show on my face because Honey squeezes my hand, "I meant my place."

"Oh. Thanks." The stinging in my index finger returns, so I stick the digit into my mouth. It tastes coppery, like blood.

"What are you doing?" Honey's eyes are on my finger as her face grows pale.

"Paper cut from the marriage certificate," I say in a strained voice. "It wasn't enough to make me bleed metaphorically. It had to do it for real, too."

Upon hearing the word "bleed," Honey turns ghostly white. "Can I ask you a huge favor?"

I blink at her. "Sure. What is it?"

"First, promise you won't ask any questions."

I nod. I don't have the energy to interrogate anyone anyway.

"I don't want to see that finger... especially if there's blood."

"Why?" I stare at her, momentarily distracted.

"No questions. You promised."

Okay, whatever. I hide my offending finger in the folds of my dress.

The only explanation I can think of is that she's got a problem with blood, but that would be strange. She's famous for cutting people who cross her. Well, she cut one girl in high school, at least. Still, you can't exactly cut a bitch if the sight of said bitch's blood would trouble your delicate sensibilities.

Under normal circumstances, I'd grill her mercilessly, but I don't have the slightest inclination to do so now. Instead, my thoughts turn to Art and his lies, and the burning behind my eyelids returns.

Don't cry. Don't freaking cry. He's not worth it.

Speak of the lying devil. Honey's phone rings, and when she glances at it, she mouths, "Him."

Huh? Oh, right. I left my phone back at "our place."

I swallow thickly. "Tell him I don't want to hear any more of his lies."

Honey picks up the call.

"Hi," she says. "Go fuck yourself." With that, she hangs up.

He calls again.

She sends him to voicemail and deletes the message he leaves.

He calls once more. I suggest she block his number or turn off her phone. She goes for the block option, and deletes his number for good measure. Just as she's finishing, the cab stops.

"Come." She jumps out and holds the door open for me.

My chest squeezes. Art would always hold doors for me, but he probably does so for his other wife too. His real wife.

As I follow Honey, I'm back to walking like a zombie.

Entering her place, I nearly trip over Bunny.

If cat glares could kill, I'd be a pile of ashes now—which might be a relief, given how I'm feeling.

"You can take my bed," Honey says, gesturing at her bedroom door.

"What? No. I don't want to impose."

She snatches Bunny off the floor and strokes his fur thoughtfully—both of them looking like Bond villains in the process. "How about this? You can earn my bed... by never mentioning that bit in the car." She looks worriedly at my finger with the paper cut.

I make a fist to hide the deformity. "The blood thing?"

She winces. "No questions either."

I sigh. "You've got yourself a deal."

Honestly, Honey has been so helpful today I'd owe her my silence on the blood issue even without the bedroom sacrifice.

"If you don't mind, I'm going to lie down," I say wearily.

"Do you want company?"

I shake my head.

She extends her cat my way. "Want to cuddle with something warm?"

I shake my head again. Firstly, I just want to be alone. More importantly, though, having my eyeballs eaten is not the way I want to go.

"Understood," Honey says softly. "Give me a shout if you need anything."

I thank her and slink away into the bedroom.

I feel like I'm holding myself together by a thread— a thread that snaps as soon as I'm alone.

Crashing onto the bed, I bury my face in the pillow and let the tears fall.

CHAPTER
Thirty~Eight

A KNOCK WAKES ME UP.

I look around groggily, wondering where I am.

Then it all rushes back, including the fact that I'm at Honey's place.

"Sis, you will want to hear me out," Honey shouts. "Chop, chop."

I get up, stumble to the door, and open it. "What?"

Honey steps back. "On second thought, you can brush your teeth first."

She's offended by *my* smell? Oh, the irony. Now that I'm not so overwhelmed, I can detect all manner of unpleasantness—like kitty litter, Honey's leather jacket, her antiperspirant, and a faint hint of Fabio's yucky cologne.

Still, fair is fair, so I brush my teeth with a spare toothbrush and splash some water on my face. Feeling a bit more human, I check to make sure that my paper cut —that horrific injury from last night—is healed enough to spare Honey's fragile mental state.

Yep. No sign of blood.

Of course, when I come out of the bedroom, I almost trip on the damned cat. He hisses at me and waltzes into the bedroom. In this, he reminds me of Woofer, who also likes to wait for someone with opposable thumbs to open doors for His Majesty.

"So," I say when I locate Honey in the kitchen. "What's the emergency?"

"This." She waves the paper Black Swan gave me. "I have reason to suspect this isn't a real document—or at least, not one as old as it seems."

I sit down into a chair, hard. "How do you know?"

She pushes a small plate with an éclair toward me. "Not sure if you know this, but I'm an expert on paper."

I bite into the éclair, but the stress hormones coursing through my veins make it taste like a fat-free, sugar-free granola bar. "You mean that literally, right? Because it sounds like you're saying you're not really an expert, but on paper, you are."

She frowns. "Do you want to hear this or not?"

"Sorry. Shutting up." I shove the rest of the tasteless éclair into my mouth, belatedly recalling the trouble Honey got into for forging coupons. Her expertise on paper must stem from that side of her life.

"Anyway, as I was trying to say, last night I was looking at this certificate, and I realized it looked much too old for the date it was issued. At first, I thought that maybe Russian paper is crappier and therefore ages extra fast, but after some testing, I'm convinced this is a fresh piece of printing paper that's been stained by coffee."

I snatch the paper from her hands, yank out my nose filters, and take a deep sniff.

Fuck.

She's right.

Underneath the repulsive aroma of Black Swan's perfume, there's tthe faint floral and woodsy tang of good-quality coffee.

I swallow the part of éclair stuck in my throat. "You think the certificate is fake?"

"Why else age it like that?"

I bite my lip. "Could it be real, but someone spilled coffee on it at some point over the years?"

"No. This was done with highly diluted coffee, or else the paper would look ancient."

There's a tingle in my chest, like swan feathers brushing against my heart. "Then why would he admit it?"

Honey cocks her head. "Did he, though? We don't know exactly what he meant when he said, 'I can explain.'"

Skunk. She's right. I should've let him speak.

"Are you sure about this?" I ask, afraid to hope.

Honey's phone dings.

My pulse leaps.

Art?

But no.

It's a text from Blue, which Honey triumphantly shows me:

Checked out the marriage certificate against **classified**.

No such thing was issued in Russia on that date. Also checked in **classified** and learned that Art never married in Russia or in the US—that is, until Lemon.

Another ding, and a second text from Blue shows up:

Speaking of Lemon, tell her that the dancing bitch got hers. For mysterious reasons, "she" filed papers to permanently change her name to "Crusty Vagina," and someone with friends in the right places made sure the name change was expedited. However, the name change reversal, should she file for one, will take as long as these things can possibly take.

Honey beams at the phone. "Just picture your nemesis handing someone an ID that says 'Crusty Vagina.' Or booking a restaurant reservation as Crusty Vagina. Or going to the doctor, where they'll call for a patient named Crusty Vagina. Or—"

I wave her away. I couldn't care less about revenge on Black Swan at the moment. Not when I'm realizing what a monumental ass I must have seemed to Art.

I didn't give him a chance to explain.

I ran out of our wedding reception in front of everyone.

Fuck. Fuck.

He must be so pissed.

I would be if I were him.

"I need to call him." I grab for Honey's phone.

She yanks it away, out of my reach. "I blocked him and deleted his number, remember? Let's see if Blue can help."

She fires off a text, and a minute later, Blue texts us

Art's number. She also informs us that Art was asking about me last night, and that she told him I was okay.

"How did she know I was okay?" I ask Honey.

"No idea." Honey scans her surroundings as if looking for hidden microphones or cameras.

"Anyway," I say. "Call him. Now."

Honey dials the number and hands me the phone.

The call goes to voicemail.

My heart sinks.

"Art, pick up, please."

He doesn't.

I call back.

Same result.

Damn it.

I must speak with him now. I'll burst if I don't.

I type out a message to Blue to ask if she can locate him using her spy juju. Thanks to auto-correct, the text reads as:

Can you citrate Art musing his lumber?

Somehow, she understands me because she replies with:

I'll need some time.

Grunting in frustration, I call Mom.

"Namaste, sunshine," she says. "Are you—"

"Mom, where is Art?" I demand.

"I have no idea," she says. "After you left, your father and I booked a hotel and moved into it before Art came home. We didn't want to be in the middle of a—"

"Thank you. Talk soon." I hang up.

Well, that was a dead end, and Blue hasn't come through.

Leaping to my feet, I say, "I'm going home. He's probably there."

"I'm coming with," Honey says.

I shake my head. "I've got this. I'll let you know what happens after it happens."

She gives me a crisp salute. "Go get him."

I stick my nose filters back in. "I plan to."

———

When I rush into our place, there's no sign of Art anywhere.

I walk over to Fluffer's mansion, and the little guy looks at me warily.

Why do you look and smell like a grumpy cat? Are you finally going to eat me?

The good news is that the chinchilla has been fed recently, so Art did get home last night.

I grab my phone off the charger and call him.

Voicemail.

I text him.

Nothing.

I text Blue to see if she finally knows where he is.

No reply.

I sprint into Art's office and use the "Baryshnikov" password again.

Okay, I'm in. Now what?

Oh, I know. I type in "find my phone" and click the first link that pops up.

Eureka. The phone is at an address in Brighton Beach, and I bet Art is there too.

My phone pings.

It's Blue, who's discovered the same thing I just did but a few seconds too late.

Okay. That settles it. I book a ride to Brighton Beach.

———

I approach the building that is my destination, and my heart sinks. The sign above it says "Easy Fume," but I have been mentally calling this "the *taranka* place" and then gagging afterward.

In hindsight, it makes sense he'd be here. He said this is where he goes when he's stressed. Also, his not picking up his phone or answering texts makes sense now. He probably left his phone in a locker.

Maybe I should wait here?

No.

I have to fix this, ASAP. He could be in there, spanking another woman right now.

Not on my watch.

I take deep breaths in an effort to saturate my blood with oxygen. Hopefully, I can hold my breath for a while and thus not smell the horror as I rush in.

When I feel almost lightheaded from the crazy breathing, I open the door.

Now or never.

I stride into the fishy stink.

CHAPTER
Thirty~Nine

Fuck me. Somehow, I can smell it without even taking in breaths.

Better make this quick.

I run in, ignoring the worried calls of the hostess. What does she think, that I'm trying some sort of swelter-and-dash maneuver?

Thirty seconds into the banya's interior, I can't help but suck in a breath.

My eyes water, and it takes all my willpower not to puke.

It's official.

Taranka smell is worse than putting your nose under the tail of the stinkiest skunk in the history of skunks. Worse than rotten eggs, onion bread, and Black Swan's (or should I say Crusty Vagina's) perfumed armpits —combined.

My legs feel heavy from the lack of oxygen.

With the heroic effort of a triathlete approaching the finish line, I keep going.

In the distance, I spot a towel rack. Behind me, the hostess is still shouting in Russian.

Okay. If I can just make it to the towels, maybe I can survive this olfactory assault.

The shouting behind me intensifies.

Skunk.

I force myself to jog, which makes me breathe faster, which pulls more stench into my poor nose, which makes me want to fall down and curl into a ball.

No.

I'll make it.

Somehow.

Gritting my teeth, I head toward the towels.

Almost there.

Just another foot.

Finally.

I grab a towel and try breathing through it. The stench is dampened, but breathing is much harder this way.

"What are you doing?" the hostess screams, switching to accented English.

I don't answer. That would be wasting precious oxygen.

Towel pressed to face, I pass the nearby pool and rush toward what must be a *parilka* door.

The handle is hot enough to burn my hand, but I pull the door open and shout into the steamy depths, "Art, are you here?"

No reply, and the steam makes it hard to see if he's in here or not.

I shut the door and turn.

There. On the other side of the pool, a tall, athletically built man stands with his back to me, wearing only swim trunks. Is it Art?

It's the best lead I've got. Holding my breath, I sprint that way—which is when the hostess tackles me.

Splash.

I land in the pool.

Fucker.

I begin flailing and gasping for breath—the last thing I want to be doing in this place.

Somehow, I'm surviving. The stench of chlorine from this pool would usually kill me, but it covers the *taranka* so I'm grateful for it—at least until I accidentally swallow some of the nasty pool water.

Now I'm not grateful at all, and afraid for my life.

"Hold on, *kislik*," an achingly familiar voice says, and then strong hands grab me and pull me out of the water like a wet doll. In an eyeblink, I'm being transported through the banya in a bridal carry.

Wiping pool water from my eyes, I feast on Art's gorgeous face. His dark hair is wet, and droplets of water cling to his lashes, highlighting their thickness.

"Hi," I gasp.

"Don't breathe. I'm going to get you out of here." He speeds up, and in a few seconds, we're out of the horrid place and on the street.

I inhale my first *taranka*-free breath and nearly have an orgasm.

Art doesn't set me down. He carries me across the street and onto the boardwalk.

Oh, the ocean air. It's as welcome as the hands holding me.

Seeing color return to my face, Art finally sets me on my feet.

"Can I breathe *now*?" I ask.

His lips quirk. "I guess that's okay."

I pointedly fill my lungs with luxuriously salty air, then let it out with a whoosh. "I'm sorry. I shouldn't have—"

"No, I'm the one who's sorry." He grimaces. "I should've told you."

"That's just it. I have no idea what it is that 'you should've told me.'"

He frowns. "But I thought Alisa—"

"She made me think you were married to another woman."

His eyes widen. "She what?"

"She gave me a marriage certificate that stated you were married back in Russia."

His jaw tightens dangerously. "That's a lie," he says in a low, hard voice. "I was never—"

"I know that now." I squeeze about a gallon of pool water from my hair. "The document she gave me was a fake."

"Oh." He grabs my hand. "So she didn't tell you what really happened?"

My hand should feel warm in his palm, but it doesn't. What if "what really happened" is worse than the "secret wife?"

"She didn't tell me much," I say cautiously. "But you should."

He sighs and releases my hand to shove his fingers through his wet hair. "Remember when I told you about a couple of casual encounters with ballerinas?"

Oh, skunk. I think I see where this is going. "The ones that led to so much drama that you now avoid ballerinas like the plague?"

He nods solemnly. "One in particular made me take that stance—and, as you might have guessed, it was Alisa."

I resist the urge to smack my forehead. That makes so much sense. Now that I know, I can't believe I didn't suspect it sooner. He slept with her and drama ensued —and she's clearly still pining for him. Violently. And hey, having slept with him myself, I can sort of understand her—but not forgive.

"Are you mad?" he asks.

Am I? A bit. I hate the idea of him with another woman. Then again, it happened long before we met, and he's paid for it by having to deal with her brand of crazy.

"I'm more confused than mad," I say. "If she's your ex of sorts, why invite her to our reception?"

He sighs again. "I didn't. She crashed the party. I didn't want to make a big scene in front of the whole company." His nostrils flare. "Had I known about the stunt she was going to pull, I would've had her escorted out by security."

Is this a good time to tell him her name is about to become Crusty Vagina? Nah. Might sound like I'm being petty.

I narrow my eyes at him, mostly in jest. "Swear you

don't have feelings for her anymore, and I'll forget this whole thing."

"I never had feelings for her in the first place," he says. "But, speaking of feelings... I need to tell you something."

CHAPTER

Forty

"What?" I whisper and wait with bated breath for him to speak.

He steps closer to me and cradles my face in his palms.

As if waiting for this moment, the ocean breeze picks up, making me recall just how wet we both are—and in my case, in multiple ways, thanks to his touch.

"Everything I said during that toast at the ceremony is how I really feel," Art says, his eyes locked on mine. "I wanted you from the moment I caught you in my dressing room. I think that's why I asked you to be my green card wife. I had to get to know you, and that was the best pretext I could think of to bring you into my life."

I feel like I'm about to take flight as I cover his hands with mine. "You mean you weren't looking for a fake wife?"

"Not until I met you. The idea came to me right then

and there, in that dressing room. Before that, I was considering other ways to get the green card."

I bite my lip as he drops his hands. "Why didn't you say something sooner? Tell me it wasn't all fake?"

He winces. "I wasn't sure how you'd react. I didn't want to push for more and lose you. You were so dead set on your rules about us not sleeping together that I thought all you wanted out of our arrangement was the money—and I knew I'd rather have you in my life as my fake wife than not have you at all."

"So… you're saying you like me?"

He shakes his head. "Me and you, we just fit, like banya and birch trees. So, no. I don't merely like you." He pulls me closer, his eyes warm and soft. *"Kislik…* I love you."

My heart explodes into swan feathers.

"I fell for you, hard," he continues. "I—"

"Wait," I gasp. "There's something you have to know. The day we met, I wasn't there on a dare. I saw you on TV long before that and got so obsessed with you that I snuck into your dressing room, like a stalker."

I stop breathing, scared that my admission will make him push me away.

Instead, he grips my hands in both of his. His voice is husky. "I'm flattered, *kislik*. And so glad you did."

Whew. Should I tell him the rest? In for a *kapeika*, in for a *ruble*. "I sniffed your dance belt because I wanted you out of my system," I blurt.

A smirk curves his lips. "And how did *that* go?"

"It backfired—and made me believe in love at first sniff."

He pulls me closer. "You mean—"

"I love you too," I say solemnly. "I want to remain your wife. Be your main squeeze. Be your—"

He shuts me up with a kiss.

A sweet, devouring kiss that promises a million tomorrows.

Epilogue

ART

"I'M TELLING YOU," Lemon says, her voice muffled by the gas mask. "I smell an alcohol swab."

The doctor—or Ava, as she insists on being called—rolls her eyes, but only so I can see. "Impossible," she says. "Your husband made it crystal clear that you have a smell sensitivity, so I personally made sure there were no open alcohol swabs in this room. Or lunch leftovers. Or any hint of perfume. Or—"

Lemon grunts in frustration inside her gas mask. "The swab is in a nearby room."

Ava looks at me pleadingly.

"My *kislik*." I lovingly pat the part of Lemon's belly that isn't covered in gel. "The sooner this ultrasound can start, the sooner I can get you into fresh air."

"Right." Lemon turns to Ava. "Do it then. Quickly."

Ava does her thing—and to her credit, she doesn't blink an eye when it comes to the ONLY 4 MR. BIG tattoo.

I stare at the results on the screen, where *something* is happening.

"There." Ava points at a wriggling blob. "A heartbeat."

My chest fills with pure joy.

A baby.

Our baby.

"Wait a second," Ava says, scaring me half to death. "There's another one."

I gape at the screen.

Lemon rips off her gas mask, revealing her radiant complexion. Pregnancy has done wonders for her already-beautiful face. "Can you say that again?" she says in a choked voice, like she's trying not to inhale. "I think the mask muffled my hearing."

Ava grins. "You're going to have twins. Congratulations."

And just like that, my joy doubles.

In one fell swoop, my new family has gotten bigger —and a big family has been my dream for as long as I can remember.

"Twins," Lemon says, sounding stunned. She seems to have forgotten all about the alcohol swab. Instead, she looks at me accusingly. "You put two babies in there?"

Uh-oh. I grab her hand. "You're not happy?"

I thought she'd make lemonade out of this situation as quickly as I have. Was I wrong?

She blinks, then squeezes my fingers. "Yes. No. I don't know. I'm shocked, but probably shouldn't be. Twins are a part of Hyman DNA."

I grin. "And now they're part of Skulme DNA too."

She blinks again, shakes her head, and then a slow, gorgeous smile spreads over her face, making her green eyes sparkle. "Twins," she says softly. "Yeah, I think I've made up my mind: I'm happy."

By the time she stops speaking, however, she looks a little green. I help her tug the mask back on before the smells make her puke, as they did on the way here. And this morning at our house. And last night. And each time she thinks of banya or skunks or chlorine.

She takes a few deep breaths, and when her face is back to its usual pale shade, she turns to Ava. "It is just two, right? Not six?"

"Nope. Two," Ava says. "Now go. Get that fresh air."

———

As soon as we enter our apartment, I make sure Lemon eats something. She lost her breakfast to the cab air freshener, and she's eating for three now.

After she's done with her plain toast, she looks visibly better, so I bring her a fruit tart.

"Will you share this with me?" she asks.

I gladly reach for a spoon.

Half of her desserts are fruits nowadays, and she really enjoys them, especially the more exotic, sweeter ones like mango and cherimoya. The other half are sugary concoctions like this tart, and since I don't dance professionally anymore, I occasionally indulge as well, especially when she invites me to share. Not that she's been in much of a sharing mood lately, with her appetite so unpredictable.

"Is the beast hungry?" she asks when we've demolished the dessert.

She means Fluffer, but my mind goes elsewhere and what she calls Mr. Big stirs. Her lush new curves have been driving me insane, and it's all I can do not to attack her twenty-four-seven. Maybe I should join a support group? Or start one? HAPWA—Husbands Addicted to Pregnant Wives Anonymous.

With effort, I wrench my mind away from thoughts of tangled sheets and soft, deliciously full breasts. "I fed him earlier, don't worry."

Fluffer has been much more tolerant of her company as of late, but he still prefers it when I take care of him. I can't say I mind.

"In that case, I'm going to go write a post," she says.

Should I tell her to wait, so I can finally reveal my big news? It's an announcement that pales in comparison to the twins, but still.

No. Her work is super important to her, especially now, thanks to the huge success that is her partnership with Bella.

We settle together on the couch, and I check my stock positions on my laptop as she writes on hers.

Sometime later, she clears her throat.

When I look at her, she wrinkles her nose. "I smell dog breath again."

"On it." I close the laptop and head over to the apartment across the hall to ask the neighbor to brush his pooch's teeth.

At first, the neighbor thought Lemon was imagining his dog's bad breath, but then he and I started keeping track of her complaints and realized that she only says something when he forgets to brush his pet's teeth.

I knock on his door, and as soon as he opens it, I hand him a bottle of wine. "Thanks for understanding."

He grins. "When my wife was pregnant, she was also sensitive to smells."

Yeah, but his wife didn't have a borderline super-hero nose *before* the pregnancy.

When I return, Lemon beams at me. "Much better. Thanks, darling."

"You're welcome. Are you done with your post?"

She sets her computer aside. "Just finished. Why?"

I grab the all-important envelope and hand it to her.

She looks inside, eyes widening. "It came?"

I nod. "I'm a proud owner of a green card."

"Already?" She jumps up and gives me a big hug. "Yay! I thought it was going to take longer."

I hug her back, inhaling her sweet scent, and Mr. Big goes on alert again. It takes everything I have to keep things platonic, but I manage. Somehow. I also don't tell her that it was her sister Blue who helped expedite things, since Lemon is very proud of how she aced that government interview.

"It was even quicker than you think," I say when she pulls away. "I got it a week ago, but I was waiting for a good moment to tell you."

She gives me a sweet Lemon smile that never fails to make my heartbeat speed up. "So that's it, right? You're staying here with me?"

Damn it. Keeping up the fight against Mr. Big is getting more difficult by the second.

She leans in and sniffs my neck.

That's it.

The fight is over. Mr. Big has won.

"Yes," I growl. "I'm staying with you. Forever."

And for the next hour, I show her exactly how much staying power I've got.

Sneak Peeks

Thank you for participating in Lemon and Art's journey!

Looking for more laugh-out-loud romcoms? Meet the Chortsky siblings in *Hard Stuff*:

- *Hard Code* – A geeky workplace romance following quirky QA tester Fanny Pack and her mysterious Russian boss, Vlad Chortsky
- *Hard Ware* – The hilarious story of Bella Chortsky, a sex toy developer, and Dragomir Lamian, a potential investor in her next big business venture
- *Hard Byte* – A fake date romcom featuring Holly, a prime-number-obsessed Anglophile who makes a deal with Alex Chortsky (aka the Devil) to save her dream project

And if you can't get enough of the Hyman sisters, you

should also check out:

- *Royally Tricked* – A raunchy royal romance featuring daredevil prince Tigger and Gia Hyman, a germaphobic, movie-obsessed magician
- *Femme Fatale-ish* – A spy romcom starring aspiring femme fatale Blue Hyman and a sexy (possible) Russian agent
- *Of Octopuses and Men* – An enemies-to-lovers romcom about Olive, an octopus-obsessed marine biologist, and her sizzling hot (and infuriating) new boss.

We love receiving feedback from our readers, and we are always interested to know what you'd like to see in books to come. Want your favorite side character to have their own book? Mention it in a review! We take all suggestions into consideration, and if you sign up for our newsletter at www.mishabell.com, you'll be the first to know who will be featured next!

Misha Bell is a collaboration between husband-and-wife writing team, Dima Zales and Anna Zaires. When they're not making you bust a gut as Misha, Dima writes sci-fi and fantasy, and Anna writes dark and contemporary romance. Check out *Wall Street Titan* by Anna Zaires for more steamy billionaire hotness!

Turn the page to read previews from *Femme Fatale-ish* and *Of Octopuses and Men*!

Excerpt from Femme Fatale-ish

BY MISHA BELL

My name is Blue—insert a mood-related joke here—and I'm a femme fatale in training. My goal is to join the CIA. Unfortunately, I have a tiny issue with birds, and the closest I've come to my dream is working for a government agency that's disturbingly up-to-speed on everyone's sexts, rants in private Facebook groups, and secret family chocolate-chip cookie recipes.

I know I'm a spy cliché, that agent who works at a desk but craves fieldwork. However, I have a plan: I'm going to infiltrate the secretive Hot Poker Club, where I've spotted a mysterious, sexy stranger who I'm convinced is a Russian spy.

And once I'm in? All I have to do is seduce the presumed spy without falling for him, so I can expose his true identity and prove my femme fatale bona fides to the CIA. I never lose concentration at work, so that'll be an absolute breeze for me. Oh, and did I mention he's sexy?

I'm doing it for my country, not my ovaries, I pinky swear.

WARNING: Now that you've finished reading this, your device will self-destruct in five seconds.

———

I stick my finger into Bill's silicone butthole.

"What the hell?" Fabio exclaims in a horrified whisper. "That's poking. You have to be gentle. Loving."

Grunting in frustration, I jerk my hand away.

Bill's butthole makes a greedy slurping sound.

"See?" I say. "He misses my finger. It couldn't have been *that* bad."

"Look, Blue." Fabio narrows his amber eyes at me. "Do you want my help or not?"

"Fine." I lube up my finger and examine my target once more. Bill is a headless silicone torso with abs, a butt, and a hard dick—or is it a dildo?—sticking out, at least usually. Right now, the poor thing is smushed between Bill's stomach and my couch.

"How about you pretend it's your pussy?" Fabio's nose wrinkles in distaste. "I'm sure you don't jab *it* like an elevator button."

"I usually rub my clit when I masturbate," I mutter as I add more lube to my finger. "Or use a vibrator."

Fabio makes a gagging sound. "You're not paying me enough to listen to shit like that."

With a sigh, I circle my finger seductively around Bill's opening a few times, then slowly enter with just the tip of my index finger.

Fabio nods, so I edge the finger deeper, stopping when the first knuckle is in.

"Much better," he says. "Now aim between his belly button and cock."

I cringe. I hate the word "cock"—and everything else bird-related. Still, I do as he says.

Fabio dramatically shakes his head. "Don't bend the finger. This isn't a come-hither situation."

I pull my finger out and start all over.

My digit goes in rod straight this time.

"Huh," I say after I'm two knuckles deep. "There's something there. Feels like a walnut."

Fabio snorts. "That *is* a walnut, you dum-dum. I shoved it in there for educational purposes. The prostate—or P-spot—is around where you are now, but the real one feels softer and smoother. Now that you got it, massage gently."

As I pleasure Bill's walnut, Fabio shakes the dummy to simulate how a real man would be acting. Then he starts to voice Bill as well, using all of his porn-star acting ability.

"Bill" moans and groans until he has, as Fabio puts it, "a P-gasm to rule them all."

I remove my finger once again. I have mixed feelings about my accomplishment.

Fabio grabs my chin and tilts my face up. "Show me your tongue."

Feeling like I'm five, I stick my tongue all the way out.

He shakes his head disapprovingly. "Not long enough."

I retract my tongue. "Long enough for what?"

"To reach the walnut, obviously." He sighs theatrically. "I guess I'll work with what I've got."

Ugh. Can I slap him? "How about we work on his peen?"

With another sigh, he turns Bill over. "Did you take those lozenges, like I told you?"

Not for the first time, I field doubts about my instructor. The goal for this training is simple: I want to be a spy, which means gaining skills as a seductress/femme fatale. Think Keri Russell's character in *The Americans*. According to her backstory in that show, she attended a creepy spy school that taught seduction. In fact, such schools are common in movies about Russian spies—the latest was featured in *Anna*. Alas, these schools are harder to find in real life. So I figured I'd hire a professional instead, but the prostitute I solicited for help refused. Ditto with the female porn stars I reached out to on social media. As my last resort, I turned to Fabio, a childhood friend who's now a male porn star. Being in gay porn, he claims he's able to please a man better than any woman can.

"Yes, I sucked on the lozenges," I say. "My throat is numb, and I can barely feel my tongue."

"Great. Now get that whole shlong down your throat." Fabio points at Bill.

I scan Bill's length apprehensively. "You sure about this? Wouldn't the lozenges make the penis numb? If Bill were real, that is."

He lifts an eyebrow. "Bill?"

I shrug. "Figured if I'm having relations with him, he shouldn't be anonymous."

Fabio pats my shoulder. "The lozenges are just to give you some confidence. Once you see that it fits, you'll be more relaxed for the real thing and won't require numbing. Don't worry. I'll teach you proper breathing and everything. You'll be a pro in no time."

"Okay." I take off my sexy wig and put it on the couch. Before Fabio says anything, I assure him I'll keep it on during a real encounter.

Now comfy, I lean over and take Bill into my mouth as far as I can.

My lips touch the silicone base. Wow. This is deeper than I was able to swallow any of my exes—and they weren't this big. My gag reflex is sensitive. Typically, even a toothbrush gives me issues when I use it to clean my tongue. But thanks to the numbing, the silicone dildo has gone in all the way.

This is interesting. Could lozenges also help one withstand waterboarding? If I'm to become a spy, I need to learn to withstand torture in case I'm captured. Of course, waterboarding isn't my biggest concern. If the enemy has access to a duck—or any bird, really—I'll spill all the state secrets to keep the feathery monstrosity away from me.

Yeah, okay. Maybe the CIA did have a good reason to reject my candidacy. Then again, in *Homeland*—another one of my favorite shows—they let Claire Danes stay in the CIA with all of *her* issues. Which reminds me: I need to practice making my chin quiver on demand.

Fabio taps my shoulder. "That's enough."

I disengage and swallow an overabundance of saliva. "That wasn't so bad. Should I go again?"

He shakes his head. "I think you need a motivation boost."

I know what he's talking about, so I take my phone out.

"Yeah." He rubs his hands like a villain from the early Bond films. "Show me the picture again."

I pull up the image of codename Hottie McSpy.

An undercover FBI agent took this photo because he was after one of the men in it, but not my target. No. Everyone thinks Hottie McSpy is just a rando—but *I* believe he's a Russian agent.

Fabio whistles. "So much premium man meat."

It's true. In the image, a group of extremely deli-cious-looking men are sitting around a table inside a Russian-style *banya*—a hybrid between a steam room and a sauna—wearing only towels and, in the case of Hottie McSpy, a pair of non-reflective aviator sunglasses that must have some kind of anti-fog coating. With the sweat beading on everyone's glistening muscles, they look like a wet dream come to life.

"They're playing poker," I say. "That's why I've been taking poker lessons."

362

"Yeah, I figured as much, since the picture is called Hot Poker Club." Fabio giddily enunciates the last three words. "You realize that sounds like the title of one of my movies?"

I shrug. "An FBI agent named this image, not me. They were after another guy who was in that room, and I was helping out as part of the collaboration between the agencies."

Fabio taps on the screen to zoom in on Hottie McSpy. "And he's the one you're after?"

Nodding, I drink in the image once more. Hottie McSpy has the hardest muscles of this already-impressive bunch, and the strongest jaw. His chiseled masculine features are vaguely Slavic, a fact that first made me suspicious of him. His hair is dark blond and shampoo-commercial healthy. Not even my wigs are as nice.

If I were to learn that this man was the result of Soviet geneticists trying to create the perfect male specimen / super-soldier / field agent, I wouldn't be surprised. Nor would I be shocked to find out that he was the inspiration for the Russian equivalent of a Ken doll (Ivan A. Pieceof?). Even if I didn't think he was a spy, I'd infiltrate that poker game just to rip those stupid glasses off of him and see his eyes. Though I picture them—

"You're drooling," Fabio says. "Not that I can blame you."

I nearly choke on the treacherous saliva. "No, I'm not."

"Yeah, sure. Be honest, are you going after him

because he might be a spy, or because you want to marry him?"

"The first option." I hide my phone. "Spy or not, marriage is out of the question for me. My current attitude toward dating shares an acronym with the name of the agency I work for: No Strings Attached. But that's not what this is about, anyway. If I single-handedly expose a spy, the CIA is bound to take notice and rethink their rejection of my candidacy. And even if they don't take me, I will have made America safer. Russian spies are still among the biggest threats to our national security."

"Sure, sure," Fabio says. "And his hotness has nothing to do with you focusing on him, specifically."

I frown. "His hotness is why he's the perfect agent. Think James Bond. Think Tom Cruise in *Mission Impossible*. Think—"

Fabio raises his hands like I'm threatening to shoot him. "The lady doth protest too much, methinks."

I gesture at the silicone phallus. "Should I go again? I think the numbing is wearing off."

For some unknown reason, I feel super motivated to deep-throat someone.

Fabio takes out his phone. "Sure. You work on that, but I've got to run. My Grindr date awaits."

He shows me a dick pic.

"Dude," I say. "Don't you get enough action at work?"

Fabio playfully flicks at Bill's erection, and it swings back and forth like a naughty pendulum. "This is why I thank heavens for being attracted to men. Their sex drives are so much stronger."

"That's sexist. Just because women don't hump everything that moves doesn't mean we have weak sex drives."

He flicks Bill's manhood—or is it his dummy-hood? —again. "If your cock and asshole aren't always sore, your sex drive is lacking. That's all there is to it."

I cringe again. What do roosters—killing machines that they are—have in common with penises? Why not call the male organ a python, a bratwurst, or a honey dipper? Any of those would be more appropriate.

Fabio grins and flicks the appendage in question once again. "Sorry for saying 'cock.' I'm such a—"

Before he can finish, a blur of fur streaks by. A giant feline lands on Bill's washboard abs and swats razor-sharp claws at the pendulum-like phallus.

Screaming in falsetto, Fabio pulls away from the scene of the unfolding hate crime.

The owner of the claws is my cat, Machete, and apparently, he's not done—because he rakes his claws over what's left of Bill's dummy-hood.

"That's just obscene." Fabio stands crossed-legged, as if he needs to go tinkle. "You should get your cat to a therapist."

As if he understands what my friend has just said, Machete shoots him a feline hate-filled glare.

As usual, I can picture what Machete would say in a nightmarish world where cats could talk:

The silicone male couldn't escape Machete. The softer, fleshy one will be next.

"Come here, sweetie," I croon and swoop down to grab the cat.

Machete must be feeling extremely magnanimous today because he lets me hold him and keep my eyes.

Fabio chuckles, and I give him a quizzical look.

"Your cat was trying to kill Bill," he explains.

Machete hisses at Fabio.

Machete is not amused. Uma Thurman has a lot of range, but she can't play Machete.

I grin. "He must've heard you call that a cock." I gesture at Bill's misfortune. "My sweetie protects me from birds." I pet Machete's silky fur and get rewarded with a deep purr. "When I first got him, he killed what turned out to be a goose pillow for me."

Fabio eyes the door. "All I know is he looks like he'd fought in a lot of illegal street fights before you adopted him. And lost a lot."

It's true. Machete actually looked even worse when I came across him at the shelter. It was also the only time I can recall seeing him vulnerable in any way.

Needless to say, I used my work resources to track down his prior owners, and soon after, they mysteriously ended up on a no-fly list... just before a big vacation.

I stop the petting for a moment, and Fabio gets hissed at again.

"I'd better go," Fabio says, backing away.

I follow him. A videocall window pops up on one of my wall monitors. Yes, I have multiple wall monitors. My home setup is inspired by all the movies where spies watch someone from a surveillance room.

Forgetting the cat danger, Fabio stops and looks at the screen. If my friend were one of Machete's kind, his curiosity would've killed him long ago.

"It's my video conference with Gia and Clarice," I explain. "You can go."

Fabio purses his lips. "Who's Clarice?"

"My poker teacher," I say. "Go."

He looks on the verge of stomping his foot. "But I want to say hi to my girl Gia."

"Fine." I accept the call, and both Gia and Clarice show up on the screen.

———

Go to www.mishabell.com to order your copy of *Femme Fatale-ish* today!

Excerpt from Of Octopuses and Men

BY MISHA BELL

My grandparents' grumpy neighbor is as hot as the lethal Florida sun. And like the sun, he's bad for me. My taste in men is the worst—just ask my ex and his restraining order.

What am I doing in Florida with my grandparents, you wonder? Well, my best friend is an octopus, and he needs a bigger tank, so I took a job at an aquarium in the Sunshine State.

I didn't expect that sexy, long-haired grump to try to buy my octopus for some nefarious purpose. Nor did I expect to make out with him during a late-night swim at the beach.

And the last thing I expected was to run into him on my first day at my new job… where he's my boss.

"Ah, Caper. What are you up to?"

I grin. My name is Olive (my parents are evil in their hippie-dippie-ness), and when Grandpa calls me Caper, he means "little olive," which makes me feel like a little girl again. Obviously, I'll never tell him that his nickname for me is botanically incorrect: capers are the flowers of a shrub, while olives are a tree fruit from an altogether different species.

"Taking Beaky out for a walk," I reply, nodding at the tank.

Grandpa squints at the glass, and Beaky chooses that exact moment to make himself look like a rock—as he does every time Grandpa tries to look at him.

Grandpa rubs his eyes. "Is there really an octopus in there? I feel like you and your grandmother are trying to make me think I'm going senile."

"No. It's Beaky who's messing with you."

I can't blame my grandfather for not spotting my eight-armed friend. When it comes to camouflage, octopuses blow chameleons out of the water. Also, if a chameleon was literally in the water, no amount of camouflage would save it from becoming an octopus's lunch.

Grandpa shakes his head. "Why?"

I shrug. "He's a creature with nine brains, one in his head and one in each arm. Trying to puzzle out his thinking would give anyone a headache."

Grandpa squints at the tank again, but Beaky stays in his rock guise. "Why do you walk him, anyway?"

"To keep him from being bored. What he really

needs is a bigger tank, but for now, he'll have to make do with a change of scenery."

"Bored?"

"Oh, yeah. A bored octopus is worse than a seven-year-old boy hopped up on caffeine and birthday cake. In Germany, an octopus named Otto repeatedly shorted out the Sea Star Aquarium's entire electrical system by squirting water at the 2,000-watt overhead spotlight. Because he was bored."

Grandpa lifts his bushy eyebrows. "But don't you make puzzles for him? Let him watch TV?"

I nod. Making puzzles for octopuses is actually what I'm famous for, and how I got my new job. "Toys and TV help," I say, "but I still get the sense he's feeling cooped up."

Grunting, Grandpa delves into his pocket and pulls out a handgun the size of my arm. "Take this with you." He thrusts it at me.

I blink at the instrument of death. "Why?"

"Protection."

"From what? We're in a gated community."

He thrusts the weapon at me with greater urgency. "It's better to have a gun and not need it."

I don't take the offering. "The crime rate in Palm Islet is ten times lower than in New York."

Grandpa takes the clip out of the gun, checks it, shoves in an extra bullet, and snaps it back in. "It would give me peace of mind if you took it."

"By Cthulhu," I mutter under my breath.

"Bless you," Grandpa says.

"That wasn't a sneeze. I said, 'Cthulhu.'" At Grandpa's blank stare, I heave a sigh. "He's a fictional cosmic entity created by H. P. Lovecraft. Depicted with octopus features."

"Oh. Is that him in your grandmother's sexy cartoons?"

"Absolutely not." I shudder at the thought. "Cthulhu is hundreds of meters tall. He's one of the Great Old Ones, so his attentions would rip a woman apart as quickly as they would drive her mad."

"Fair enough." Grandpa attempts to shove the gun into my hands again. "Take it and go."

I hide my hands behind my back. "I don't have any kind of license."

"You're kidding." He regards me incredulously. "Tomorrow, I'll take you to a concealed carry class."

I fight a Cthulhu-sized eye roll. "I'm kind of busy tomorrow, starting a new job and all."

With a frown, he hides the gun somewhere. "How about this weekend?"

"We'll see," I say as noncommittally as I can before grabbing my handbag from the back of a nearby chair and pressing the remote button again to roll the tank into the garage.

My grandparents, like other Floridians, prefer to leave their houses this way, instead of, say, through the front door.

As soon as my grandfather is out of sight, Beaky stops being a rock, spreads his arms akimbo, and turns an excited shade of red.

"You should be ashamed of yourself," I tell him sternly.

We are the God Emperor of the Tank, ordained by Cthulhu. We shall not bestow the glory of our visage upon the undeserving. Hurry up, our faithful priestess-subject. We want to taste the sunshine on our suckers.

Yup. Ellen DeGeneres talked to a fictional sentient octopus in *Finding Dory*, while my real one speaks to me in my head. And I'm not alone in having these imaginary conversations. Ever since my sisters and I were kids, we've given animals voices. In my mind, Beaky sounds like nine people speaking in unison (the main brain and the eight in his arms), and his tone is imperious (octopuses have blue blood, after all). Oh, and his words come out with that faint gargle-like sound effect used in *Aquaman* when the Atlanteans spoke underwater.

I open the garage door.

It's super bright outside, despite the ancient oaks that provide plenty of shade.

With a sigh, I take a big tube of my favorite mineral-based sunblock from my bag and cover myself with a thick layer from head to foot. The UV index is 10, so I wait a few minutes, and then I cover myself with a second layer. I do this furtively in the garage to avoid my grandparents teasing me about taking a job in the Sunshine State while being paranoid about sun exposure.

And no, I'm not a vampire—though my sister Gia looks suspiciously like she might be, with her goth makeup and all. Avoiding the sun makes legitimate scientific sense given the harmful effects of UV rays, both A and B, as well as blue light, infrared light, and visible light. They all cause DNA damage. This issue got on my radar a couple of years back when Sushi, my pet clownfish, developed skin cancer, probably due to her aquarium being by a window. I've been careful ever since, even going as far as gluing a triple layer of UV-protective coating over Beaky's tank.

Now, do I realize that I worry about the sun a tad more than anyone who isn't a paranoid dermatologist? Sure. But can I stop? Nope. I think some level of neurosis is programed into my DNA, at least if my identical sextuplet sisters are anything to go by. But hey, when I'm in my eighties and look younger than all my sisters, we'll see who has the last laugh.

Sunblocking finished, I throw on a lightweight zip-up jacket that's coated in UV-protective chemicals, a wide-brim hat, and giant sunglasses.

There. If I were really taking this too far, I'd be wearing one of those Darth Vader visors, wouldn't I?

My heartbeat picks up as I follow Beaky's tank out into full sun, but I calm down by reminding myself that the sunblock will do its job. When the tank rolls down the driveway and onto a shady sidewalk by the lake, my breathing evens out further.

So far so good. Now I just hope I don't get too many annoying questions from nosy neighbors.

A pair of herons take flight nearby as we stroll along the lake shore. Beaky stares at them intently and changes his shape a few times.

We wish to taste those things. Be a good priestess-subject and deliver them to the tank.

I pat the top of the tank. "I'll give you a shrimp when we get back."

We both spot a raccoon digging in the grass by the lake, likely looking for turtle or gator eggs.

We wish to taste that too.

"I'll give you a shrimp without the puzzle," I tell him.

Usually, I put his treats into one of my creations, making the meal extra fun for him, but if he's worked up an appetite by watching all the land animals, I don't want to delay his gratification.

A five-foot alligator slowly crawls out of the lake.

Yup, we're definitely in Florida.

Spotting it, Beaky picks up two coconut shells from the bottom of his tank and closes them over his body, appearing to the world—and to the gator—like an innocent coconut.

"That thing can't get you in the tank," I say soothingly. "Not to mention, it's scared of me. Hopefully."

The statistics on alligator attacks are in our favor. In a state with headlines like "Florida man beats up alligator" and "Florida man tosses alligator into Wendy's drive-through window," the gators have learned to stay far, far away from the insane humans.

Because Beaky doesn't read the news or check online statistics, his eye looks skeptical as it peeks out from the coconut shells.

I return my attention to the sidewalk—and spot him.

A man.

And what a man.

He could've starred in *Aquaman* instead of Jason

Momoa. If I were casting the leading man for my wet dreams, this guy would definitely get the role.

The thought sends tendrils of heat to my nether regions, specifically the part I privately think of as my wunderpus—in honor of *wunderpus photogenicus*, an amazing octopus species discovered in the eighties.

By the way, I once took a picture of my wunderpus, and it's also *photogenicus*.

But back to the stranger. Strong, masculine features framed by an impeccably trimmed beard, cyan eyes as deep as the ocean, a tanned, muscular body clad in low-riding jeans and a sleeveless top that shows off powerful arms, thick, blond-streaked hair that streams down to his broad shoulders—he'd look like a surfer if it weren't for the broody expression on his face.

Beaky must've forgotten about the gator because he's out of his coconut and looking at the stranger with fascination.

Figures. Aquaman has the power to talk to octopuses, along with other sea creatures.

I realize I'm also gaping at him and tense as he gets closer. Unlike back in New York, where it's customary to pass a stranger without acknowledging their existence, here in Florida, everyone at the very least greets their neighbors.

What do I say if he speaks to me? Do I even dare open my mouth? What if I accidentally ask him to have his way with me?

Wait a second. I think I've got it. He's also walking a pet, in his case a dog of the Dachshund breed, a.k.a. a hotdog dog, the most phallic member of the canine species. All I have to do is say something about his wiener—the one wagging its tail, not his Aqua-manhood.

When the man is a dozen feet away, he seems to notice me for the first time. Actually, his gaze zeroes in on Beaky's tank, and his broody expression turns downright hostile—jaw clenched, mouth downturned, eyes flinty. The insane thing is, he looks no less hot now. Maybe more so.

What is wrong with me? No wonder I end up dating assholes like—

His deep, sexy voice is the kind of cold that can create a wind chill even in this humid sauna. "How much for the octopus?"

I blink, then narrow my eyes at the stranger, my hackles rising like spikes on a pufferfish. He wants to buy Beaky? Why? Does he want to eat him?

This *is* the state where people eat gators, turtles (even the protected species), bullfrogs, Burmese pythons, and key lime pie.

Gritting my teeth, I point to the tail-wagging dog at his side. "How much for the bratwurst?"

A sneer twists his full lips. "Let me guess... a New Yorker?"

Aquaman? More like Aqua-ass. "Let *me* guess. Florida man?" I can picture the rest of the headline: "...steals octopus in tank and tries to have sex with it."

Given what my grandmother said about Rule 34 and where I am, it's not that far-fetched. I once read an article about a Florida man who tried to sell a live shark in a mall parking lot. What's sex with an octopus in comparison?

His thick brown eyebrows snap together. "The stories you're alluding to are about transplants. They're never about actual Floridians."

"Oh, I've read what you're talking about," I say with a snort. "'Florida man receives first-ever penis transplant from a horse.' I'm pretty sure the article said that the brave pioneer was born and raised in Melbourne—that's two hours away from here."

Oops. Have I gone too far? Everyone does seem to carry a gun here. And since I found him attractive earlier, with my dating track record, he might well turn out to be dangerous.

Instead of pulling out a weapon, the stranger rubs the bridge of his nose. "Serves me right for trying to argue with a New Yorker. Forget the news. That tank is too small for that octopus. How would you like to live your life inside a Mini Cooper?"

I suck in a breath, my stomach tightening. "How would *you* like to be walked on a leash?" I jerk my chin toward his wiener, whose tail is no longer wagging. "Or to be forced to ignore your screaming bladder and bowels until your master deigns to take you for a walk? Or to have your reproductive organs messed with?"

He glowers at me. "Tofu isn't neutered. In fact, he—"

"Tofu?" My jaw drops. "As in, a tofu hot dog? Talk about animal cruelty."

The veins popping out in his neck look distractingly sexy. "What's wrong with the name Tofu?"

Before I can reply, Tofu whines pitifully.

"Great job," the stranger says. "Now you've upset him."

"I'm pretty sure you did that." *By naming the poor dog Tofu.*

"This conversation is over." He turns his back to me and tugs on the leash. "Come, Tofu."

Tofu gives me a sad look that seems to say, *I don't like it when my daddy and my new mommy argue.*

With a huff, I roll Beaky's tank in the opposite direction.

————

Go to www.mishabell.com to order your copy of *Of Octopuses and Men* today!

About the Author

We love writing humor (often the inappropriate kind), happy endings (both kinds), and characters quirky enough to be called oddballs (because… balls). If you love your romance heavy on the comedy and feel-good vibes, visit www.mishabell.com and sign up for our newsletter.

Printed in Poland
by Amazon Fulfillment
Poland Sp. z o.o., Wrocław

52099R00217